Aris Rising

The Court Of Vampires

"A surprising twist on the vampire trend...Author Morgan weaves together the thrilling history with a contemporary love story that comes together in an action-filled climax—and an enticing cliffhanger—that will leave readers thirsty for more. Blending sensual fantasy and the supernatural, this vampire saga takes a welcome turn."

— Kirkus Reviews

"This sophisticated vampire romance with a twist takes readers on a compelling journey deep into...the pull of hypnosis...the possibility of past lives...and the power of dangerous desires."

— Kindle Nation

"This is a very grownup Vampire story that is just as sensual as it is supernatural. The reader will not be disappointed with the denouement or the inevitable cliffhanger that entices one to look forward to the next book in the series. Devin Morgan will be one to watch in this genre."

— Amazon

"Eloquent imagery and vivid detail--the author does a wonderful job of harmonizing two different worlds together. She brings you into the story quickly and doesn't let you go until the end. Unpredictable (in the best and most refreshing of ways) and delightful."

— Amazon

www.TruLoveStories.com
Where Passionistas Play!

BroadLit

February 2013

Published by

BroadLit ®
14011 Ventura Blvd.
Suite 206 E
Sherman Oaks, CA 91423

ISBN 978-0-9887627-8-7

Produced in the United States of America.

Visit us online at www.TruLOVEstories.com

To the memory of my cherished friend, Bea Greenwood.

A hearty thank you to my publishers and editors, Nancy Cushing-Jones and Barbara Weller, without whom Aris would have been kept in hiding in the Catacombs for all eternity. Their patience, understanding and confidence have enabled me to now call myself "author." And thank you to their wonderful staff: Michelle Clark, Jeff Kongs and Rod Keller, who take such wonderful care of all the details that are so important in the day-to-day marketing of a novel.

Aris Rising

The Court Of Vampires

by Devin Morgan

AN
INFINITY DIARIES
NOVEL

A BROADLIT BOOK

Prologue

Night after night Aris climbed through the window of Sarah Hagan's high-rise apartment in Chicago. The soft amber night light on her bedside table cast odd shadows on her sleeping silhouette. Standing at the foot of her bed watching her sleep, his heart ached to hold her. In her slumbering presence he was transported back in time to the court of Henry VIII and his beloved Elizabeth whose death brought him such anguish.

His wretchedness was the same though the centuries were different. The same separation he felt so long ago from Elizabeth, he now felt from Sarah, despising he was not human. His only desire was to wake her, to hold her, to make love to her, knowing the only way he could express his love was if she were to change, to become one of the undead. Could he ask her such a thing? Long ago he questioned her as he spoke of his friend Sebastian and his human love, Emily. Emily gave her life to become one of the Immortals before their mating. Aris questioned Sarah if she would do such a thing for love. She had no answer for him then. Would she now? He survived in torment.

Each night when he came to watch her he felt as if he were a thief, stealing unrealized moments alone with her. He loathed himself for it yet could not control his need to simply be near her. How long could this continue without her knowledge and would she be repelled when she knew?

CHAPTER 1

"I miss having Gorgeous come in here every week. He hasn't been around in a while. I guess since he's off parole, he's decided not to keep up his therapy sessions." Sarah's assistant, Maggie Fisher, stood in the door of Sarah's office, an expectant look on her face. "Seeing that hunk last thing on Friday always set me up for a great weekend." Maggie laughed as she handed her boss a huge paper cup filled with hot coffee.

"Well, I'm pretty sure he'll stop in once in a while. We couldn't let him deprive you of your fix." Sarah laughed but her heart was in turmoil. Carlos Havarro, the beautiful young man Maggie spoke of was dead, shot in a drive-by shooting, yet everyone thought he was alive and well. In his place and in his body lived Aris, a vampire that had been in existence for thousands of years. The death of her client and friend broke her heart but she couldn't show it. No one would believe her if she told them that an Immortal had taken over his body just as he breathed his last breath. And if she did tell anyone, they would decide she was insane. There were moments she wondered if that were true herself.

As his therapist, during her hypnotherapy regression sessions with Carlos, Aris had made himself known. She had grown accustomed to their conversations and looked forward to them. He gave her glimpses into times long past and had actually known historical figures she had only read about. Now that he possessed a human body and was able to walk the earth again, not just occupy Carlos' mind, he had almost disappeared from her life. Her logical mind told her to be glad the vampire had abandoned her, had once again become a mythological creature. The whole situation was more than any human could understand yet she missed him, their intimate conversations, his passionate convictions. They shared a strange kinship she felt with no one else, a closeness of spirit.

And she missed her human friend, Carlos, terribly, his easy banter, his warmth and affection. She felt more alive since knowing him than ever before. When he was taken away just as he was beginning to find himself outside of his gang-banger life, inexplicably, she felt a piece of her heart die with him.

Her grief for him was solitary. No one except her knew that he was gone forever. His soul, his personality vanished into some nameless oblivion. She missed him very much. His death was a secret she shared only with Aris and now he, too, had deserted her in her mourning.

"Hey boss, are you okay? You've been really quiet the last few weeks." Deep concern for her friend filled Maggie's voice as she broke the silence.

"I'm fine, Maggie. It's just been such a confusing time." She paused a moment. "At least Carlos is still alive." She knew she was telling Maggie a lie but there was no way around it. "There's always a chance he'll come back to his sessions. He's been through a lot and I'm sure it's a big adjustment, even losing that gang-leader scum, Manu. I know that creep had Carlos shot, but Carlos felt they were like brothers for a long, long time. His whole life revolved around that gang and now the sun of his previous solar system doesn't exist anymore. His whole orbit is misfiring. It's like he's lost the only family where he felt he belonged." It wasn't just the gang members who disappeared into some dimension of Infinity.

"I don't get it. Why did Manu try to have him killed anyway if they were so close?"

"Manu was just using him all the time. Once Carlos found out Manu instigated a drive-by shooting where a rival gang member was killed, he became dangerous. They were safe while he was still a part of the gang but once he went straight, they were all afraid of him turning them in. He was the only one who had ever left the gang and I guess because he was no longer of use to them, they figured he was better off dead."

Maggie sat comfortably in the chair opposite Sarah. "Boy, the tables really turned on them in the end. Did the police ever get any leads on who took out Manu and the other two leaders?"

"No, they just closed the case as a gang vendetta. I think everyone is glad to just let the whole thing cool off."

"Has Colleen heard from him? After all she was his parole officer?"

"Every once in a while he'll check in. She said he has his own place to live now; he's not at the half-way house any more. His father disowned him once and for all, and his mother is too weak and frightened to see him. They sent his brother to live with his grandmother in Mexico to make sure he doesn't get involved with the wrong people like Carlos did. He really is on his own."

No one except Sarah knew just how on his own he was, a being out of his time, his element, separated from his own kind, living a lie. A noble vampire in a not-so-noble human world.

\#

She sat in her car outside the market watching the rain come down in torrents. The gray, empty parking lot matched the heavy feeling in Sarah's heart. There were times when she was able to bear the grief of losing Carlos with quiet resolve. This simply was not one of them. She sobbed uncontrollably, trembling with sorrow. She missed him so dearly. Thoughts of his determination to be a better person, his great sacrifice to keep his family and her safe from harm ripped her apart. How long could she grieve in silence? How long must she continue the charade that he was alive, just out of reach? She knew the answer. For always. Her thoughts brought a new onslaught of tears.

CHAPTER 2

A heavy autumn rain splashed showers of water on the floor of her balcony. It bounced with a "ping" onto the sliding glass door. Black ominous clouds coiled around one another in the sky. A gust of wind rattled the glass as Sarah sat on the sofa bundled under a cream colored afghan staring into space. The cover of the book propped on her knees held the likeness of Henry VIII, the wine in the glass resting on the coffee table was a soft merlot.

A sudden ring of her telephone shocked her from her sixteenth-century reverie, reminding her she was sitting in her condo in Chicago. Glancing at the caller I.D., she saw it was Colleen Stevens-Drake. Had it been anyone except her best friend, she would have ignored the call.

"Hi C." Sarah could hear the sound of traffic and windshield wipers. "What in the world are you doing out in weather like this?"

Colleen laughed. "I like it. There's hardly anybody on the road. Besides, I'm on my way to the police station. One of my parolees has screwed up and I'm trying to save his butt."

"Sounds familiar." Sarah took a sip of her wine, placing the glass back on the coaster.

"I know what you mean but, trust me, this guy isn't like Carlos. I've never been assigned a con who is as good a guy as Carlos. He's really turned his life around." She laid on her horn. "I wanted to tell you, he called."

"Carlos?"

"Yeah.

"When?"

"This morning. He sounded strange but genuinely glad to talk to me."

"Yeah?" Sarah wanted to ask her friend for more information but she controlled her desire.

"He asked if I thought you would see him. I thought that was pretty weird; he knows how you feel about him. Anyway, I told him I knew you'd be glad to see him and I think he's going to call you. I just wanted to give you a head's up so you won't be surprised."

"I'll be waiting for his call." Her heart raced as she said goodbye to her friend and hung up the phone. Now her greatest wish and her biggest nightmare was about to happen. She was going to see Aris again.

CHAPTER 3

Sarah had barely stepped into the elevated car when the doors snapped closed behind her. The seats and aisles were filled with commuters just beginning their workday. Some of them sipped coffee, some read newspapers and some just slept with their eyes wide open focused on some netherworld just outside the smudged, fogged window. A chilly wind had blown across the platform as she waited for the train, making her grateful for all the heat from the bodies jammed into the narrow compartment.

Just as she settled in, holding tightly to a strap to keep from being tipped over, she noticed a tall, dark man. He was amazing looking and she couldn't take her eyes off him. Almost a full head taller than anyone else standing in the car, his dark eyes and golden complexion reminded her somehow of Carlos. His features were more mature, refined, chiseled, and his coal black hair lay in soft waves on his turned up coat collar. She thought she saw a tinge of gray in the perfectly trimmed hair at temples.

As he turned fully to face her, his eyes locked onto hers and held them. Unable to tear away, she had no idea how long they stood fixated in the middle of a crowd, seeing only each other.

Suddenly the train stopped. Sarah heard the name of her station over the P.A. A strange confusion overtook her as she turned to hurry out the door. Embarrassed by the feelings she was having at the thought of the stranger, she felt the color rise high to her cheeks as she made her way up the stairs and into the morning light.

#

Sarah knew that in most cases it was almost impossible for a client to have social interaction with their therapist. She was glad that it was different with Bonnie Petrillo and her. They began their relationship as colleagues sharing an office together. When Sarah went through her divorce, it was only natural that Bonnie was the one to assist her. As they learned more about one another, they began developing a closer kinship. Then when Sarah decided she needed to start going to the gym to lose her fifteen marriage pounds as she called them, Bonnie joined her. Before long they became great friends.

The two women had just finished their dinner and the waitress cleared their table as they sipped their wine. "Why do you want to come back now? I'm not talking you out of it mind you, Sarah, you just always felt you didn't need to do any further past life regression sessions."

"I know, but things have changed. I don't want to do it for therapeutic reasons. I've really gotten hooked on sixteenth century history lately and I'd like to see if there's any connection to a past life during that period hidden somewhere in my subconscious." Bonnie would never understand if she shared the truth. Sarah was actually beginning to believe the story Aris told her; she might have lived a different life during the time of Henry VIII. She might have known and loved Aris in a time long past. "I'd just like to explore the possibility. And besides, past life regression sessions are a lot more fun than reading a book. Okay?"

"Of course, I don't have my schedule with me, but I'll call you tomorrow when I get to the office and we'll set things up." Bonnie signaled for the waitress to bring two more merlots to the table as the friends settled in for a long over-due girl's night.

#

Sarah's palms began to perspire every time she thought of seeing Aris at one o'clock that afternoon. She could almost see her breath in the air as she stepped on the elevated platform hoping their unseasonably cold autumn didn't herald a freezing cold winter. Snow and slush were one thing, but sub-zero weather chilled her to her very bones.

She was traveling to her office a half hour early to catch up on some work before Maggie arrived. She couldn't sleep anyway. Her heart had been out of sync ever since Maggie told her he had called to make an appointment for a session.

She realized in the middle of her sleepless night, whenever she thought of Carlos she thought of him as he was before, a man and a messenger for an other-worldly being. He was no longer that man. He was the other-worldly being, the embodiment of something older than she could conceive. It frightened and excited her at the same time. Their time together since the transformation had been brief and they hadn't been alone. How would she feel sitting across from a vampire? Something deep inside her knew she was physically safe with him. But what of her emotions? Where would they take her? She felt her knees go weak at the thought of his great power and wisdom. With Carlos, she had been the teacher and now their roles would be reversed. If there were roles. Would they continue . to see each other? What did she want? That was the question that kept her awake at night. What did she want?

Suddenly the doors slid open and the mysterious stranger with the turned up collar she had seen the day before stepped onto the train. Sarah's eyes raced to the floor to keep from acknowledging his presence. He knew she saw him and he smiled a slow smile as he stepped to the other end of the car.

#

They heard the outer door of the office open.

"Hello ladies."

Maggie turned and gave him her most welcome smile. "Hello Carlos, great to see you." Sarah couldn't help see her assistant look him up and down as he crossed the room to her office.

"How are you Maggie?" He touched her shoulder gently as he passed. Maggie grinned as she winked at Sarah, touching her forefinger to her tongue and then to her hip signifying "hot" as she watched him walk into Sarah's office.

He hesitated in the door for just a moment.

"Have a seat." She motioned to the chair across from her desk.

He closed the door behind him then sat. His tight jeans and black leather boots were new. She scrutinized him. He looked like Carlos. The features were the same. But that is where the similarity ended. His mannerisms were different. He carried himself with the easy assurance of someone who is always in control of their environment, of someone without fear. There was a deeper magnetism beyond his physical beauty. She knew his black eyes held the sorrows and joys of hundreds of years. From some unaccountable place inside herself, she was again reassured without a doubt she was safe with him; she knew he would never hurt her. She stood behind her desk and moved to the chair by the window. He joined her. They sat across from one another, the coffee table keeping a safe distance between them.

Neither of them wanted to speak first. Silence hung heavy in the room. When an interminable amount of time had passed, she was the one to break it, her voice matter-of-fact, clinical.

"So, you took over Carlos' body."

"Yes."

"You have been living through him since that day in the hospital."

"I have been living instead of him. Carlos died that day, Sarah. You know he did. His life force departed and I transferred my consciousness into his body before it could begin to deteriorate. I swore to you I would never hurt Carlos and I did not. He breathed his last living breath before I entered this body. I can only enter the body of a dying human, Sarah. I have not taken the life of an innocent since the time of Katherine of Aragon and I did not take Carlos' life."

"Really? What about Manu and his friends?"

"Sarah, Manu Silva was not an innocent. He would have killed Carlos' brother or you without thought. The fiend had Carlos shot when he lost power over him. His fear that Carlos would betray his thievery and murder to the police drove him to take the life of a good man. I delivered Manu a painless death, a clean kill. I did not touch a drop of his blood nor the blood of his cohorts."

"I suppose you think that makes it alright?"

"Alright? Of that I am not sure. But it was justice."

"And you were judge and jury?"

"Yes. I was judge, jury and executioner."

She shook her head in abject frustration. "How do you think knowing that and not ever being able to tell anyone makes me feel? How do you think knowing this whole bizarre, insane story makes me feel?"

He leaned forward as he spoke, "Sarah, I do not know what the future holds for either of us. I am a being out of my time." His eyes were tender as he gazed into hers. "I know how awkward, how strange, this must be for you. You do not even know who I am." He stood. "May I come closer to you?"

After a tense moment, silently she nodded her head. He moved to stoop next to her and held his hands toward her. Reluctantly she placed her palms on his. She was surprised at their warmth.

"I am Aris. Carlos is no more. This body is a vampire body

possessing all of the supernatural abilities of my kind. I am here because I have searched for you, my beloved from the past. I found you and now I must know you. All that I ask is that you will allow me to see you, to spend time with you."

He waited for her answer. When it didn't come, he continued. "I will never harm you. I vow to never take the life of another innocent for the rest of my existence. I will not kill to sustain myself. There are other ways to quiet the hunger for human blood in your modern times. All I ask is the opportunity to show you who I truly am."

She drew her hands away from his, stood, then turned away. "It's an almost impossible situation. Even if I can accept the whole vampire concept, when I look at you I see Carlos. I will always see Carlos. How will I ever be able to separate the two of you?"

He rose, stepping closer. Reaching to turn her toward him, he felt her stiffen as he touched her shoulder. "Look into my eyes, Sarah. Look deeply. Is it truly Carlos you see?"

Silence filled the room. Suddenly she realized the only sound she heard was the sound of her own breath. The man standing next to her had no need to breathe. She grew pale and began to tremble. Not wanting to frighten her, he removed his hand quickly. He stepped away.

"Come, Sarah, let us sit." He guided her back to her desk chair, seating himself with the large piece of furniture between them. "We will take this slowly, as slowly as you see fit. I will live now as Carlos. It has taken me hundreds of years to find my love from the sixteenth century, my Elizabeth. I found her in you and as I have come to know you, Sarah, I have found my love of the present time. I will wait for as long as it takes for you to remember our past, for you to look upon me as a friend. My one hope is that one day you will grow to love me as you once did. I have all eternity to wait." Looking up at her under his long black lashes, his eyes pled for her acceptance. "And if you never love me, I pray you will allow me to remain as your friend, your champion. My fondest dream is you will give me the good fortune simply to allow me to share your life."

Folding her hands in her lap, she dropped her gaze. "I can't begin to think about the future. The present is freaking me out sufficiently at the moment." There was a long pause before she spoke again. "I hope you can understand. I just have to have some time to digest this. I need some time alone to just think it through."

Sensing that she was afraid of his other-worldly life, he withdrew his devoted attention. Speaking simply as a friend, his voice was soft and kind. "I understand, Sarah, and I am here whenever you find yourself ready to know me as I truly am. I will leave you now to your solace and your thoughts."

He rose and silently left the room, closing the door without a sound. She could faintly hear Maggie laugh at something he said to her as she folded her arms on her desk, buried her face in them and began to cry softly.

She was shaking, afraid of what would happen if she allowed Aris into her life. He had been just a phantom being living in Carlos' brain, but now, he was alive, a vampire. He wasn't human. She knew he believed she was connected to his past, his soul mate. She was terrified and afraid of being terrified. She thought she would burst if she couldn't talk to someone about him, but she knew no one would believe her if she told them. She dried her eyes then turned her chair to gaze out her office window, losing herself in the Chicago skyline.

#

The hour was late as she let herself into her apartment. Turning on the light and hanging her coat in the closet, she looked forward to a warm cup of tea. She glanced through the mail in her hands before she laid it on the hall table next to her purse.

Turning, she made her way to the stove then set the kettle on the burner. It had been a long day and she couldn't get Carlos out of her thoughts. No, it was Aris. But he looked like Carlos. Sometimes she thought she would lose her mind at the impossibility of her present reality. She stood, staring into space, immobile, while her thoughts raced at break-neck speed. She tried to put a halt to them, or at least slow them down as she opened the cupboard to find a cup.

She brewed her tea, stirred a huge tablespoon of honey into it and crossed to her bedroom. Turning on the light, she yawned. She almost dropped the mug when she looked toward her bed. Lying on her pillow was one long stemmed blood red rose. She gasped as she realized someone had been in her apartment. Reaching for the phone, she called the lobby. The doorman answered in two rings.

"This is Sarah Hagan, Tom. Has anyone been here asking to see me this evening?"

"Why, no, Miss Hagan. It's been quiet all evening."

"Have you been away from the desk at all."

"No Miss, I've been glued to this seat since five o'clock. My relief had an emergency and he's late. I haven't moved since I got here."

"Thank you, Tom."

She hung up the phone with one word on her lips. "Aris." She knew if he were still there, he would have shown himself.

It took everything she had not to call him and let him know it wasn't okay to sneak into her apartment without telling her. Not now, not ever. She caught herself just in time, deciding to wait until their next session. She couldn't allow herself to think about it. If she thought about it, she would explode. She turned off the light and in full denial; she went into the bathroom to prepare for bed. "I'm exhausted. I'll think about it tomorrow."

CHAPTER 4

The recliner in Bonnie's office felt familiar and comfortable as she leaned back into the soft leather cushions. After her divorce she visited Bonnie for weekly therapy sessions to work through all the steps of finding herself as a single woman again. That painful part of her life seemed so distant now and her reason for these current sessions so absurdly different.

Decorated in beige and taupe, the room promoted an atmosphere of relaxation, a sense of well-being and peace. Sarah desperately needed the respite from her confusion. She needed to let go of her tumultuous present, to have a moment in a different reality. She sighed deeply as Bonnie began the familiar induction. Her muscles grew soft; she felt her consciousness was floating a few inches above her body. Bonnie's well-defined words took her back through space and time to a century long ago.

SARAH HAGAN, transcript, session 1
"In your imagination, look at your surroundings. Absorb them." She was quiet for a moment allowing her friend time to adjust to the hypnotic state. She spoke quietly. "Where are you Sarah?"

"Cotswold in the manor house of my father, Sir Henry Wyatt."

Sarah's voice was soft, her words slightly slurred, as if she found it difficult to speak.

"I am standing in the great hall as the servants light candles against the twilight. The flames dance in reflection on the pale green mullioned windows."

"What year is it Sarah?"

"It is 1530."

"What season?"

"It is autumn and there is a chill in the air. It is near the time of All Hallows Eve and the manor is bustling with wonderful smells of harvest pies and cakes baking in the ovens of the kitchen."

"What else do you see Sarah?" Sarah lay silent for a few moments as Bonnie watched the movement of her eyes beneath her eyelids.

"The room is large, long with a high, high ceiling. The great gray stones of the walls are covered with enormous intricate tapestries. Deep, rich, colorful carpets are piled high against the cold of the stone floor. My father's pride rests in these carpets brought from the East, the bright colors and thick weave legendary in King Henry's kingdom."

"What is your name?" Silence once again. "Can you tell me your name?"

She spoke with reluctance, stumbling through the words. *"Elizabeth Wyatt, oldest daughter to Sir Henry, one of the King's knights, older sister to Jane who is fourteen and James who is eight."*

"How old are you Elizabeth?"

"I am just seventeen and well past marriageable age yet my father is opposed. He wishes me to go to King Henry's court. He hopes for a husband that will care well for me that I may know the luxury of court life."

"Can you tell me about your life?"

As she spoke, the words rolled off her tongue as if she finally was able to communicate easily as Elizabeth. *"My life is glorious, full of forests and meadows, horses and riding. My father is much different than most fathers. He cares deeply for his daughters, treating them as treasures, not burdens or possessions to be used to better the family standing. My sister is quite lovely and very musical. I much prefer the out-of-doors. I would rather ride to the hunt than eat or sleep. My father* takes great pride in my hands on the reins and my ability with the bow. My mother admonishes me for such masculine traits and works tirelessly to find a position for me in the Queen's court. I have no desire to leave my home to travel to London, to be bound by all the pomp and tradition of the royal house. Here, in the country, I am free."

"Does your freedom mean a great deal to you Elizabeth?"

"My freedom is all to me. My father says my high spirit must not be fettered by any man."

Bonnie smiled as she thought how peculiar it was to hear Sarah speak with a distinct British accent, to hear her speak of prized traits so dissimilar to her dear friend. "Is there a man in your life? Are you in love, Elizabeth?"

"What is love to a woman of my station? If I am sent to court, even with my father as an advocate, the King will be the one to choose my husband. And from tales that are told of Henry, one does not want to be too fair in his presence or he will snatch you up like a cat with a mouse." She shook her head vehemently. "No, I choose to stay in the country and remain free."

"What more can you tell me?"

"My father calls. There are guests to greet. I must say farewell."

Bonnie turned off the recorder and closed her laptop. It seemed their trip to another time was at a close for the day.

#

Sarah remained silent for a few moments after Bonnie brought her back to real time.

"It went very well. Your subconscious mind slid easily into Tudor times and you found an identity immediately. What do you think? How did it feel to be Elizabeth Wyatt?"

"Very strange. I could feel the sensations of cold from the stones and smell the wonderful fragrances of things baking. Bonnie, isn't hypnosis just the most amazing thing?"

"You are preaching to the choir, remember? It's what I do all day long." She leaned forward. "Do you want to continue with the sessions?"

"Oh yes. I'm looking forward to our next one. What an amazing way to learn about the past. Same time next week?"

Bonnie laughed at her eager friend. "You're on, Lady Elizabeth. Don't forget to journal any memories that might come up or any dreams you might have."

Sarah realized she hadn't had one of her darkly erotic dreams since Carlos was killed. She wondered why.

CHAPTER 5

Aris telephoned her to reschedule the time of their next session needing to delay it a half hour. He reached her on her way to work. The cold wind whipped around Sarah's ankles as she hurried from the elevated train toward Saul's Deli for breakfast. It reverberated through the receiver of her cell phone making it difficult for Aris to hear her clearly. There was no problem with the new appointment time and once it was settled, she decided to tell him about her regression with Bonnie. She knew he would be interested.

As she began to speak, a huge gust of wind made it impossible for him to hear what she said. He heard only bits and pieces of words and asked her to repeat her statement.

"I said I did a past life regression with Bonnie. It was pretty amazing. I went immediately to Tudor times and Elizabeth Wyatt."

"So now perhaps you will see that I tell you the truth about our past."

"Perhaps, but I wasn't at the King's court. I was in my father's manor house with my family. The session didn't last very long but I remember everything. I'm so looking forward to having my next one."

"It is possible through your sessions you will go to Henry's court and you will remember me. Us. It is my hope."

She ignored his comment as she spoke. "I'm seeing Bonnie again next week. We'll just see where it goes."

"Yes Sarah, we will see."

"I'm at the restaurant. I'll speak with you soon."

"Goodbye, Sarah."

"Bye." She closed her phone as she pushed the heavy glass door open and walked into the warmth and noise of the restaurant.

#

Sarah was sliding into her favorite booth ready for coffee and a quick breakfast when she looked across the room and there he was, the mysterious stranger. "This is getting kind of creepy," she thought.

He rose from his seat and wound his way toward her through the crowded tables. He moved with grace that was uncommon in a man so masculine.

"Good morning. It seems we are destined to meet." He extended his hand. "I am DeMarco Brassi."

His hand was large, the fingers long and artistic. His voice was deep, resonant with a slight accent. From his name, she decided he must be of Italian descent.

"Yes?" Her tone was questioning, her voice a bit nervous.

"Are you Sarah Hagan? I just read a book on past life regression and you look very much like the photograph on the book jacket."

Relieved, she smiled at him. She had only been recognized a few times and it both embarrassed her and made her feel proud. "Yes, I'm Sarah Hagan."

"I, too, am a psychologist. I am visiting your country from Italy to attend a meeting of the International Society of Psychology. I know this is quite irregular, however I just read your book and I find your theories quite fascinating. When I first saw you, I actually had your book with me."

He smiled as he spoke and she felt she had seen him somewhere before their few encounters on the elevated train. After a moment she realized it must be because he looked much as Carlos would have looked had he lived another ten or fifteen years. "*Must be the tall, dark, handsome thing*," she thought.

"I apologize for intruding on your breakfast; however, I would very much like to ask you a few questions about your hypnotic theory. Would you mind if we spoke while you finish your coffee?" She thought, "*This guy is either full of old world charm or he has a brand new come-on I've never heard before.*" She was surprised when she heard herself say, "Won't you sit down for a moment, Mr. Brassi?" She wasn't accustomed to inviting strange men to have coffee with her.

"I would like that. And please, do not be so formal. Please call me DeMarco."

"And you may call me Sarah."

"Sarah. I will be brief so as not to take too much of your time. In your book, you never decisively describe the induction used to take the subject to another time. Was there a specific reason you withheld that information?"

"Very good question, DeMarco. Yes, each therapist develops their own induction so it changes from person to person. I didn't want to give my reader some specific words to expect. It might make them question the validity of the induction being used. I wouldn't ever want to add a subconscious wall between the working therapist and their client." She slid into her coat, alerting him to the fact their meeting was coming to a close.

"Thank you for taking the time for me." He stood when she did. "I have a few more questions I would like to ask. Would it be possible to meet again?"

She hesitated.

"Would you have breakfast with me here tomorrow? About the same time?" His voice was more confident than questioning. He was obviously a man who received most everything he requested.

She thought about it for just a moment. Not much harm could come to her at Saul's Deli. Besides, if anyone ever appeared to be a gentleman, DeMarco Brassi did. "Yes, I'd be glad to meet you and answer more of your questions." She thought that perhaps being in the presence of a startlingly handsome man who was obviously interested in her work might make her feel more normal. She knew she needed a bout with normalcy. And soon. "Tomorrow then."

He watched her as she slid out of the booth and left the restaurant.

"Tomorrow then." He spoke softly as he turned his collar up before he left the restaurant and stepped out into the Chicago wind. He smiled as he watched her walk away, yet the look in his eyes was angry, dangerous.

CHAPTER 6

She was always startled by Aris' appearance. As Carlos he had been handsome. Now he was glorious. As she sat behind her desk Sarah tried to pull her eyes from his, but she couldn't. She was locked in his gaze. The shape of his eyes, his eyelashes, all were pure Carlos. The fire, the love, the passion all were new. There was more intensity in his changed body than she knew existed. Gasping for air as she turned away, she realized she had once again been made breathless by Aris. Was it fear or exhilaration? She wasn't sure but she would be careful. She wouldn't allow him to lead her into anything except friendship--that is if a friendship is possible with a vampire.

He sat quietly, waiting for her to speak, knowing full well the power of his eyes.

She brushed the hair away from her face and smoothed her skirt as she turned toward him. "There is something I must ask you." Her tone was grave as she spoke. "Have you been in my apartment without my knowing?"

He dropped his eyes to the floor fully aware he owed her the truth. "Yes, I have."

"Please don't do that again. It's an intrusion on my privacy."

"I am truly sorry." He spoke to the floor. "Please believe me; I will respect your wishes. It will never happen again."

With his face cast down, all Sarah could see was the black thick hair on his head. On some level she understood why he needed to be near her. She was the only other person on the planet who knew who he was. He probably was aware she might be frightened. Perhaps that was why Colleen told her he asked if she would see him again.

Her tone softened. "Alright. You are forgiven."

He looked at her with a smile in his dark eyes.

"How did you get in without the doorman seeing you?"

Looking a bit embarrassed, he spoke. "Just like I got into castles in the sixteenth century, up the side of the building." He grinned and the grin was every bit Carlos. "Super powers, remember?"

She couldn't help but laugh. "Right, super powers. Just please remember, you don't have to do that. You're welcome to visit me in a more conventional way."

"Telephone to make an appointment?"

"No, telephone to ask me if you can visit me?"

"If you are willing, there is no purpose in waiting. May I see you this evening, just for a little while?" His voice was hopeful.

She sat quietly as she made her decision. As he waited, he was strangely aware of human time. It seemed to him hours passed, yet it was only a moment.

"Alright, this evening. Just for a little while."

He stood, sliding his arms into his black leather jacket. "Is eight o'clock too late?"

"Eight o'clock will be fine."

She rose from her desk chair to see him out. "This evening then." As she closed the door behind him, she realized her heart was racing in her chest. "*What's up with that,*" she thought. "*I'm not afraid of him.*" She leaned against the door for a moment. "*Is it possible I'm afraid of myself?"* The answer came instantly. *"More than possible, it's probable."* How could any woman resist such an irresistible man? *"But,"* she told herself, *"He isn't a man. He's an Immortal."* She shook her head disconcerted for a moment at her own decision. She crossed the room to sit at her desk and stare out the window.

#

She heard Maggie enter her office, but she didn't look up from the file she held in her hand. All she could think about was what she had just done--made a date with a vampire.

Maggie spoke softly. "Are you feeling alright?"

She wasn't sure how she felt about anything except nervous when she thought Aris was picking her up at eight o'clock. Why had she agreed to see him?

"Boss?" Maggie touched Sarah's forehead to see if she had a fever. "Sarah, are you okay?"

"Oh, yeah, I'm fine. Just thinking about Friday afternoons."

#

She changed her clothes three times, but she still wasn't sure it was right. Sarah was nervous. Anxious. Elated. All at the same time. She hadn't felt giddy in the pit of her stomach for years and she liked it. She felt a bit out of control and it excited her. At the same time, it also worried her to feel so out of her element. After the pain of her divorce, she regained control of her feelings and maintained her emotional equilibrium by building safe, secure walls around her heart. She wondered if the handsome Immortal had the power to break down her defenses.

She stepped in the bathroom to look at herself in her full-length mirror. She was finally satisfied. Her dark jeans and knee boots suited the crisp autumn air and the cream colored turtleneck sweater would keep her warm beneath her jacket. She wondered where Aris would take her.

The doorbell rang.

She quickly pulled a brush through her hair, turned off the light and crossed the living room to open the door.

He looked taller than usual as he stood in her hall. *"Must be his invincible thing,"* she thought as she stepped aside to let him in.

He didn't cross the threshold. "Are you ready for our first evening together?" He raised his hand, motioning toward the elevator.

She only paused a moment before she answered. "I'm ready. Let it all begin."

#

Lake Michigan lapped gently against the breakwater as they strolled slowly along the top of the huge rocks forming it. Sarah was enjoying the crisp dark night and the light sprinkling of stars above them. There was no horizon line, just a solid darkness as far as the eye could see.

They stopped to look behind them at the city. Lights glowed from the windows of the skyscrapers, creating a glowing aura surrounding the tall buildings. A sudden cool gust of wind blew off the lake sending a chill through her. She shivered noticeably.

"Are you cold?" He moved closer to her.

"A little." She stepped back, looking up into the darkening sky. "Look, what a bright star. Or is it a planet?"

His eyes followed her direction to the heavens. "Stars twinkle, planets shine. I believe you are right. It is a star. Is it not your custom to make a wish on a star?" He wanted to hold her but he was afraid she would bolt if he strayed too close so, in Carlos style, he jammed his hands into his pockets.

"When I was a little girl, I always said the 'Star light, star bright' poem. I made the same wish every time."

"Now I must know, what was your wish?" He caught her eye and smiled.

"Well, I wished I'd grow up to do something that would help

people." She smiled in return.

"So, your wish came true?"

For a moment, the evening air was silent except for their breathing. He realized early on that she was more comfortable with him when he breathed. Their eyes locked. She was the first to stir, to step away. Hesitantly, they returned to their walk leaving the skyline behind them. The sky was a deep indigo blue, the color of her romantic dream skies as the couple looked out over Lake Michigan. A few more stars began to twinkle.

"Do you suppose I might make a wish?"

Sarah smiled and nodded yes. "First you must repeat the poem." She spoke the age old lyric. "Then you just wish. But you can't tell anyone what you wish or it won't come true." She laughed the lightest and happiest laugh. He felt assured for the first time she was truly comfortable with him, no longer apprehensive.

"I am ready." He stood very still, scanning the sky for the most brilliant star. When he found it, he closed his eyes. She heard him mumble under his breath. Soon even that ceased. The only sounds were the gently lapping waves and the murmur of the city behind them. He opened his eyes, staring down at the dark water and the swirling white foam on the breakers as they crested against the rock.

As Sarah stepped closer, he caught hold of her arm. Turning her to him, he placed his cool hands on either side of her face. His touch was tentative, light. She could feel his warm breath as he touched her lips so softly she wasn't sure he was really there.

He released her and stepped away. "A wish, sealed with a kiss. A perfect end to a lovely evening. Are you ready to return home? The hour is growing late."

"Yes, you're right, it is getting late. It's best you take me home." She decided to act as if nothing had happened between them, but her lips felt warm and her legs trembled as he held her arm and guided her to the street to call a taxi.

CHAPTER 7

Of all mornings to oversleep, this was definitely the wrong one. Her thoughts had been so full of Aris when she crawled into bed, she forgot about her breakfast plans with the handsome Italian doctor. She neglected to set the alarm.

"*I hope he doesn't leave,*" she thought as she hurried out the door to the elevator. Glancing at her watch, she anxiously waited for the familiar ding.

Half walking and half jogging, she hurried through the crisp, clean smelling morning air while wrapping her light weight muffler more securely around her throat. The elevated platform was hardly crowded; most of the morning commuters were already on their way downtown. She tried to telephone the deli to tell him to wait for her, but the phone was busy each time she rang. "I hope he waits, I hope he waits," her mind chanted in time with the clicking of the train over the track. Dialing again, the familiar irritating beep-beep of the busy signal was her only answer. She muttered under her breath, "*What in the hell is going on with that phone?*"

After an interminable time, the train entered the station. Sarah tried the deli's phone again then gave up realizing, at last, lunch deliveries to the near-by offices were scheduled in the morning so the phone was incessantly in use. Rushing down the street toward the restaurant she wondered, *"Why am I being so neurotic about this?"*

The tables were still crowded when she entered. He caught her eye smiling a greeting as he waved to her from the back of the restaurant. She was surprised to see he was even more appealing than she remembered, dressed impeccably in a dark business suit and navy blue cashmere coat. *"Incredibly handsome and he's even human,"* she thought.

"I'm so sorry I'm late." She was a little out of breath from her hurried trip from the train station. "I tried to call the deli several times, but the phone was busy."

"That's quite alright. I understand, however, I just received a text from a colleague. I have a meeting scheduled this morning, which I forgot and I must rush. I hope you will forgive me." They stood, her face lifted to meet his eyes; he was a whole head taller than she was. "I know we've just met and you don't know me at all, nevertheless I must ask. Would it be possible that we meet for drinks or dinner this evening, your choosing? I find the subject of past-life regression most interesting and you are the first expert I have met."

He tipped his head toward her in a gesture that reminded her, once again, of Carlos. What could happen in a restaurant? The truth was she wanted to see him again. It had been so long since she was out on a date with someone of her own species, she wondered if she would know how to act. Hastily, she responded. "Yes. Let's meet at The Bistro. It's just a few blocks south of here."

"Six o'clock?"

"Yes, six o'clock will be fine. I'll be on time."

Smiling what seemed a grateful smile, he turned toward the door. His teeth were straight and white against his golden Italian skin. Sarah was puzzled at her immediate reaction of acceptance. She wasn't accustomed to meeting strange men for dinner.

As he crossed the restaurant toward the door to the street his cell phone rang. Turning to wave goodbye to Sarah, he answered. As he stepped through the door onto the sidewalk, he spoke. "Yes, I just met her." He was silent as the voice on the other end of the telephone spoke. When he replied, his tone was angry. "Leave it to me. She suspects nothing. If I need your help, I will ask for it." Without waiting for a response, he ended the call, dropped the telephone in his coat pocket and hurried down the street.

#

"So, have you heard from him?" It was past the noon hour and the lunch crowd had thinned. There were just a few late comers still in the restaurant. The mid-day noise of the busy diner had quieted, making for an easy conversation. Sarah was hungry and dived into her salad without hesitation as soon as the waitress placed it on the table. That morning she left Saul's immediately after her Italian doctor without eating, missing her breakfast entirely.

"Colleen, if you don't quit living on burgers, you're going to have cholesterol that is over the moon." Sarah eyed the double burger and fries her best friend was wolfing down practically whole. "At least chew, for heaven's sake. That baby you're carrying is going to come out crying for a quadruple burger on a toasted bun with extra pickles instead of a bottle."

"Give me a break." Colleen laughed. "First my husband is on me about what I eat and now you. Bob nags me constantly about food and vitamins and exercise. I'm a saint at home so cut me a little slack once in a while, okay? Besides, I've been so sick the last few weeks, I couldn't eat much of anything." So saying, she dipped a huge French fry into an enormous glob of ketchup and popped it into her mouth. "And, you didn't answer me. Have you heard from him?"

"I assume 'him' means Carlos." Sarah wasn't quite sure how to answer. "He's been in touch and he seems to be doing fine."

"What the hell does that mean? After spending a couple of years trying to keep the guy straight, 'doing fine' doesn't cut it."

"Well, he's still gainfully employed and he's still in his own apartment."

"That guy has sure had some hard luck." Colleen shook her head as she spoke. "And some amazing luck. I still get freaked out when I think how that bullet wound in his gut just disappeared. I'll never figure that one out."

"Neither will the doctors." Sarah finished eating the last bites of her salad, stacked her silver on the plate and pushed it to the side of the table. *"And I'm damned glad of that,"* she thought as she waved the waitress to bring some more iced tea. She added an additional sugar packet to the remnants of the amber liquid and ice cubes pooling in the bottom of her glass.

"I'd sure like to see him. If you speak to him soon, why don't you ask him to come with you to Thanksgiving dinner. I know Bob would like to see how he's doing. He saw a lot of good in Carlos and for my hard-nosed cop husband to see anything good in a con is really amazing." Colleen dragged her last remaining French fry through the dregs of ketchup on her plate and ate it, licking the final drop from the tip of her forefinger. "What do you say? Will you ask him? It'll just be us."

"Alright, I'll ask him if I talk to him before the holiday." She stood, ending their conversation. "Now come on, I've got to get back to work." After sliding her arms into her trench coat, she gathered her purse and scarf.

Colleen wondered if anyone noticed her tiny pregnancy bulge. She realized she was the only one who would notice such a small change; her waist had barely thickened. It made her happy to think she might already be showing a little bit. After the deep sorrow of losing her first baby when she was hit by a car, she was doubly excited to be expecting again. Patting her stomach with a smile, she put on her knitted jacket and gloves. Picking up the check, she reached in her pocket. As she withdrew a wad of crumpled money, she spoke. "I've got this one. Come on; let's go before the wind blows any harder." She wrapped her muffler around her neck as she dragged Sarah toward the door of the restaurant. The two friends hurried into the street just as the heavy dark clouds covered the mid-day sun.

CHAPTER 8

"Alright Sarah, lean back in the recliner and relax."

Sarah found Bonnie's suggestion difficult to follow. She was restless at the thought of her appointment that evening. She felt she was doing something she wouldn't want Aris to know about and she didn't understand why. Why did she need to keep her dinner engagement a secret from him? There could never be a romance between them. She and Aris were just friends. It had been their mutual decision to allow their relationship to evolve slowly of its own accord. She was irritated with herself for feeling she was doing something behind his back. It wasn't necessary for her to report in to him.

"Would you like to do this on another day? You seem a bit agitated."

"No. No, just give me a minute to breathe and clear my mind." Closing her eyes, she leaned against the cool leather. Focusing only on where she was in the moment, she began to relax.

Bonnie watched her friend grow more calm and when she felt all was well began the induction into hypnosis.

SARAH HAGAN, transcript, session 2

Bonnie led her back in time, back to the manor house in

Cotswold. "What's happening today?"

"It's the morning of All Hallows Eve and the maids are scurrying around, lighting the huge fireplace in our chamber. My sister, Jane, and I share a bed. We are huddled close waiting until the fire warms the air before we open the bed curtains. We love to lie in bed eavesdropping on the gossip of the two girls who serve us. They always know exactly what is about in our household and speak in loud whispers. If we listen closely, we can hear every word."

"There are gypsies in the forest. Have ye' heard?"

"I did hear. Head cook told the footman as I gathered kindling this morning. The footman told her his wife went last night to find the sex of their unborn child. An old woman with an eye patch covering her evil eye told him it was a male child."

"When I heard they were here, I hoped there was someone who read fortunes. Let's sneak out tonight. They might not be long in the forest."

"Nay. Tonight is All Hallows Eve. I wouldn't go into the forest for all the gold in the King's coffers." They finished lighting the fire and left the bed chamber.

"Elizabeth," my sister whispered as she pulled the covers over our heads so no one might hear us. "Let us, you and I, go tonight." While my sister was younger than I, she was more fearless and secretly craved dangerous excitement. "There will be fires and music and fortune telling. We shall ask when you will be married." She giggled as she spoke the words.

"We shall do nothing of the kind. Father would be mad with worry if he should find us missing."

"He will not find us missing. Rolled bedding under our covers will appear as two sleeping girls. Please, Elizabeth. It will be such a lark."

"No," I said. But she could tell from the sound of my voice, I was intrigued. Gypsies. Never in my life had there been gypsies in our forest. I wondered if this would be our only hope of seeing them and I so wanted my fortune read.

All during the day she pled to see the gypsies. She could see me weaken at each request. At last, at early twilight, I agreed. When the evening fire burned low, we would sneak through the kitchens to the stables. We would walk our horses until out of earshot of the inhabitants of the great house then ride like the wind to the forest.

It seemed forever before the household was quiet. Silently we crept to the stables. The horses responded as if they were knowingly involved in our clandestine outing. They were calm as we walked them from the stable and through the great gates of the courtyard. Once on the outer road, we mounted and galloped toward the forest trail. It seemed just a short time before we heard music and saw the glow of the fire of the camp.

Tying our horses to a tree, we crept through the remaining woods toward the sounds. As we approached the clearing we were mesmerized by the strange vision of these vagabonds in our country. Primitive wooden wagons formed a circle around a blazing campfire; the firelight danced on the colorful flowers painted on their outer walls. Overhanging roofs made tiny porches where some of the dark-skinned, dark-eyed women sat smoking pipes, tapping their bare feet in time to the drum and violins being played. The music was passionate and wild.

Suddenly a man leaped from one of the porches to land whirling in a spirited dance. He was magnificent, golden and muscular, his tightfitting black pants tucked into tall boots, his long black hair swirling around his beautiful face. Hoops of gold suspended from his ears glittered as he spun.

The tempo slowed, growing melancholy, dark. He stopped short, his arms raised above his head, wrists crossed. He appeared as a statue. His bare chest glistened with sweat as he seemed to halt even his breath. Then one foot stomped quietly into the soft earth. Then the other. His chin and chest raised high, he began to clap his uplifted hands in time with the drum. His feet met the tempo. His hips moved enticingly as the tempo increased until his steps were pounding the earth keeping pace with the increasing rhythm of the drumbeat. At the same moment the music ended, he leaped high in the air and landed on one knee, his chin tucked into his chest, his black hair wild around his shoulders. There wasn't a sound from anywhere in the camp. Both Jane and I stood frozen, trance-like, unable to speak or move. Such raw beauty, such grace and power. Never in our young lives had either of us seen such a sight.

At last he stood, laughing, pulling his damp hair away from his face, tying it with a scarf he drew from his pocket. His movement broke the spell and the camp came to life. The women applauded and began to chatter, the men clapped him on the back, handing him a huge goblet to ease his thirst. A dark-haired beauty moved from the shadows and placed a red rose in the belt of his trousers. He smiled, his perfect teeth white against his dark swarthy complexion.

"Come, Elizabeth, let us explore. We must find the woman with the patch to have our fortunes read."

The sound of her voice startled me. I was lost in the beautiful man that stood in the clearing. She took my hand and led me into the camp. As we circled the edge of the clearing making for the largest of the wagons, I could see him follow us with just his eyes. I felt I was wearing only my chemise as we climbed the steps. My face glowed red. I could not ascertain if the flush was from the heat of the bonfire or the unfamiliar sultry flame that filled my belly.

We paused at the doorway. There was no door; a simple embroidered shawl covered the entrance. "Come inside, my ladies." Her voice was old yet sprightly. "Come in."

Jane moved the shawl aside as we crossed the threshold. The interior of the wagon was lit by one small lamp and there sat the woman with the eye patch in a beautifully carved chair behind a table laid with large cards. So large that I could see they were filled with strange markings.

"Sit." She motioned us toward two barrels drawn close to the table. "Which maiden shall be first to have her fortune read?"

"I will," Jane spoke quickly. The crone held out her palms. With a tentative motion, Jane reached to touch her hands. The gypsy closed her eyes and appeared to go into a trance. I watched her. She was enchanting. Old and wrinkled, a life of work without luxury etched upon her face. Her hair gray and wispy, yet she had a dignity that even my own mother was without, dignity that only living a life to its fullest could produce. Questions began in my mind. How was it possible that this poor woman without a home, her life lived moving from place to place, was able to find such obvious peace? I listened with only half an ear as she told my sister lovely things. A long life. A good marriage. Children. Jane glowed with her every prediction.

She released Jane's hands then reached for mine. When my palms touched hers, a jolt shook my body. I tried to pull away but could not. It was as if we had become one. Staring at her over the lamplight, I watched as she closed her good eye. Tension flew from my body as I became relaxed and passive. It seemed a very long time yet I knew it was only moments before she looked upon me once again. She was still silent as she watched me. When she spoke, her voice was clear, all the aged tremor gone.

"My lady, your life will be wrought with mystery and danger, with love and death. Fear not, for in the end, all will bring you great joy."

With that she dropped my hands, rose and left the wagon. Jane and I sat, unable to move. The air around us seemed heavy, ominous.

"Come Elizabeth, we must go. We must return before we are missed." She laid a few coins on the table.

My legs felt weak as I stood and descended the few stairs to the ground. As we hurried from the camp, I could feel the eyes of the beautiful dancer follow us into the trees.

#

"This is great stuff." Bonnie shuffled in her chair as she adjusted her position. "I'm stiff as a board. I couldn't move while you were talking. I didn't want to miss a word."

"There are very clear pictures of what is happening to me. It's like

I really am right there. Wow, what an experience!"

"Sarah, it appears you have already made the connection you hoped to make. Is there anything else you'd like to share about the session."

Dazed, Sarah sat for a silent moment as she mulled over what had just happened in her subconscious. "No Bon, I really feel as if I'm still a little out of it."

"Why don't you just lie back and rest for a few more minutes. I don't have another client for a half an hour so take your time."

She was glad for a moment to herself in the quiet of Bonnie's office. She was amazed and delighted by the ease of the regression, the depth of the hypnotic state. She was anxious for the next session, hoping to see the bewitching man once again.

#

Performing her nightly grooming ritual, she allowed her mind to wander through her extraordinary day. Strange yet wonderful, overflowing with new experiences. Her missed breakfast, her amazing session with Bonnie. Cocktails with the Italian stallion. She wasn't sure why she was becoming involved with a man who didn't even live in the same country as she did but she couldn't deny there was an overwhelming physical attraction she felt for him. They had spent a delightful evening together. Their conversation over a glass of wine had been refreshing. His questions caused her to rethink her theories and rephrase them many times. His mind was stimulating in a way that was new to her. They laughed and enjoyed each other's company to such a degree that when he asked her to join him for dinner, it only seemed natural. He was a perfect gentleman, showing respect for her intellect as well as somehow making her feel like a desirable woman without putting any moves on her. When he asked if he could see her again, the only logical answer was yes.

Yet now that she was home in familiar surroundings, the

confusion set in once more. What was she doing? Should she tell Aris about DeMarco? Why was she even wondering if she was being deceptive? For God's sake, Aris was a vampire and he could only ever be her friend. The only way she could have any kind of a romantic relationship with him was to give up her human life to become an Immortal. She couldn't even imagine what that meant much less begin to contemplate doing it. Besides, DeMarco lived in Italy. Their relationship could never be more than a long distance friendship. Did she have to announce to Aris every new friend she met? That was out of the question.

In addition, she couldn't understand why she felt saddened at the thought of the good doctor returning to his home country? They had just met. Yet she did feel sad at the thought of never seeing him again. There couldn't possibly be any connection between the two of them so soon, but she was drawn to DeMarco. At least he was human.

What was happening to her well-ordered life? It was going to hell in a handbasket. She felt torn, yet exalted. And, somewhere, sandwiched in between the two, vampire and man, was the image of the fiery gypsy dancing around the fire. For the first time in a long time, Sarah was finding pleasure in the unfolding complexity of what had been a very staid life.

She smiled as she crawled into bed, pulling the covers close against the chill of the night. *"Just like Scarlett O'Hara, I'll think about it tomorrow."* She turned out the light as she closed her eyes.

#

A loud sound in her room woke her from a deep sleep. Sitting up quickly, her heart racing, she reached to turn on the light. Nothing had fallen and the room was empty except for her. *"Must have been dreaming,"* she thought, yawning as she stretched her arms over her head. She shook off the groggy feeling of being suddenly awakened at five o'clock in the morning.

"I'll never get back to sleep and it's so close to time to get up, if I do, I'll never wake up in time." She mumbled under her breath. "Might as well do some journaling."

She reached in the drawer of her bedside table and pulled out her journal and a pen. She propped her pillows into a huge pile against the headboard, then went to the kitchen to brew a cup of coffee. When she was snuggled back in her warm bed, steaming black liquid resting on the table beside her, she bent her knees to make a desk to lean the notebook against.

Where to begin? Sipping from the mug, she smiled. "I guess the session today is a good place to start." She leaned her head against the makeshift head rest, closing her eyes. She could see the clearing and the fire just as vividly as she had during her session. She remembered the gypsy in complete detail down to the light sheen on his damp, nude, muscular chest. Allowing herself to drift in and out of a gentle state of self-hypnosis, she was in a netherworld between sleep and wakefulness when the vision changed. She saw herself as Elizabeth Wyatt in the clearing with him, her golden hair loose, hanging below her waist. She wore bangles on her wrists and ankles, a full, colorful skirt whirled about her as she enticed him to dance. Her feet were bare as were her shoulders beneath her thin cotton top. Her breasts were free, unbound, and as she moved, the soft fabric caressed them gently, causing her nipples to stand firm and erect. The fire blazed brightly as he moved toward her. His arms went above his head, his wrists crossed. As if on signal, the violin and a concertina began to play from the dark night just outside the circle of firelight.

Turning, he caught her eyes with his, then slowly began side stepping closer to her, his hands clapping with each movement of his feet. He gazed down at her underneath his long, black lashes, his dark eyes flashing with passion.

Grasping her skirt in her hands, she lifted it high, showing her beautiful legs as she danced. She began to match her movements to his. It was as if they had been dancing together for a lifetime. The music grew more provocative, their dancing more uninhibited. They whirled around each other, reaching out yet not quite touching. Her heart raced in her chest, her breath came in gasps. He stopped short, his large hands wrapping around her small waist. Lifting her high, he buried his face in her soft belly, breathing in the fragrance of her. She thought she would burst with desire. Slowly he slid her over his body until they were thigh to thigh, abdomen to abdomen. She could feel the hardness of his manhood straining against his tight black pants. Arching her back, she pressed herself into him. He held her tightly, supporting her back with his strong arms; he leaned her backwards, his lips resting on her throat. He felt the beat of her heart pounding in perfect rhythm with his. Dropping her head back, she exposed her long beautiful neck, vulnerable, seductive. The music stopped. Hands clapped and feet stamped from the darkness that surrounded them. They stayed still, their breaths panting as one.

Suddenly he swept her into his arms, quickly carrying her through the camp and into his wagon. The only illumination was from a single candle burning on a small battered table. He laid her on a soft pallet on the floor.

She watched him as he undressed, stripping his black pants from his perfect body. He stood above her nude. He was erect. Strong.

When he stooped to her, the exotic male fragrance of him surrounded them. She reached her arms to him. Kneeling beside her, he began to undress her. First the skirt, then the lacy chemise that covered her breasts. Her body was pale in the candle light, enticing. His dark hands caressed her. Even in her desire, she noticed the deep contrast in their skin. It made him appear even more fascinating. He watched her as he began to stroke her body with his strong fingers. His touch was gentle as he held his passion in check. He didn't want to rush.

The glow of the candle made a halo of light around his dark head as he bent to kiss her breasts. His lips were cool, his tongue warm, exploring. She felt him with every fiber of her being. Winding her fingers through his hair, a deep ardent moan escaped from her throat. The sound unleashed the great passion he held in check.

Sliding his hands beneath her, he grasped her bottom lifting her legs to wrap them around his muscular back. She cried out with desire as he entered her.

They moved together as they had in the dance by the fire; uninhibited, as if they had shared this fiery passion all of their lives. First one then the other led; he was the master, then she.

As she sat astride him, he found his release. His back arched, his beautiful chest glistened in the candle light, moist from their effort. His chin raised, his eyes closed as his breath and movement halted; he looked like a perfect Greek statue frozen in time. After only seconds passed, an intense guttural sound escaped from his beautiful mouth. And then her name whispered over and over again. He raised up, wrapping his arms around her, kissing her lips, her throat, her breasts. Her body convulsed as he, once again, took control, rolling her on her back. His body responded instantly to her movements and he was once again hard, ready to deliver pleasure.

And so he did. Such pleasure that tears of joy poured from her eyes as she cried out.

The sound of her own voice in her Chicago bedroom and the sound of her breath coming in loud gasps brought her awareness back inside her body. She had been neither awake nor asleep but somewhere just in-between; a place where fantasy and reality joined in a perfect melody.

She slowly opened her eyes and glanced at the time. Six o'clock. "I really have to re-think this provincial attitude I have. It isn't

working too well right now." She laughed as she sipped her coffee.
It was cold and bitter.

CHAPTER 9

DeMarco sounded out of sorts when they spoke on the telephone. She wondered what was going on, but had the feeling he would tell her at lunch. He wanted to meet at Saul's for a quick bite at noon.

Hurrying down the street, she felt early light snow flurries melt against the warmth of her cheeks. Why did she always seem to be running behind schedule lately? She never before in her life had an issue with punctuality. Why now? Shrugging her shoulders inside her coat she wrote it off to all the life changes she was going through. *"Who is this masked woman,"* she thought. She laughed at herself as she opened the door to the warmth of the restaurant.

Scanning the bustling room, she saw him just as he stood to get her attention. He always seemed to arrive ahead of her no matter where they met. It was a bit disconcerting at times, but she told herself she liked a punctual companion.

"Hi." Her words caught in her throat and her blood rose to her cheeks as he reached across the table, resting his large warm hand on top of her small cold one. *"Must be the hot Latin blood,"* she thought with a smile.

"Hello Sarah." They each sat at the same time but he kept her hand in his. "Thank you for meeting me today."

He never looked more handsome than when he turned to speak with the waitress. He had the profile of a Roman god, the gray at his temples lending more mystery and magic to him than any one man deserved. He ordered warm tea for both of them, then turned to her once again.

Taking her hands in his, he removed her gloves. He rubbed her cold fingers in his warm ones, smiling at her with his eyes. Suddenly she was overwhelmed with intense desire. It took everything in her power to not reach across the table to kiss him. *"What the hell was that?"* Thoughts raced through her mind as she tore her eyes from his and glanced down. It took a few deep breaths before she regained her composure. DeMarco was signaling the waitress to fill her tea cup. She was glad he was looking away and hadn't seen her turn beet red.

He waited until he was facing her again before he spoke. "I have some good news and some not so good news. Which first, Sarah?"

"The not so good."

"I will be returning to Italy just before your Thanksgiving holiday."

She felt her shoulders sag at his words. "And the good?"

"I will be coming back to the states after the first of the year. I am thinking of joining a firm in your country and working here for part of the year studying hypnosis. What would you think of that?"

Elated that she wasn't losing him permanently, she replied, "I think it would be wonderful."

He stood, pulling her to her feet. Wrapping his arms around her, he kissed her long and hard right there in the middle of Saul's Deli. His lips were soft yet demanding. She yielded to him, wrapping her arms around his shoulders. When the kiss ended and she finally opened her eyes, she saw the entire corps of waitresses standing in front of the coffee machine watching them, huge smiles on their faces. She released him and smoothed her skirt, embarrassed by her public passionate response to him, but thrilled in spite of it.

#

Bonnie was lost in the song blasting through her earphones, shaking her head to the beat as her legs pumped the elliptical. Sarah laughed, reaching to touch her shoulder. Jumping, grinning sheepishly, she turned the music down to greet her friend.

"Hey Sarah. Wow. It seems like weeks since I've seen you here. Welcome back to the world of cardio."

"I know," she said, climbing on the treadmill, draping a towel around her neck, and placing her bottle of water in the rack on the front of the machine. "I can't believe how busy I've been."

"Colleen said she hasn't seen you much lately either. Is everything okay?"

Sarah took a deep breath. "Well," she hesitated a moment. "There's this guy."

Bonnie's legs stopped pumping and she removed the headphones completely. "What guy? Tell me."

"There's not a whole lot to tell yet. He's a psychologist from Italy here for a convention. He's interested in past life regression." Her cheeks colored. "And it looks like he's also interested in me."

"Don't stop until you've told me absolutely everything." Bonnie stepped to the floor, moving closer to Sarah to hear better over the loud music playing throughout the gym. She didn't want to miss a word.

"I've only seen him a couple of times, but I really like him. He's a little older than I am. Sort of a young old-world gentleman--not to mention absolutely gorgeous."

"Come on, more. What's his name?"

"DeMarco Brassi."

"No one is named DeMarco Brassi. It sounds like some fairy tale prince."

"Yeah? Well, he looks like some fairy tale prince. But he's a lot more than good looks. He's bright and attentive and interested."

"Are you sure he's not just some figment of your imagination."

"Nope, he's real." She glanced at her watch. "And I've got to get going or I'm going to be late for work. Don't tell Colleen. I want to tell her myself."

Bonnie climbed back on the elliptical and started to pump. "DeMarco Brassi. Wonder if there are any more at home like him?" Bonnie grinned at the thought as she placed the little earphones in her ears and started to hum along with the song.

#

"It seems like forever since we've all just hung out. Is Bonnie coming when she finishes work?" Colleen sipped her herb tea, leaning back into the soft cushion on the sofa, stretching her legs, her feet propped on the pillow at the other end.

"Lean forward, honey." Bob moved to fluff the cushion, placing it lower to support his pregnant wife's back. "Okay, now relax." She kissed him lightly on the cheek. It was a delight for Sarah to see them so happy. After miscarrying their first child, Colleen's second pregnancy was moving along without a glitch. Her best friend looked radiant as pregnant women were supposed to look. Bob beamed as he patted his wife's barely visible tummy. "Got to keep the two of you fat and happy."

Sarah sipped her wine. "Yeah, I spoke to Bon just before I got here; she said she'd be along as soon as she could close down for the day. She's been really busy lately."

"What about you, Sarah? We haven't seen you in too long. What's up?"

Sarah had been looking for the perfect opening to tell them about DeMarco; it appeared this was that moment. "There's kind of this new man in my life. Well, not exactly in my life." She wondered silently how old she would have to be to stop blushing. "Sort of in my life."

Colleen sat up, swinging her legs off the sofa and leaning forward. Bob settled in next to her. "Tell us, we're waiting."

"There's not too much to tell. We haven't been seeing each other very long but I admit I do like spending time with him." Sarah described her new friend to her old ones. As she listened to herself describing their relationship, she realized she really was glad he was considering working in the states for a while. She would miss their camaraderie if he left. He was a comfortable companion, sharing the same profession, having so many of the same interests. Not to mention his lips were delicious, he smelled wonderful and she was powerfully attracted to him. She grinned as she thought, *"It's also great being the same species."*

The ringing of the doorbell ended their questioning. "I'll get it." Bob stood.

A chilly autumn wind stirred the living room curtains as he opened the front door. "Carlos, hey. Come in." Stepping aside, Bob showed the man he thought to be Carlos into the living room. It was the Immortal's first interaction with the small group of friends since Carlos died and Aris took over his body. Sarah was nervous the group might sense the difference in him. A moment of discomfort at their reunion surrounded them all until Colleen stood, walked to him and gave him a huge bear-hug.

"It's so great to see you." She stepped back, holding him at arms-length. She looked him up and down then whistled. "Hey dude, you look great."

He grinned. "So do you." He reached his hand toward Bob. "Congratulations, man, about the baby, I mean." As he shook hands with him it was one hundred percent Carlos, no Aris anywhere to be seen. He flopped down on the sofa and leaned back, folding his hands behind his head. "It's great to see you guys." They all suddenly felt quite at ease. The awkward moment passed. They were just friends together again.

Sarah was very much relieved. She felt anxious when Colleen told her he would be there. She didn't know what to expect of him. When they were alone, she knew a very different person. One that was mysterious and wise, sensual and deep. One that had the experience of ages behind him and an eternal future ahead of him. She felt glad and sad at the same time as she looked at the dark, handsome man sitting on the sofa. She missed her young friend yet here he was, appearing to be alive and well.

"Sarah, hon, Bob asked if you'd like another glass of wine. You looked like you were far away."

"No C, I'm right here." She grinned as she reached her glass forward for a refill. "Right here."

CHAPTER 10

Colleen was less than enthusiastic when Sarah suggested she and Bob have dinner with Sarah and DeMarco. She would have much rather been out with Sarah and Carlos, but she agreed anyway just to satisfy her curiosity about the new man in Sarah's life. She was glad she did when the smell of Thai food stirred her taste buds as she and her husband walked in the door of the Thai Palace. They had never eaten there but Bob said he had read great reviews on the internet. The restaurant was packed and noisy even on a Thursday evening. DeMarco and Sarah sat at a table in the only semi-quiet corner in the room, clearly deep in conversation.

"Hi. Are we late?" Colleen slid into a chair across from her best friend.

"No, we were early." Sarah smiled as she made introductions. DeMarco stood, leaning over the table to shake hands with the couple.

"I've heard so much about you." The dark Italian doctor spoke softly, his deep resonant voice easily heard over the racket made by the patrons enjoying their evening meal.

Colleen laughed as she spoke. "Well, Doc, I haven't heard nearly enough about you."

Shaking her head, Sarah spoke, exasperation clear in her voice. "C, I thought I told you, no cross examinations tonight." She turned toward DeMarco. "She's so accustomed to being in a courtroom, she forgets herself sometimes."

"Hey, I didn't forget myself. I don't know nearly enough about this guy." She grinned making her words light, but she meant it. She was protective of her friend.

Bob took the lead smoothing a moment that could have become uncomfortable. "We've got all evening to get to know one another. Let's order a bottle of wine and look at the menu."

DeMarco looked relieved as he reached for the wine list.

#

"Well, I wasn't sure at first, but I ended up liking the guy okay." Colleen spoke over the sound of her windshield wipers as she drove home from the court house. "Just okay, I guess I'm still not sure."

"What are you not sure of?" Sarah sat at her desk doodling infinity signs on a yellow-lined tablet. Rain pummeled the office windows, causing the lights in the office building across the street to twinkle in the early twilight.

"Well, to be honest, he seemed pretty stuffy at first."

"C, has it ever entered your mind that you might be just a little bit overwhelming to a normal person?" Sarah teased her friend.

"Me? Never. Anyway, Bob says he's okay too. I think he's just glad to see you doing something besides work. And he wants you to have someone special in your life." Their conversation halted as a fire engine drove by Colleen's car, the siren blasting. When it had passed, she continued. "We were hoping for Carlos, but since you seem to be in complete denial about him, the Italian Stallion will have to do."

"I'm glad you approve." Sarah laughed. "I like him a lot." Her voice was light, happy.

"My question to you, my perky little friend, is could this possibly be a man who just might have the key to open the chastity belt you've been wearing for way too long?"

"We'll just have to see, won't we? We'll just have to wait and see."

CHAPTER 11

All of Sarah's friends teased her for getting ready for Christmas the weekend before Thanksgiving arrived, but she couldn't help it. She looked forward to the holiday season all year and when it finally was upon her, she welcomed it joyfully.

She dragged the four large green plastic storage bins that held her Christmas decorations out of her guest closet. After stacking them neatly in the living room, she methodically removed lid after lid, eyeing her collection of ornaments. She reminisced about her childhood years with her parents and her married years with her ex-husband, Jeff. She thought long and hard about her present, the unreal ordinariness of it all.

In some insane corner of her mind, all of the past few months made sense. She no longer questioned the reality of Aris. She knew Carlos was gone but, somehow, she was unable to grieve for him any longer; she felt him so strongly in the presence of Aris. She adored her time with him. The stories he told of the past, the vampire lore about his kind that he shared. Finally, she felt comfort being with him. Delight. He touched her infrequently, almost shyly. He kissed her rarely, sweetly and without passion, holding true to his promise to simply be her friend.

As she sifted through her ornaments, she found a colorful Murano glass sphere. As she held it up to the light she thought of DeMarco. She was glad he decided to return to America for a few months to work. He had become a welcome companion and new friend. Their time together was so stimulating intellectually, not to mention how wonderful it was to look at his handsome face. He, too, had kissed her yet with more hunger, more passion. Surprisingly she found herself returning DeMarco's kisses with a deep yearning even though she wasn't ready for a more intimate romantic relationship with him, with anyone, regardless of what Colleen and Bob thought. She was simply enjoying being in the company of two glorious men.

The sound of knocking on the door brought her attention back to the present. She hurried across the room to answer,

"Hello. The air is quite brisk this afternoon." Aris entered the room, brushing melting snowflakes from his dark hair, his leather jacket zipped to his throat and a black, soft muffler wrapped carelessly around his neck. She stepped back to usher him into the living room.

The large green containers caught his attention. He smiled. "Ah, Christmas. I told you long ago I wanted to share your Christmas and, at last, here we are." He began to examine the sparkling ornaments in the cases before him, lifting one after another, examining each one as he turned it in the light.

"So shiny and beautiful." He bounced each one on the palm of his hand. "Yet no substance. I have noticed that in your time, most humans seem very much like these decorations." He turned toward her, "Yet you, Sarah. You are not. There is depth and intellectual weight to you. There is truth in the very core of who you are. It is that truth that draws me to you."

A slow smile covered his face. If she didn't know better, she would have thought it was the old Carlos as he looked at her from head to toe. "And, I must confess, some other parts as well."

Sarah felt a heat inside her as his eyes trailed the contours of her body. She was confused by her own reaction. She was pleased he found her attractive, not frightened, not put off. She was so drawn to him. Even as she fought the attraction, she wondered how long she would be able to hold out against his charm. Then she remembered, she would have to become an Immortal to share anything other than friendship with him. His actions just seemed so human sometimes she forgot what he was. *"How can you possibly forget that,"* she thought then immediately put it from her mind.

"Are you ready to find the perfect Christmas tree? I saw several vendors as I walked from the bus stop."

"I thought we might go out into the country to cut one. There are Christmas tree farms west of the city. I haven't done that since I was a little girl and I think it might be more fun for you, a little less current day commercial."

"Wonderful." Lifting her light-weight white down coat from the sofa, he held it for her. Standing behind her, he slid it over her arms then wrapped it around her waist. His face nestled in her sweet smelling hair and for just a brief moment, he touched his lips to the base of her neck. She shivered as she drew away from him.

"Great, we'll take my car and be out of the city in an hour or so." As she closed the door behind her, the tingling on the back of her neck where his lips had rested ignited a fire somewhere in a dark place deep inside her. She put that, too, immediately out of her mind.

\#

A light dusting of snow covered the ground and their boots left a dark path of footprints through the trees.

"These trees are grown for the express purpose of being cut to the ground?" His eyes were busy assessing the pines that surrounded them. "Some of them have been growing for several years." It was hard for him to believe such a sacrilege was a part of modern society.

"Well, it's a Christmas tree farm." Sarah didn't know why she felt embarrassed to have brought him here. "There were farms in England, weren't there?"

"Yes, of course. But farmers grew food and crops to make cloth and rope. Not farms for trees." Realizing just how critical he sounded, he stopped walking. Turning to face her, he gently rested his hands on her shoulders. "Sarah, I am so sorry. I did not intend to offend you. I think your Christmas tree farm is a splendid idea."

She chuckled at his feeble attempt to apologize. She was growing much too fond of this strange being.

"Come." He took her hand and began walking quickly down the path. "Let us find the perfect tree."

She hurried to stay a pace with him and felt a strange disappointment that he hadn't kissed her. She could have sworn he wanted to. "*Why,*" she asked herself, "*would I want him to kiss me?*" She answered her own question. "*Could it be I'm falling for him? No, I can't be that crazy. That just can't happen.*"

#

The ringing of the telephone was barely audible over the sound of Sarah's electric toothbrush. She heard it, lifting the receiver just in time.

"Hello?"

"DeMarco?"

His laugh was clear as he answered. "Si. DeMarco. I am calling to tell you that you are in my thoughts and to wish you well on Thanksgiving."

She didn't tell him she was just thinking about him, wondering if she would hear from him while he was in Italy. "Thank you. It's great to hear your voice. How are you?"

"All is well here, but I do miss your smile."

"Are you with your family?"

"No. I am taking care of some business in Milano before I travel to be with my family. It seems so long since I have spent much time with them. Our home is in the country and it is very beautiful." He paused. "Perhaps some time you will visit."

Sarah was glad she didn't really have the option. She certainly didn't have any intention to travel with DeMarco to visit his family, yet she wondered what they were like. He hadn't told her very much about them except that there were a lot of them. *"Like most Italian families, I suppose,"* she thought.

"When will you return to the states?"

"I will be back soon after New Year. I will telephone you again before I leave my country."

"It will be great to see you again."

"Yes, I miss you, Sarah. Have a lovely holiday. Buona sera."

"Goodnight, DeMarco." She held the receiver to her ear a moment longer until she heard dead air at the other end.

CHAPTER 12

The waiter left the table and the three friends settled in for their traditional pre-holiday dinner. They sipped their wine and ate bruschetta as they chatted.

"Okay Sarah," Colleen spoke, exasperation clear in her voice, "what took you so long to fess up about this Italian guy?"

"C, there's not that much to 'fess up' about. We've been seeing each other for a while, that's all?"

"But what about Carlos?" Bonnie rested her elbows on the table as she leaned toward her friend.

"I don't get it. Why is everyone asking me about Carlos?"

"Come on," Colleen grinned. "We all know you've got the hots for each other. It's been obvious for a long, long time."

"We're just friends." Her words sounded hollow as she spoke and she knew it. "Okay, so I'm not quite sure what we are; we've never really talked about it much." "*Hell,*" she thought, "*if they only knew I'm not even quite sure what he is much less how I feel about him.*" She spoke out loud once again, "We just enjoy being together."

"That's pretty obvious, so what about him? Does he know about DeMarco?"

"I told you, DeMarco's just a friend."

"You sure have an over-abundance of friends these days." Colleen giggled before she picked up her iced tea.

"Okay ladies, my turn." The two other women turned to give Bonnie their full attention. "I've met a guy."

"Where? Tell us everything?"

"I hate to admit it, but on the internet and he's a really nice guy. He's a fireman and knows how to cook." Bonnie laughed.

Colleen gave her a hug. "Never under estimate the power of a man who knows how to boil water. I married me one, didn't I?"

"I don't know if I'll marry Jack Dixon, but he can sure whip up a great dinner in record time. And he actually likes doing it?"

"I say do not pass go, do not collect one dime, grab this guy and run." Colleen was happy to see Bonnie meet someone after a long, dry spell of not dating.

"It hasn't gotten that far yet, we just seem to really get along and laugh a lot. And the really cool thing is we're from similar backgrounds."

"*Similar backgrounds,*" Sarah thought about the two men in her life. "*How about similar continents or similar species.*" She shook her head and chuckled to herself as the waiter brought the pasta to the table.

#

Aris enjoyed driving Sarah's car and having her as a passenger. The trees whizzed past them, their black trunks clearly sculpted against a cloudy, gray Thanksgiving sky. Driving was one of the added benefits of the twenty-first century. He looked forward to the day when he would own a really fast car. He remembered riding the swiftest horses in the king's stable through the English countryside. The exhilaration he felt in those long gone days would pale in comparison with one hundred miles an hour and many, many horses under the hood of a shiny black sports car.

He slowed down as he turned into a residential neighborhood.

Aris pulled the car in front of Colleen and Bob's front walkway and parked. He jumped out and walked around to the passenger side to help Sarah lift a huge bag of food out of the back seat.

"Is it traditional to bring such massive amounts of food to a Thanksgiving dinner? This is my first, you know."

"Yes, I know, but do your best to not be so obvious about it. You're supposed to be a Mexican-American who has been doing this for more than a quarter of a century." He took the shopping bag from her and held her arm as they walked down the icy sidewalk. "We all expected you would be different after a near death experience, but so far you've been all Carlos."

"Do not be afraid." He laughed as he let go of her arm to ring the doorbell. "Baby, I'm so down with it." He winked at her as he pressed the buzzer

CHAPTER 13

Sᴀʀᴀʜ HAGAN, transcript, session 3

I was sleepless throughout the night. Only he filled my thoughts. Even memories of the old woman's prediction of mystery and death could not erase the image of his golden skin and flying black hair from my mind. I moved quietly from the bed so as not to disturb my sleeping sister. "I must see him again." The thought chewed at me without ceasing, giving me no peace.

There was a moment of silence as Sarah paused, deep in trance. In that brief instant, her romantic dream from weeks before flashed through her mind in its entirety. She gasped as she remembered the intensity of their passion as he made love to her.

At last, she groaned as she spoke a name. "Diego."

"Who is that Elizabeth?"

Bonnie was alert, a bit shocked by the sound of desire etched into the voice of her friend. "Tell me more of him Elizabeth."

I rode alone, away from the hunt. A wild boar ran in front of my horse, frightening it. It reared and as it bolted, I was thrown onto the ground. As I stood, a masked rider appeared as if from nowhere lifting me in front of him onto his mount. He rode like a whirlwind, carrying me off into the wood. Her breath was short, almost panting as she recounted the experience. *There, on the forest floor, he ravaged me. I fought as a demon at first yet even as I struggled, his lust ignited a never-before-felt yearning inside my young virgin's body. I was unable to withstand the fervent demand from him; at last, I succumbed with all my heart and with a heat I was not even aware existed. His lust wrapped us in a blanket of wanton abandon. Who was I? Who was he? I disappeared into him as he loved me with his body, his soul. I became his in that moment knowing naught about the past, the future. Not caring. Each caress, each kiss burning a raw, aching need into my yielding flesh. There was pain and blood and ecstasy.*

At last when we were spent, he held me, covering my nude body with the thick strands of my long, golden hair. "I have taken you. Now you are mine. I pledge my life and my love to you always."

I reached to untie his mask, to see the rest of his beautiful face. He grasped my wrists moving my arms to rest on the ground above my head. I whispered, "Who are you?"

He was silent, staring into my eyes. As I opened my lips to ask again, he covered them with his own. "No, do not speak. My name is unimportant. But, your name? Your name is Beauty, Belleza, Belleza de Oro. My beauty of gold," he murmured into my trembling mouth.

I know not how many hours we lay on the forest floor. He covered us with my voluminous skirts to keep warm as the twilight crept among the trees. A sliver of a moon peeked from behind the sheltering leaves and branches when, at last, I recognized the lateness of the hour. I knew I must return to my father's house. If I were gone longer, a search party would be sent for me. I did my best to make clear to him who I was and the great danger there was to him and to his people if my father found us.

He shook his head and drew me more closely into his arms. Promising to come to him the following day, I persuaded with words and caresses to be allowed to rise. We gathered my clothes, doing our best to arrange them. Filthy and wrinkled, yet I knew I could explain it away. My horse must have returned to the stable hours ago. The household would know I had an unfortunate occurrence. It would easily explain my distress. I felt their concern for me even in that very moment. I knew I must make haste to protect my love, to protect the esteem of my family. My actions of the day had dishonored our household. I must not let on. They must not know.

Once dressed, he lifted me onto his horse and we rode to the edge of the clearing where he found me earlier in the day. Kissing me roughly, he set my feet on the ground. Looking deeply into my eyes, he spoke. "I am Diego." He reached to untie his mask and as he removed it from his face, I gasped. It was he, my beautiful gypsy dancer; he who I was unable to forget. I knew unbounded joy as I hastened to my father's manor house, arriving just as the dogs and horses entered the courtyard, home from their search.

My father's arms wrapped around me. I could hear my mother's sobs of relief. I told the tale of being thrown and lying, senseless for most of the day. An easy lie for it was true. Entranced in a stupor of love, I had spent my afternoon. I felt no remorse for my story as I was led into the house and taken to my room.

All was quiet in the office as Bonnie finished her notes then sat silently, waiting for her friend to continue. When she didn't, the therapist questioned her further. "Did you see him again?"

Again and again I crept away while my sister slept. I danced and laughed and loved as the gypsy camp became as my second home. The married women stayed far from me; the young, unmarried ones despised me for entering their world. The crones and the men delighted in me, in my differences. It was a time of great joy and adventure. The old ladies brushed my long blond hair and dressed me like a gypsy doll every time I visited.

One morning, just before dawn as I crept up the stairs to the room I shared with my sister, I was seen by one of the kitchen girls. Now frightened less she make it known I was away from the manor during the night, I hurried up the stairs to my chamber.

Sitting in the middle of the bed, very awake and very cross, was my sister. Arms folded across her chest, her mouth set in a straight, demanding line, she spoke. "Where have you been, sister? What mischief have you wrought? Father came to our room last night and found you gone. He is furious. He rode out with his men to search for you. It seems luck was with you he did not find you. Now, where have you been?"

"Oh Jane, you must help me. He must never know. I have been at the gypsy camp."

"The gypsy camp?" Her tone was incredulous. "Why the gypsy camp? What have you done?" She gasped. "The gypsy dancer. You have fallen in love with the gypsy dancer. Oh Elizabeth, whatever will you do? Father will send you away."

"He will do worse than send me away. He will send me to the royal court and I will never see Diego again. I love him, Jane."

The younger girl covered her ears with her hands. "No. Do not make me a part of your charade. I will not alibi you, sister." Her eyes grew round and her mouth hung open. "Has he touched you," she whispered. "Have you given him your maiden-head?"

Casting my eyes to the ground, I nodded my head yes.

"Oh my Lord. What will Father do to you? What have you done? Can you be with child?"

"I do not know."

Sounds of feet stomping on the stones of the great hallway making haste toward our chamber caught my attention. "They come, silly girl. What will you do now?"

"Oh Jane, I know not." I hid my face in my hands as I sank to the hard stone floor. "I know not."

The door burst open. My father yanked me from the floor, slapping me hard on my face. I had never been touched except in love and my heart was crushed with the blow.

"I know where you have been," he roared. "It is over. Their wagons *are burned. They are turned off this land and if I see another gypsy they know I will strike him dead."* He threw her on the bed. *"Gather your things. You go to court in the morning, position or no. You are no longer welcome in this house. You are a disgrace to me."* He spun on his heel, slamming the great door behind him.

I crumpled into a ball of sorrow and shame. My sister left me quietly to sob into the pillows of her virgin bed.

Tears poured from Sarah's eyes as Bonnie slowly brought her back to real time. She stared blankly at the ceiling as Bonnie handed her a damp towel to wipe her face. "Come on honey, sit up and have a sip of water. You'll feel better in a minute."

Sarah swung her legs off the recliner, placing her feet flat on the floor. She was silent for many minutes before she spoke.

"Good heavens, Bonnie, what was that?"

"That, my friend, was a past life regression lived like reality."

"I need some time to digest this, Bon. I think I'll go home and we can discuss it next week. Is that alright with you?"

"Perfectly. Just be careful going home and if you need me for anything, call me. I'll be close to the phone."

Sarah stood, hugging her friend good-by. Buttoning her coat, she silently left the office.

CHAPTER 14

Curled on her sofa, the ritual mug of evening tea steaming in her hand, Sarah prepared to write in her journal. What in the world happened to her? Her session with Bonnie had been astonishing. She had fully expected to return in her mind's eye as Elizabeth Wyatt, to meet and love Aris at Henry's court, but a concubine for a wild, Spanish gypsy? Never would she have dreamed such a thing. Yet she did. Her whole body flushed white hot as she remembered it again. The passion of her dream. Never had she remembered there being such passion in her present life, such yearning. What in hell could it all mean?

Writing in her journal became a task that was impossible. Her mind was too wild and out of order to make one word follow another into even a semblance of a complete thought.

"Bed. Sleep. Tomorrow morning it will all make more sense." Methodically running water into her mug then turning it upside-down in the sink, Sarah made for her bedroom.

As she clicked on the light, she caught sight of a blood red rose, once again on her pillow. "Enough! He promised!" Furious hands reached for the telephone as she dialed Aris.

After two rings she heard his voice. Without a greeting she

began. "What the hell are you doing? You gave me your word you wouldn't sneak into my room again and you did it tonight. With me sitting right in the living room."

His tone was shocked. "What are you talking about, Sarah?"

"You and your nighttime climbing up the side of my building. The red rose on my pillow. You gave me your word."

"Sarah, calm down. Just calm down. I have not been in your home without invitation since the first time I came back to your office. And, I never left a red rose on your pillow."

She gasped,then all was silent.

"Sarah, what is it? What has happened?"

"I don't know. This is the second time it's happened. I go into my bedroom and there's a long stemmed rose on my pillow. I checked with security the first time and they didn't show a record of anyone coming upstairs so I assumed it was you. You said you had been here without my knowing."

"Yes, at the very start of my life as Carlos. To be close to you while you slept. I never came when you were not there. Are you in the apartment right now?"

"Yes."

"Get your keys and leave. Go to the lobby and wait for me. I am on my way. Take your cell phone with you. Leave that apartment this instant."

"I'm in my pajamas."

"I do not care if you are naked, leave the apartment now, lock the door and wait for me in the lobby. I will be there as soon as I possibly can be." She could hear the rustle of him getting into his jacket and closing his door. "Do it now, Sarah, do you hear? Now."

Quickly she changed into the sweats lying on the chair by the bed. She rushed out the door. Shaking, she entered the elevator, watching the door close behind her.

"Tom," her voice was shaking as she spoke to the security guard behind the desk. "Has there been anyone asking for me this evening?"

"No, Miss Hagan. No one I know of."

"Someone has been in my apartment without my knowledge." She took a few deep breaths to regain control of herself before she continued. "Is it possible to see the footage from the security cameras." As a full security building, there were cameras trained on all the entrances and exits of the building at all times.

"I don't know how it's possible for someone to get past me. I was here all evening, Miss, but I'll call my supervisor right away and get the okay to check the camera footage. You want to just stay here until I get someone to go through your apartment and make sure it's safe?"

"Yes." She shivered, not because she was cold. She was very frightened. "Yes, I'll wait here. I have a friend coming over to stay with me but until then, I'll just sit in the corner there and wait." She pointed to the grouping of chairs near the elevators.

"I'll get you some water."

"No, Tom. I'd feel better if you just stayed within view until my friend gets here if you don't mind."

"Not at all, Miss Hagan. Not at all." He helped her settle into a comfortable chair.

She felt a little more calm as she sat in the well-lit lobby with the well-muscled security man standing close to her. She would feel much more secure when Aris arrived and they figured out who or what had been in her apartment. She grinned sardonically at her thoughts. What kind of convoluted world did she live in where she felt less danger in the presence of the undead than she did alone? There was no sane answer to the question. Time seemed to stand still as she waited.

It took every bit of control she had to keep from crying out in relief when she saw Aris come through the revolving door. He wrapped his arms around her protectively and she began to relax a little. "It will be alright. Everything will be alright. I am here now. You are safe. You will always be safe with me, Sarah." He stroked her hair as she rested her cheek against his strong chest. "You are fine. No one is going to harm you, I will see to that." He kissed the top of her head then settled her back into the over-stuffed chair. "Stay here. I'm going to talk to the guard." He approached the man behind the security desk.

"You saw no one this evening?"

"No, sir. No one even came into the building after Miss Hagan. It's been like a tomb here all night. I called my supervisor to get a release to go through the security tapes and to send someone over to go through her apartment. I'm waiting for him to call me back right now."

"You needn't send for anyone else. I am going to her apartment now. Please watch her until I return."

"Glad to, sir. We all really like Miss Hagan around here. I don't know what's going on, but we'll get to the bottom of it."

"Thank you." He returned to Sarah. Bending down, he spoke softly. "Are you feeling better?"

"A little."

"Please, may I have your keys?"

Panic lit her eyes. "Where are you going?"

"To your apartment."

"What if they're still there?"

He tapped his chest lightly as he smiled. "Invincible, remember?"

"I hope so." Her hand trembled as she relinquished her keys.

It was as if she was physically pushing the hands of the clock on the wall, forcing the minutes to tick by. At last the elevator door opened and Aris stepped out. He hurried to her side. "There is no one there and no sign of any forced entry. Sarah, who has a key to your apartment?"

"Colleen and Maggie both do."

"Let's go upstairs. I'll stay with you tonight. We'll tuck you into bed and check with your friends tomorrow. Maybe one of them left you the rose as a joke and you didn't notice it before." She stood, taking his hand. "I'll be with you. Nothing can happen to you as long as I'm there. You know that, don't you?"

"Yes. I trust you with my life." And she meant it.

#

When at last sleep found her, it was fitful. Her chaotic dreams were fragmented and frightening, leaving her with a semi-conscious feeling of being somehow threatened. Each time she called out, he was there, stroking her hair, speaking soft reassuring words to her. As the first light of dawn stole through the window she sat up. "Aris?"

"Right here." He sat beside her in the chair by her bed. "Always right here whenever you need me." He moved closer to her, fluffing her pillow and laying her back into it. He covered her to her chin with her soft blanket. "Relax. I'll make you a cup of coffee. Just close your eyes. I'm right here."

Familiar noises of coffee brewing came to her from the kitchen. When he returned, a wonderful aroma filled the bedroom from the steaming cup. Placing it next to her on the table, he sat close, taking her hand in his.

"It's too early to call your friends. Enjoy your coffee; take a shower. You will feel much better after washing off the fright of last night. See?" He pointed toward the window. "The sun is going to be bright today." He was silent a moment before he spoke. "Things always seem better in the light of day."

#

He sat quietly, waiting until he heard the water in the shower running. When he was sure she wouldn't come out of the bathroom, he stood, crossing to the spot below the window that had caught his attention. There, just below the sill, was a dark smudge. It appeared to be from the heel of a shoe. He knew Sarah would never let a dirty mark remain on the wall. "Where did this come from? When? And most of all, who or what left it there?"

#

In the daylight, Sarah was able to deal with the phantom florist with a lot less fear. There had to be some logical explanation for the rose. Neither of her friends had any idea where it came from, but Colleen insisted Sarah stay with her and Bob until they could investigate. At first they thought it might be one of Manu's gang members, however Bob did a thorough check and none of them had been around for months. It appeared they had all returned to Mexico. The security tapes showed nothing. No one entered or left the building who didn't belong there. In complete denial, Sarah refused to think about it further and in spite of her friends cautioning her, she returned home. She waited for the holidays all year and she wanted to put the whole mystery behind her and simply "deck the halls."

Aris didn't write it off quite so easily. He watched over her from the roof of an adjoining building every night without telling her. He wasn't sure exactly what was going on, but there was only one kind of being he knew that could climb a wall. He didn't want whatever it was alone with Sarah. Sarah alerted the security staff to be extra wary; she made arrangements so that Aris could enter without them checking with her first. Somehow, she was able to put it all out of her mind in a frenzy of holiday spirit. Besides, she had someone with "super powers" watching out for her. She knew he would never let anything hurt her and she couldn't imagine anything that could ever hurt him. Her imagination wasn't broad enough.

CHAPTER 15

The fire in Sarah's fireplace burned brightly; the flames leaped and bowed, adding to the colorful glow of the tiny lights that decorated the Christmas tree. They sat on the sofa enjoying a comfortable evening together. Sarah sipped from a glass of merlot she held in her hand, an untouched glass of wine sat on the coffee table in front of Aris. He could sip it if he wanted to but, at the moment, he had no need or any desire for either food or drink. He partook from time to time in social settings. Otherwise it was rather like breathing, a possibility rather than a necessity.

It had been difficult at first to understand that most of the legends about vampires that had been passed through the centuries were false. Fables. Vampires could walk out during the daylight. Sunshine didn't burn them. Crosses didn't frighten them. They reflected in mirrors the same as anyone else. Garlic didn't bother them. They didn't need to sleep in a coffin or out of one. They simply didn't need to sleep. But they could. They could do all the things that human beings could do. Eat. Drink. Sleep. Breathe. If they chose, they could live in a human society without anyone ever knowing they were Immortal. Sarah had begun watching people on the street and wondering if they, too, were Immortals like Aris.

He had just finished telling her a story about a Christmas he had spent in the Tudor court with Henry VIII and Anne Boleyn. Sarah was mesmerized. She was always enthralled by his stories. Those stories were what had drawn her to him the first time he appeared during a session with Carlos.

Aris' tale that she was his beloved from a past century had been difficult for her to accept, yet through her sessions with Bonnie, it became more and more a possibility her mind could not deny. If she honestly believed her own theory of past life regression, it was most definitely more than a possibility. She knew Aris believed it without any doubts.

"Sarah?" He leaned toward her. "Where were you just now?"

The sincere questioning look on his face caused her to laugh as she reached to pat his hand. He turned his wrist to interlace her fingers with his. The heat from his hand warmed her. His eyes locked on hers and she could see little reflections of the dancing firelight in the black circles of the iris. Sarah felt his other worldliness, the inherent seduction in the gaze of an Immortal.

Moving even closer, he kissed her tenderly. His lips barely brushed hers. They were softer than she remembered. He rested his full mouth on hers and the feel of his breath, a breath he breathed just for her, was warm and sweet on her skin. She hungered for more of him and without thinking she reached to wrap her arms around his neck.

His hands grasped her wrists with the greatest of care as he stopped her from holding him. He placed her hands in her lap and kissed her sweetly on the forehead. "Don't get up. I'll show myself out." He looked down at her in the glow of the firelight. "You are so beautiful." He slid into his jacket as he walked to the door. She heard a soft click as he closed it behind him.

Sarah drew her legs close to her chest, wrapped her arms around them and rested her chin on her knees. She was silent a moment then spoke softly to no one except herself. "Absolutely. No doubt about it. My feelings for him are getting out of hand. Where can this possibly go?"

She leaned back on the sofa and thought of the two men in her life. When DeMarco left the country she thought she would get over him, but he had already been gone a few weeks and she still felt heat when she remembered his kisses. His attention to her was so much more demanding than Aris. Of course, she and DeMarco could actually have a sexual relationship --something she could never have with Aris while she was human. Her decision was made long ago, she would never give up her human life to become an Immortal. So a sexual relationship with the vampire was impossible. Her dreams had made her aware that she wanted and needed to be intimate. It had been way too long since she had felt more than a dream man in her bed.

CHAPTER 16

The children's furniture store was exploding with plastic elves, reindeer and an enormous red and white Santa Claus ho, ho, ho-ing and moving its arms up and down. Sarah supposed the decorations were to make the shoppers feel festive enough not to mind spending more on an infant's crib than on their own beds.

"So," Colleen questioned, "are you ready to finally admit what I've known all along?"

Sarah held a tiny pair of jeans to show them to her friend. "How about these? They're as unisex as you can get." The prospective mother and father chose not to know the sex of their unborn child so all of the tiny clothes they bought would fit both boys and girls.

"Sarah, answer my question. What's up with Carlos? Even Bob said it's obvious you two are nuts about each other."

"C." Sarah lifted her palm toward her friend in an attempt to quiet her inquiring mind.

"Don't do that to me Sarah. It's clearly apparent. Why can't you just admit that you care about him? And don't give me that age crap. I don't buy it."

Sarah paused, keeping her thoughts to herself. *"If you knew the real age difference, you most certainly wouldn't buy it."*

When she spoke, it was the truth. "I honestly don't know what is going on between us. You keep asking me and I keep telling you, I have no idea where it's going. The only thing I'm sure of is that we really enjoy spending time together."

"What in the world do the two of you talk about?"

Sarah laid the little pair of jeans on the counter as she thought, *"If you only knew C. If you only knew."* But there was no way to explain Aris' true nature to her friend.

Colleen guided the shopping cart as the two women moved toward the checkout counter. "So?"

"We talk about all kinds of things. What do you and Bob talk about?"

Colleen laughed. "For the past couple of months, nothing but little Eggbert in here." She patted her round stomach. "What about the Italian doctor? Is he still in Italy?"

"Yeah."

"When is he coming back?"

"After the New Year." They crossed the store in silence.

"Is that all you've got to say? 'After the New Year?' I'd like a little more info if you don't mind."

Sarah sighed. "There isn't any more info, C. He calls. We chat. He's coming back to the states. We'll see each other again. That's all. We're just friends."

"Hon, as a good looking woman who is in the prime of her life, it's time for you to find a man who is just a little bit more than a friend, don't you think? You better use what you've got before nobody wants it anymore. If you know what I mean."

Sarah shook her head and laughed at her friend's words as they got in line, but she knew that Colleen was more right than she cared to admit.

#

Sarah placed her keys and purse on the small table by the door. She removed her coat then sifted through the day's mail. A few bills, some advertisements and some holiday cards. She opened an envelope that she knew was from Colleen and Bob. It was a wonderful photograph of the two of them in Santa Claus hats and fake, cottony white beards. Sarah laughed out loud at the silly looks on their faces.

The next card she picked up had a strange looking stamp on it. She noticed it was international mail and her heart skipped a beat. It was from DeMarco. With him so far away, it had been relatively easy to keep him out of her mind, to pretend her feelings for him · were just a fantasy, to concentrate on Aris. Yet, now that she held a message from him in her hand, read his greeting written in his own handwriting, he was once again very real to her. Suddenly she missed him. Missed their conversation, the gray on his temples, the way he held her hands in his. Knowing he would return excited her. "No, I won't go there. I'll think about him later. After the holidays. Now, I'll just focus on Aris and our strange friendship."

She slid the card back into the envelope and placed it at the bottom of the stack of mail.

CHAPTER 17

The hour's drive from the city to her mother's home in the northwest suburbs was uneventful. A light snow fell as they left her parking garage, but by the time they reached their destination the flurries had stopped completely.

The outside of the house and all the trees in the yard were decorated with twinkling white lights. It was still late afternoon but the gray cloudy sky created the perfect contrast as they blinked on and off. Aris carried a stack of colorfully wrapped packages as they hurried up the walk. Sarah slid her hand under his arm when she nearly slipped on a hidden piece of ice on the sidewalk.

As they stepped onto the porch, the door opened in welcome. The smells of Christmas dinner cooking and the warmth of the house enveloped them. "Merry Christmas." Sarah's mother drew them out of the cold into the entrance hall. She hugged and kissed her daughter. "I'm so glad you could join us, Carlos." She took the packages from him, placed them on a nearby table and shook his hand. "It's good to see you again. Please, come in."

The dinner was intimate. An old friend of the family and a couple that lived down the block were the only guests other than Aris. They laughed and joked as they sat around the dining room table after dinner, enjoying the conversation and each other's company.

"John has a gallery, Carlos." Delores Hagan patted John Marshal's hand as it rested on the table. "Sarah mentioned that you sketch and you are quite good at it. Perhaps you might show some of your work to John."

"Why, yes. I'm always looking for new artists to showcase." At middle age, the gallery owner was tall, handsome and had a head full of thick gray hair. "Stop by and see me and bring some of your work." He reached into his suit pocket, withdrew a business card and handed it across the table to Aris. "We're having a winter finale at the gallery. I can't promise, but let's see if you have anything we might display."

"I'll do that. Thank you." He tucked the card in his shirt pocket. "I'll telephone you this week to set an appointment."

As he spoke, Sarah's grandmother brought in a flaming Christmas pudding. "Dessert anyone?"

#

"He really is a lovely young man, Sarah. It's hard to believe he's a criminal. But don't you think he's a bit young for you?" Sarah and her mother rinsed the dishes before placing them in the dishwasher.

"First of all, he isn't a criminal. He made some mistakes when he was younger but that is all behind him now. And the age difference? I hadn't thought about it," she lied. "Besides, we're just friends. That's all."

"I find that hard to believe. I saw how he looks at you." Mrs. Hagan added the dishwashing liquid, shut the door of the appliance, and pushed a button to turn it on. "And how you look at him. I'm not making any judgments, Sarah. I just don't want to see you get hurt again."

The sound of a piano echoed from the living room as Sarah's

grandmother played Christmas carols. Soon voices were singing about decking the halls.

"Don't worry, Mother. I'm not going to get hurt." She dried her hands. "Come on, let's go sing with them." She took her mother's hand to lead her out of the kitchen as the dishwasher hummed along with the song.

#

"You spoke of my sketches to your mother?" He drove through the falling snow. The wipers made a steady clicking sound as they erased the tiny wet marks made by the flakes as they landed on the windshield. The heat of the defroster warmed the glass and the flurries melted instantly as they touched it.

"Well, yes." Sarah was a little embarrassed and she wasn't sure why. "I told her about them before. I guess she remembered." She turned to look at him. His handsome profile was outlined by the lights of the oncoming cars. "You can still draw, can't you?"

"Of course. It was my influence that inspired the sketches Carlos created. It is a natural talent I inherited from my human mother. She was quite the artist and I watched several other well-known painters through the years." He grew silent as he reflected on his human life with his human family so many, many centuries past. Christmas carols played softly on the radio. Sarah hummed along.

Aris remembered his vampire life at the court of Henry VIII. His sketches had been prized by Anne Boleyn. After his trial in the Catacombs, his vampire home, the death of his human body and the banishment of his essence, during the years he floated though time and space as consciousness only, he witnessed many of the great masters as they created some of the most treasured paintings in the world. He watched and he learned. Monet. Da Vinci. Picasso. So many great artists. His present artwork was a combination of so many of the masters' talents.

Aris exited the tollway just as the snowplows were beginning their tedious work. The accumulation in the city was so much greater than it had been in the surrounding area where Sarah's mother and grandmother lived.

"The weather people said there is going to be at least four inches falling tonight. I'm glad tomorrow is Saturday and I don't have to go anywhere." She leaned her head against the headrest and closed her eyes.

"Sarah, I heard your mother mention your birthday next month. May I spend the day with you?"

"I hadn't planned on even celebrating this year." She understood that each year as she grew older, this man beside her would remain the same. Each year as her hair grew white and her skin grew wrinkled, he would still be young and vibrant. She detested thoughts of an aging body and mind. "Birthdays just aren't that important anymore."

"Yours is to me. Your birthday in this life has made it possible for me to find you, to share some of the things with you that were taken away from us in our past life together. Cardinal Wolsey took you from me in Henry's court. He separated us and sent you to your death." Anger touched his voice as he finished his sentence.

"I don't know about any of that, I'm just glad that you're here now and that I have gotten to know you." She reached to gently place her hand on his.

He held his tongue. The promise he made to himself weeks ago kept him from proclaiming his affection, his desire to have her with him. She would have to be the one to instigate the conversation. She would have to be the one to speak of love. He had waited hundreds of years and he would continue to wait.

"Aris, tell me more about the Catacombs and the Immortals, about your friend Sebastian." She was afraid to ask herself why but she wanted to know more about Sebastian and Emily, the vampire and the human who mated.

"I suppose you could say Sebastian was the closest to a true friend I ever had. He and Richard.

"Sebastian is brilliant and kind. He is the first Immortal created by Queen Akira. When Akira and Khansu came to earth with the star voyagers, they had no intention to colonize. They came solely for research. But when it was decided that the voyagers should return to their own world, Akira and Khansu decided to stay. They decided to make earth their home.

"The star voyagers were blood drinkers. On their home planet, colonies of feeding stock were bred for their blood. I don't know how to say this, Sarah, but the stock was humanoid by nature. Mutes. The minds of children, but humanoid. They were well cared for and allowed their freedom. The society's system was much like your barter system here on earth. The stock was fed, clothed and given places for shelter. Each time they were bled, they healed stronger than they were before the bleeding. The bleeding was painless, even pleasurable to some. The stock had a life expectancy of about a quarter-century and then they expired. But while they lived, they lived contented lives.

"Akira and Khansu wanted to understand the differences in the humanoids on earth and the humanoids on their planet. They experimented with humans and devised a way to create an earthling super race. Blood drinkers. The Immortals. Through the millennia Akira has grown more gentle. More understanding. She has grown to respect earthlings. She understands they are different than the stock of her home planet. The humans of earth have consciences.

"Her first changeling, her first creation was Sebastian. She treated him as if he were a true son. He and his newly made brothers and sisters of the coven assisted in the building of the Catacombs. He has served the royal couple since the beginning and I am quite sure he serves them still.

"I have thought about the mental torture he must have endured when he defied her order to end my existence for breaking the law, for killing out of hate. He placed himself in jeopardy by hiding my staked and dead body and only banishing my essence. My sentence was stake and fire. I was to be eliminated. It was only Sebastian's love of a brother that saved me. It could have only been for love. I miss our talks and our silences.

"Sebastian fell in love with a human, Emily Brown. He petitioned the Council for permission to marry. After many meetings and much pleading, it was finally allowed. Emily became an Immortal. They were joined by Akira and Khansu." He smiled as he thought of his friends. "I feel sure they still are living below ground with the royal couple."

Aris pulled into the parking garage and parked. He leaned against the car door and looked at Sarah. "Any other question?"

"What about the woman he took for a mate, Emily?"

"Yes, Emily. A human with such a deep soul, a profound love and a brave heart. She chose to be an Immortal. There are few who have made that choice. She lived, died and was reborn for Sebastian. When my essence left the Catacombs after my trial and my body's execution, I never returned. I do not know what their life was after their mating. My only hope is they found joy as great as their love."

Sarah leaned against the passenger door of the car, facing the vampire. The air inside the car was still warm from the heater and the atmosphere was cozy. "What about Richard?"

"Richard and Gabriela, two wonderful friends. They were the first of my kind that I ever met and I believe it has made us more of a family. While I still worked for the Spanish Emperor, they traveled to London to find the Catacombs. It took them some time before their petitions to the Council were heard. At long last, they convinced the Council they would swear and live by the Blood Oath and they were allowed to join the coven."

"Blood Oath?"

"Never take the life of an innocent. Never take a life through the drinking of blood for retribution or spite. Never take a life through the drinking of blood to gain power."

"That isn't the kind of law people think about when they think 'vampire'."

Aris laughed. "I know. So many myths." His expression became more somber as he continued. "But there are evil vampires like those that changed me and those that changed Richard and Gabriela."

"Aris, let's go upstairs. The car is getting cold." They gathered their things and left the parking garage. They continued their conversation as they stepped on the elevator and rode to her floor.

"I've wondered something for a long time. Why did you wait so long to find a human body?"

"Sarah," he sighed deeply before he continued. "Few Immortals have a choice of a body. Other than those who are only partially destroyed such as I was when Sebastian banished me, the body that is inhabited at the time of change is the body used for eternity. But, as you see, in my case, there are rare instances when one has the opportunity to make that choice. Without a body I am nothing more than awareness and thought." He smiled. "Now, I ask you, if you had to select a body to have until the end of time as we know it, would you not be choosey?"

She spoke through muffled laughter. "Yes, I suppose you're right."

"I was able to contact you through Carlos because of his involvement with mind altering drugs, because he was in hypnosis and his subconscious was open. Had both of those things not happened, I would not have been able to contact a human through him or anyone else for that matter. I am not able to enter into a living conscious being's subconscious unless their mind is altered in some way. If my essence is without a host and present at the time of a death and I desire to inhabit that body, I am able to it. Had Carlos not died, I would still be just a thought coming through his voice and only while you had him in a trance.

"Remember, we do not take the lives of the innocent and we must take the body at the moment of death. The bodies of the wicked show their evil. I waited for the body of a good man, a beautiful man. I was given life on this plane as a gift from him. A gift not given purposefully yet nevertheless, a gift. I will honor that always."

The elevator opened and he walked her to her door. She unlocked it then turned to say goodnight.

Kissing her gently on the cheek, he whispered, "Merry Christmas, Sarah. It has been a wonderful day."

"For me too." She returned his kiss. She watched him walk to the elevator. He turned to wave to her before he stepped inside and the doors closed.

CHAPTER 18

After taking Sarah deep into a hypnotic trance, Bonnie waited patiently for her to speak.

SARAH HAGAN, transcript, session 4

Sent away in disgrace and without a bid farewell, I traveled to London. It rained as the horses made their way through the mud. It was a cold and miserable girl who arrived at Whitehall Palace in the dead of night. I was taken directly to an opulent room warmed by a blazing fire and told to sit. Waiting in silence, I sipped the warm wine brought to me by one of the servants. As the dawn began to break through the mullioned windows, the great door opened. Looking like a fat red bird, a Cardinal of the church stepped into the room.

"I am Cardinal Wolsey." He held forth his ring to be kissed. Bowing, I lowered my lips to the huge brilliant stone as I curtseyed low. "Rise, Elizabeth Wyatt." Bidding me to sit near him, he settled into a great chair close to the warmth of the waning blaze. The dimming firelight danced on the glorious red satin fabric of his robes. For a moment, he appeared more a fat devil than a paragon of the church.

"Your mother has petitioned for your acceptance at court." He neglected to tell me the small fortune that accompanied the petition.

"*After much deliberation, I have decided to intercede for you with Queen Katherine. As I am of notable influence upon her Majesty's judgment, be assured you will be accepted. He opened the great door, moving his hulk with a grand rustling of satins and silk. Beckoning a footman to show me to the chamber I would occupy for the few days I must wait until I was formally accepted at court, he then turned from me as if I had never been in the room. Frightened and exhausted I made my way into what was to become my new home. It felt huge and cold and empty. Just as did the vacant place in my heart where just days ago, there was heat and light and passion.*

As time passed, I despised court more than I dreamed possible. King Henry frightened me. He was always staring at me when Queen Katherine or his mistress, Lady Anne Boleyn, was not close by. While the Queen was kind and gentle with us, all of the maids were terrified of the King as well as of Lady Anne. If he showed the least interest in anyone, the maid disappeared from court and was sent either home or to some God awful drafty castle as far from London as the Lady Anne could manage. I did my best to hold my distance yet for some reason, I know not why, Lady Anne took a liking to me hence I was in her rooms much more than I desired. Perhaps it was that I was young, naïve and without any court connections. She began to take me into her confidence.

It seemed the bravado she displayed to the courtiers was false. She was as fearful as a child. Of course, she never let on in the beginning, even to me. Yet, in her rooms, I became acquainted with one of her musicians. The handsome young lute player, Mark Smeaton. Smeaton was free with his words and opinions and spread court gossip more rapidly than any of the ladies. Anne, it seemed, had trusted him with her worries of holding the King. She had his attention, no doubts, yet so had many before her. Holding him while Katherine was still Queen was her present task. Anne saw me as one who could report to her the goings on in the Queen's chambers; a spy who could aid her in her quest.

As she grew more loose of tongue with me, she told me her great secret. *Her uncle and father saw her as an emissary for their family to ingratiate the Boleyn clan with the King and move them forward in rank. Regardless of her pleas that she was betrothed to marry her one love, Henry Percy, she was treated as chattel. Sent to court to claim the affection of the King, her beauty and wit caught his attention in short notice.*

Suddenly, she was of great import to her family, her words and thoughts no longer taken lightly. I knew from our whispered conversations that she was still a maid, a virgin. She refused to bed the King while he was still married to Queen Katherine. Thus, the King's Great Matter became the charge of the court; ridding himself of the Queen was his only thought. I watched as Lady Anne grew more thin and nervous as time progressed, yet hold him she did.

Still, I served Queen Katherine in good spirit. She was a pious and devout Catholic who was kind and generous to her court. The King turned from her, giving his all to winning Lady Anne. I watched the Queen grow solemn and languid, her once thin waist thickening, her only distraction food and the sewing of a great religious tapestry. The King no longer entered her rooms or called for her in his. Many times I found her wiping silent tears as she sewed tiny perfect stitches in the cloth of the wall hanging. All was intrigue and subterfuge. I knew Lady Anne had no true affection for the King, yet my soul ached for her and her unrequited love of Henry Percy. I, too, knew that ache of heart.

It was at a royal banquet that I first saw him. Tall and powerfully built, he had just entered the room when he turned to catch my eye. His blond curls shown in the light and as he walked through the door, I was reminded of a great, wild cat. Lithe, sensuous, dangerous. Unable to turn away, I felt my cheeks grow crimson. I knew not if it was my blood surging in my veins under his gaze or the heat of the bodies of the courtiers in the closed, crowded room. Lady Anne beckoned for my attention; when I turned back, he was gone. Who was this magnificent man? Inexplicitly, I was drawn to him. I decided to question my cousin,

Thomas Wyatt. He knew all at court. Surely Thomas would know who he was.

Bonnie was breathless as she questioned her friend. "Who was he, Elizabeth?"

Aris, a royal knight of King Henry who would become the true love of my young life.

The office was silent for many minutes before Bonnie realized Sarah had returned to real time and had fallen asleep in the recliner. She left her friend to rest as she typed her notes into her laptop before shutting it down. Watching Sarah sleep, she felt a deep, inexplicable melancholy. What would the next session bring? And who was Aris?

CHAPTER 19

"It sucks that you've got the flu. It won't seem like New Year's eve if we aren't together." Colleen's voice sounded like she was speaking into the phone through a barrel.

Sarah's ears as well as her nose were plugged and her throat was sore. She croaked as she answered. "I feel the same, but even if I could get out of bed, I wouldn't want to be around you. I'd hate to give you something as pregnant as you are right now."

"Yeah, I know. Do you need anything? Bob's running some final errands before the party and it would be easy for him to pick up anything you want."

"No, I'm doing fine." Sarah almost told her friend that her ex-parolee was taking care of her, but she didn't have the energy to answer the innuendos that statement would bring. "I'm going to take a nap now. Thanks for calling and have a happy New Year."

"You too, hon. Call if you need anything."

Sarah placed the telephone on the bedside table, closed her eyes and waited for Aris to call. Every day her need to see him, to be in his presence, grew more pronounced. When she thought of living without him, she felt sad and alone. When she contemplated a future with him, she was both frightened and excited. His world drew her in an unexplainable way she could no longer deny.

#

Wrapped in blankets and snuggled on the sofa in front of the fireplace, Sarah sipped a mimosa. She wanted to share champagne with him for the New Year even though he thought she shouldn't. She made a bargain, orange juice with just a splash of alcohol couldn't hurt her. His glass rested on the coffee table. It was untouched except for their New Year's toast. "The first of many," his words rang in her mind. How many? Twenty, forty, forever?

"I just can't think about the future right now." She silenced her thoughts as she smiled at him.

He leaned toward her, placing his soft lips on her forehead. He hesitated a moment then looked into her eyes. "I think your temperature is normal once again. I had begun to worry. Influenza is dangerous."

Smiling, Sarah spoke. "God bless antibiotics. I don't like to take them, but sometimes they save the day."

"There are so many scientific advances in your society, yet people basically remain much as they were centuries ago. I am amazed science has moved forward while consciousness has trailed so far behind. Humans still go to war after so much history has proven the only victor in battle is death. Men still murder even though it is obvious humans who take a life lose their own humanity, their very souls."

"Is there no conflict in your world?"

"There is no conflict in the world of the Catacombs. There is only the Queen and King, Akira and Khansu, and the Immortals Akira has created. The Royal Council makes the laws and we uphold them. We have no human needs and we cannot die so we have nothing to fear. Without fear, there is no conflict. It is fear that fuels your civilization, that binds each one of you humans to aggression and hostility. It is fear that creates war and hatred.

Nothing more, nothing less."

"I do know what you mean about fear. It doesn't exist, does it, unless we give it power?" She handed him her glass hoping for a refill.

He walked to the kitchen, returning with a glass of orange juice. She wrinkled her nose when she tasted it. It wasn't what she wanted and he knew it. The champagne made her head feel less stuffed and her heart a bit more festive. "Don't you think I could have just one more mimosa?"

"Drink this first. If you still would like to have it, I will bring it to you. I have researched your illness on the computer and most accounts suggest large amounts of vitamin C."

She downed it quickly, then, smiling, handed him the glass once more.

"Alright, you win." Again he crossed to the kitchen. When he gave her the refilled champagne glass, she sniffed the contents.

"Better." She sipped then placed the glass on the coffee table. "Now, please tell me more of your society."

He leaned back on the sofa, stretching his long legs; he rested his stockinged feet on the table in front of the fire. He placed hers on his lap tucking the blanket securely around her.

"What do you want to know?"

"What do you do all day in the Catacombs to keep you busy for all eternity? Don't you run out of things?"

"We do not experience time as you do. Because we have no human needs, one moment is much the same as the next. So there is no concept of weeks or years.

"We are a studious society. We read. We have our own level of scientific research. We hunt. We are artists and craftsmen. We develop relationships. After all, we inhabit a human body Sarah. The only difference is the alien venom rather than blood in our veins. When Queen Akira realized she could create a society from the human race by exchanging our blood for her venom, she created a whole new species, neither human nor alien. We are creatures not of this earth, yet not of her planet either. It is that venom that makes us what we are." He laughed. "Other than a few small things, super powers and living eternally, we are very much the same as you are. We're just made of a sturdier stock."

The telephone rang, jolting Sarah upright. Aris lifted the receiver, handing it to her.

"Happy New Year to you both too." Sarah listened as Colleen and Bob gave her their rendition of Auld Ang Syne. She couldn't believe it was midnight. There were no minutes or hours when she was with Aris.

"Tell Carlos we said Happy New Year to him. See you guys soon." Colleen giggled as Bob's kiss cut off her words. "Bye."

"C and Bob say Happy New Year." She placed the phone on the table and as she leaned across him, he reached for her.

"Happy New Year to you Sarah." He looked deeply into her eyes as he pressed his full lips gently against her mouth. He didn't move. His warm breath caressed her cheeks as his dark eyes locked on hers. She felt she was drowning in the tenderness of his kiss.

He released her, leaning her gently against her pillows. "Now, close your eyes and rest. Nothing can harm you while I'm here to take care of you."

Relaxing completely, she knew he told the truth.

CHAPTER 20

Sarah opened the box one more time before she crawled into bed. The gloves DeMarco brought her from Italy were beautiful. Soft and luxurious, they matched her dark brown boots exactly. She realized how much she really did like him when she saw him again. She readily admitted something about him excited her, something so much deeper than his good looks and breeding. *"Possibly that you don't have to kill yourself to make love to him."*

She snickered at her own joke as she crawled into her bed. Yawning, she opened her drawer to reach for her journal. Tired but behind in her writing, she was determined to catch up. Disappointing Bonnie in doing her journaling homework was low on her list of things she wanted to do.

As she began to write, she thought of the hypnotic flashbacks she had been having when she wrote. They were not uncommon, but hers were so clear, so intensely visual. *"They're either a great imagination or an amazing subconscious memory. Either way, so far, they've been pretty damn interesting,"* she thought.

She wrote about the physical sensations she experienced in her afternoon session. The tastes and smells were so clear, so alive to her. She closed her eyes remembering the fragrance of the rosemary and thyme rushes that were spread on the floors of the corridors of the palace. The sweet scent of the pomanders the courtiers wore to mask the smells that were not so nice. She remembered the aroma of the forest floor of the gypsy camp.

She drifted in and out of sleep until a vivid dream grabbed her and held her. It was night; she had stolen away from her father's manor. She had just finished dancing with Diego and they stood in the midst of the clearing. Her long blond hair hung loosely about her hips while short damp tendrils of curls lay in soft waves about her face. He watched her, his eyes full of desire, a sensuous smile playing at the corners of his full mouth.

Without warning, a dark gypsy woman grabbed Elizabeth by the shoulders. Roughly, she threw her to the ground. "He is my man."

Elizabeth sat stunned, dust all around her, her borrowed gypsy skirt falling softly about her thighs. "Yours?"

"Mine." The dark beauty screeched as she attacked the shocked girl. Slapping her rival hard, she stood over Elizabeth, her hands on her hips and hate in her wild eyes. Firelight bounced off the halo of gold anklets dangling from her pale leg as Elizabeth swept her foot under the knee of the standing woman, knocking her into the dirt. Like a wild animal the gypsy threw herself on top of Elizabeth and sat straddling her. Entangling her hands in the blond curls, she grabbed two fists-full of hair. She pulled out a great wad, held it high and laughed wildly.

Elizabeth rubbed the tiny bald spot for only a moment before tossing her opponent on her back, returning the vicious slap that still stung her cheek. Elizabeth panted as she did her best to draw her long hair out from beneath them. The weight of their bodies as they rolled in the soil pulled and tugged at it mercilessly.

The men of the camp laughed and cheered as they formed a circle around the battling women. Arms and legs flailed as they twisted and turned. Newly stirred dust rose so thick around them it was impossible to tell the difference between the dark and the pale flesh. Female grunts and groans along with Spanish epithets spilled from the fray until, at last, there was silence and stillness. The two women lay side by side, panting, caked with a thin, pale coating of clay made of dirt and perspiration.

One of the men ventured close to the filthy, bruised fighters. He stared down at them for a full moment then reached his hands to help them up.

Elizabeth stood, smoothing her skirt, her long hair tangled with soot, leaves and twigs. The gypsy was worse for the wear. A trickle of blood coated the side of her mouth and one of her golden earrings was gone, lost somewhere in the dirt. Wiping the blood with the back of her hand, she gave Elizabeth the sign of the evil eye as she hobbled out of the clearing to her wagon. As she left the circle of light, she turned to spit at Elizabeth. She missed her mark and a small wet circle in the dust was all that was left of her rage.

Diego laughed out loud as he gathered Elizabeth into his arms, brushing dust and leaves from her fiery cheeks. "Who is that woman and what claim does she have on you?" It was a demand, not a question.

"She is a distant cousin. We were promised when we were babies. She still lives by that promise. I live by another." He turned her to him to kiss her grimy face. When his lips left hers, his mouth was smudged and sooty. His embrace calmed her. She smiled as she drew the scarf from around his head to dust his lips before she kissed him again, this time with passion.

Strong arms lifted her as dark eyes watched with hate from deep within the shadows. The lovers murmured softly to one another as he carried her into the night away from the camp.

He found a soft mound of grass beneath a tall tree so thick with leaves the moon and stars were hidden from sight. He sat her down, her back leaning against the rough bark.

"Wait here, I will return." He disappeared into the dark returning in just moments with a huge bucket full of warm water, a blanket and the clothes she had worn from her father's home. He spread the blanket beneath the tree.

"Let me undress you and bathe you." He whispered in her ear as he slowly slid her clothes from her body. She was dusty and dirty from her match with the gypsy woman. She felt the grit on her skin as her chemise and then her skirt were removed. It was so dark she could barely make out his movements, but she heard water splash and the sound of a cloth being wrung out.

The warm wet towel was welcome on her parched, scratched skin. At first the little cuts and scratches on her arms and legs burned as he cleaned them. But his gentle touch soon took the burn away. He dried her with another cloth then began to untangle her long blond curls with a comb made of horn. At first the snarls caught on the teeth of the comb and pulled, but his gentle persistence freed the waves to pool around her nude shoulders. He laid her back on the blanket.

In the distance, the plaintive sound of a lone violin filled the air. She could see the white of his smile as he drew near to her. "My beauty." He breathed her name into her ear as his hands found the warm mounds of her breasts. "My angel." His breath felt warm and sounded sweet as he nuzzled her neck. In her young life she had only thought of her neck as a place to hang jewelry. Her gypsy gave it a new purpose. First his breath, then his tongue tracing her pulse as it rose in speed until it raced beneath her skin. He kissed the hollow of her throat and laid small kisses along both of her collar bones.

Her hands went to his hair and she laced her fingers through it, pulling his kissing lips to her breasts. He feasted first on one then the other. As his tongue traced the hard mounds of her erect nipples, she began to unlace the ties that held his trousers in place.

He stood tearing the clothes from his body, tossing them in the dirt. He returned to his love nude, erect, full of desire. Unable to control her passion, lying on her back she bent her knees pressing her feet into the earth. She raised herself to him. He kissed her bare abdomen and the tender skin inside her thighs.

Her legs opened further as he kneeled in front of her. Wrapping his large hands around her legs, he lifted her and entered her. She encircled his hips with her legs and they rolled onto their sides, locked in a boundless embrace.

The distant music matched their lovemaking without fault even as they moved faster and faster. Small moans in their throats added to the symphony until at last the sounds were no longer small. A deep wrenching groan tore from her throat as she reached her peak and soon, the same from him. Their breath calmed as they lazily caressed one another and the music faded and died as the lovers fell into a satisfied sleep there under the tree near the gypsy camp.

#

Sarah opened her eyes, picked up her pen and began to document her latest vision. "I'm glad Bonnie won't ever see this journal. I'd be mortified if anyone knew what a wild gypsy heart lives deep inside this mundane, ordinary therapist." She giggled to herself as she began to write.

CHAPTER 21

Sarah didn't like to shop. The congestion and noise of malls irritated her and all the post-holiday sales brought in additional mobs of cost-conscious shoppers. All the neon lights and loud music echoing through the cavernous spaces gave her a pounding headache. Had Colleen not used the "best friend" tactic, she would still be at home enjoying her Sunday ritual instead of plodding through one shoe department after another looking for comfortable shoes for the expectant mother. After several attempts to shove her swollen feet into a size seven, Colleen finally gave up and purchased a nondescript pair of flat black leather, size eight boots.

"I've been a size seven all my life. Who would have thought having a baby would move you up a whole shoe size? No wonder all my footwear hurts my feet." They carried their loaded trays to a table in the crowded food court. As they sat down a toddler at the next table plopped down on the concrete floor, threw back her head and began to scream. The harried young mother gave the two friends an apologetic look as she gathered her packages and her howling daughter and made her way toward the exit. Sarah watched as the child pulled and tugged at her mother's hand finally sitting down refusing to move. Flailing her little arms, she kicked her feet shrieking at the top of her lungs. The embarrassed mother bent to lift her daughter, dropping all her packages. She looked like she was going to cry. Colleen watched the scene, a terrified look on her face. It took a full minute for her to regain her composure and return to her beloved burger.

Laughing, Sarah sipped her soft drink and joked, "Are you sure you want to go through with this thing, C?"

Colleen's voice had a serious tone when she finally answered. "I'll tell you the truth. Sometimes I do wish I could back out of it. It's a huge responsibility to have a child. I've never told Bob this but I would have been totally happy just being his wife. Just being the two of us. Hell, I thought getting married was the scariest thing in the world. Now, this." She shrugged her shoulders as she glanced at her round tummy. "Sometimes I'm petrified. What if I screw up and turn my kid into a basket case. I mean, look what my parents did to me."

"First of all, C, you turned out just fine. Besides, you'll be a great mom. You and Bob are not your parents." Sarah was reminded of Colleen's wedding day; her fear that she would repeat the horrors of her parents' marriage. "You're going to be so good at being a mom, maybe I'll get lucky and be your kid in the next life."

Colleen's mood lightened and she grinned, returning to wolfing down her hamburger. She spoke around a mouthful of fries, "So what's up with your two men?"

"My men?" Sarah had hoped to avoid conversation about her romantic life. There were so many secrets she must keep from her best friend; she almost slipped several times when they were talking about Carlos. It was difficult sometimes to refrain from calling him Aris to her. The Immortals were a secret that must always be kept. "My men are fine." She sipped from her soft drink. "Same ol' same ol'. Nothing new."

Colleen wrinkled her forehead in serious thought as she leaned her elbows on the table and folded her hands. "Look, I'm not sure how to say it and it's none of my business, but I just have to tell you. The more Bob and I talk about DeMarco, the more we think there's something fishy about him. Neither one of us can put a finger on what it is, there's just something that's just not quite right."

"For someone who doesn't know how to say something, you were pretty direct and to the point. What do you mean fishy?" Sarah challenged her, amazed at what she had just heard.

"Don't get bent out of shape. We don't exactly know. He just doesn't seem completely legit."

"What makes you think that?" she questioned, demanding more of an answer.

"I said we don't know. We can't figure it out. Just chalk it up to being a cop thing." She reached across the trays of half-eaten food to place her hand on Sarah's arm. "Hon, it isn't that we don't like him. I'm not saying that. He seems a good enough guy. It's just there's something we can't pinpoint that doesn't ring true."

The silence between them was uncomfortable. Colleen broke it by speaking softly to her best friend. "Sarah, we love you. We just want the best for you, that's all. And I don't want to see you get hurt again."

"I know that, C. I'm not making any life decisions here. I'm just enjoying keeping company with him." She patted the hand that rested on her forearm. "I appreciate that you and Bob care about me."

Their conversation was interrupted by the sound of a baby wailing in its mother's arms as she struggled with the stroller, packages and a toddler by her side.

Colleen gulped air, left her tray with her half eaten burger and hurried from the food court without looking back.

"C, wait up." Sarah moved quickly after her.

CHAPTER 22

"This is so exciting." The afternoon sun was just setting, turning the icicles hanging from the frozen awning a blazing shade of orange sherbet.

"Interesting is more the word." Aris wrapped his arm around Sarah, holding her close, shielding her from the freezing wind that pushed them forward.

"Isn't that the gallery on the next corner?" Curb parking was impossible and the nearest lot they found with spaces still available was three blocks away. She shivered as they hurried across the street.

The warm air hit them as soon as they stepped inside. Muffled voices joined in soft conversation were a pleasant change from the whistling wind rattling the large plate glass windows.

"Sarah? Carlos?" Maggie waved her arms to get their attention. She pointed into the next room before disappearing through the door. Sarah took Aris' hand as they walked toward the exhibit of his work.

"I didn't know you had this kind of talent." Maggie spoke to Aris over Sarah's shoulder as she hugged her boss.

Working at super speed, he had created three large oil paintings and several sketches. They were all of old England and were brilliantly rendered. Several patrons were lingering, discussing the technique and lustrous colors. It was as if pure light was shining from the canvas.

Amused, Aris leaned in toward Sarah, whispering, "A technique I learned from watching Monet." She gasped, still shocked whenever he revealed a new event from his past to her.

#

"So, what happened?" She had barely answered the telephone and the two friends hadn't said more than 'hello' to one another when Colleen questioned Sarah.

"Hold on a minute, C. I just poured coffee." Settling into the pillows on her couch, Sarah took a sip before answering. The liquid was too hot so she placed the cup on the table in front of her to cool.

"It was wonderful. Not only did everyone love his work, he sold a painting for eighteen hundred dollars. It looks like Carlos has found his niche."

Sarah moved the receiver away from her ear when Colleen whooped loudly. "That's great. I wish we could have been there, but Bob couldn't get off work and he won't let me go anywhere alone these days."

"I don't blame him. It really scared us all when you slid on the ice and fell. He just doesn't want anything to happen to you, that's all. So quit complaining."

"I'm not, just stating a fact. Back to Carlos. I bet it made him feel great to have his work so appreciated."

"I think it's a lot more than that. He sees it as a way to make his way in this world." Sarah gazed into space as she thought, "*My world. The human world.*"

CHAPTER 23

Sarah was glad she reached the restaurant not only before the lunch crowd, but before DeMarco. It was a first and it made her smile. She was relieved to have a few moments to collect her thoughts before he arrived.

He had been telephoning her almost daily since his return from Italy. They had spent more time together and the more she saw of him, the more she liked him. He really was everything she had hoped to find in a man. Kind, solicitous, intelligent. Not to mention amazingly handsome. He was a member of her own profession and they were never without things to talk about.

When he touched her, it stirred her blood. She fought hard against her own impulses. Somehow she felt if she were intimate with DeMarco she would betray Aris although she didn't really know why. DeMarco wanted more from her, but he seemed willing to allow her to take her time. She had shared things with him that amazed her, even telling him about her ex-husband and the sorrow of her divorce. He was a willing listener and seemed to want to learn more about her. She wondered what he would think if he knew what was happening in her life right now.

She smiled to herself as she thought, *"He'd be on a plane to Italy before I finished my sentence."* Or would he? There seemed to be a deep understanding between them that she couldn't rationalize.

She realized that she didn't know very much about him. All of their conversations had been about their work or about her. He was inquisitive about her background and her life. He took a deep interest in her past and her family. And she readily answered all his questions, something unusual for her.

She sipped her wine, wondering if he could be someone who could take her out of the insane world she had ventured into. Someone who could give her a normal, human life. At least that made more sense than becoming a vampire for love.

Pictures of a life with him played in her mind until, at last, he was there, standing before her. He smiled as he leaned to kiss her cheek before he sat at the table. Her entire body tingled in response to his touch.

#

"This afternoon you have an appointment with a new client. He's British or something. When he called to make the appointment, his English sure wasn't the plain old American vernacular." Maggie sat in the chair across from Sarah, dangling her shoe from the toe of her bare plump foot.

"Vernacular?"

"He sounded so refined, I thought I'd try it out." She snickered. "Doesn't work so well on me, huh?"

"Let's just say you do better as plain ol' Maggie Fisher from the north side." Sarah was always swamped with work after the holidays. Some of her weight loss people always fell off the diet wagon and they all wanted a little extra help to get back on. She looked at her schedule and shook her head. "I won't have any time for lunch today. Would you mind a run to Saul's for salads?" Pulling her credit card from her wallet, she held it out for Maggie.

"Nope boss. I got it today. I'm out of here. You want the usual?"

"Perfect. What time is this Englishman due here?" They heard the outer office door open.

"I guess right now. I'll show him in then scoot. Have fun." Maggie shut Sarah's door behind her while Sarah hunted for her own missing shoe under her desk.

"Richard Rhys-Davis to see you." Sarah grinned at the formal sound of Maggie's voice and responded in kind.

"Please show him in." She rose to greet her new client.

As he walked in the door, she hid her shock. Another gorgeous man. They were coming out of the woodwork. This one, tall and blond, with cornflower blue eyes and a smile that would stop traffic.

"How do you do?" He extended his well-manicured hand. "I am Richard Rhys-Davis. Doctor Hagan, I presume."

"Sounds like I have Sherlock Holmes in my office," she thought. "Yes," she spoke out loud. "Please have a seat."

His dark suit was without flaw and he was obviously comfortable in his own skin as he relaxed in the chair opposite her.

Her head tilted questioningly. "Where would you like to begin?"

Clearing his throat, he drew a card and a badge from his pocket. "Actually, Doctor, I am not here as a client."

She reached for his card. Reading it quickly, her gaze was full of questions as she looked up at him. "Interpol?"

"Yes, the International Criminal Police Organization. We are here in your country in pursuit of the leader of a global smuggling ring, Ricardo De Flores. I am not at liberty to tell you more than that at this time; however, we have been led to believe this Spanish national may have reason to contact you."

"Me?" Shock took her voice to a higher pitch. "Why in the world me?"

"We were hoping you could tell us that, Doctor."

"I'm not a smuggler, I'm a psychologist. What would he want

with me?"

He leaned forward in his chair. "We have records of telephone calls to this telephone number."

She started to fidget in her chair. This man obviously thought she knew something about the criminal he pursued. "I don't know this De Flores person. I don't even have any Spanish clients."

"Please, do not be alarmed. We know exactly who you are. We were just hoping you might shed some light on the subject. Perhaps you might have a client who might be connected in some way."

"No. Nothing that I know of. I did have a Latino man previously, but he is of Mexican origin and I know his family. Right now, my clientele is nothing but American citizens."

He stood. "Thank you for seeing me. You may hear from me again but as of now, I believe we are finished with any questions I might have." He shook her hand as she showed him out. "And, please, Doctor, do not be alarmed. We have no suspicions that you are in any way criminally involved."

He stepped into the outer hall. "If you think of anything further, please telephone me at the number I've written on the back of the card. It's my hotel. Good day, Doctor Hagan."

She took a deep breath as she stepped back into the office, closing the door behind her. "Good Lord, I really was talking to Sherlock Holmes. It's a shame he didn't have a hat to tip. That would have really frosted the cake."

#

Sarah was glad the Art Institute was open late on Thursday evenings. She had time after her last client to stop on her way home. One of her most relaxing pastimes was to visit the rooms that featured paintings by Monet. She remembered during Aris' art show he mentioned he learned his technique by watching Monet paint. What a life, well, un-life he had led. Being conscious during so many important moments in history; seeing and meeting people who would remain in the memory of society as long as there was a society. A life that frightened her yet continued to fascinate her. She decided she would think about all of that later.

The clock on the marble wall showed fifteen past six. Aris was rarely late, especially knowing the museum closed at eight o'clock. She was on the verge of being concerned for him when she saw him hurry through the front door. He waved when he saw her and his bright smile made her gasp. Would she ever become accustomed to this vibrant being walking across the foyer to meet her? Every woman he passed turned to look at him. He was truly a babe magnet, but he never appeared to notice anyone except her.

"*His Immortal charm,*" she thought.

She stepped to greet him. His lips were cool as they brushed her cheek lightly.

"So sorry I am late. I was detained at the gallery. It seems they would like to do another show. They find my Impressionist work intriguing." He laughed out loud. "Would they not be surprised to know from whom I learned it?"

Taking his hand, she hurried through the main hall. "Let's go visit the master's work."

The galleries were thinning as the daytime visitors left for their dinners. The evening clientele was just beginning to arrive in trickles. They found six o'clock to be a perfect time for some degree of privacy with the art.

When they reached the gallery with the Monet haystacks, they sat on the bench in the center of the room. Sometimes when she came here alone, tears sprang to her eyes at the beauty and intensity of the art that surrounded her. He held her hand as they sat in silence and just observed. It was many minutes before either of them spoke. It was Sarah who broke the silence.

"I had the strangest visitor today."

"Yes?"

"Yes, one of your countrymen. Some sort of international police force. It kind of freaked me out at first, but it turned out they just hoped I could give them some information." She snickered, "I love the last names of the British, the hyphens are great."

"Hyphens?"

"Yeah, see." She handed Aris the card the handsome policeman had given her.

He froze as he read it.

"Aris, what's wrong?"

He looked around the room making sure no one could hear him before he spoke. "Sarah, Richard Rhys-Davis is a vampire."

Her head swam, her fingers clutched the bench where they sat. He spoke hurriedly. "No fear. It is Richard from the Catacombs. He would never harm you." His voice was pensive. "But what is he doing here in America? And for what reason did he come to you?"

She took a couple of deep breaths. "I feel better now." She smoothed her skirt. "It was just a shock. How many vampires am I going to have in my life?" Shaking her head to clear it, she placed her hands on her temples and closed her eyes.

"I sincerely hope this is the last one, Sarah. But please, do not fear Richard. When he became one of the Immortals, he took the Blood Oath. He will harm no innocent human."

"But why is he here?" Her soft whisper matched his.

"What did he tell you?"

"Some story about an international Spanish criminal. Obviously not true."

Puzzled, Aris took his arm from her shoulder then folded her fingers through his. "But why you? Why would he come to you?"

"Could he be looking for you?"

"We will just have to ask him that, will we not, Sarah?"

CHAPTER 24

The Bistro was almost empty as they sat in the dim bar. They were ahead of the happy-hour crowd and, for the first time, the dark empty room appeared a bit sinister to Sarah. She had been even more nervous about the situation since Aris asked her to call Richard to set up a meeting. She had not told the strange vampire the true reason for her contacting him, simply that she needed to see him.

Aris sat across from her, spinning his glass of wine mindlessly in a slow circle.

Suddenly, his eyes shot to the door. He jumped rapidly to his feet.

The shadow of a tall powerfully built man was outlined in the doorway. Sarah willed the bartender to turn the lights brighter without success.

The man crossed the room slowly toward their table. He stared at Aris for a long moment before he spoke. "Aris?" It was a stunned whisper. "Aris?"

"Yes brother, it is I."

"But how? And when? I sense it is you, yet you inhabit a strange body? What has happened? How can this be?" Without warning, he reached his arms to encircle his lost friend in a hug between giants.

"Here, sit." Aris pulled a chair from beneath the table, motioning Richard to sit.

"So many questions, so much to tell." Sarah knew the two men could see each other clearly with their Immortal vision. She took out the glasses she so seldom wore to make sure she missed nothing in the dim indirect lights seeping down from overhead.

She listened as Aris explained his journey in a soft voice. Through the melody of their accents, it was as if she were listening to a fairy story told to frighten children on a cold rainy night. But it was reality. Her reality and impossibly, one she had begun to treasure. There was not only a surprising absence of fear, but an unexplored deep calling that came to her when she was in the presence of the Immortals.

"So there is my story." Aris finished his tale. The friends stared at each other in silence.

"I mourned you. I mourned you to this day and now, I know joy that you are here."

"But you? Richard, what are you doing here? How did you find me?"

"You are not the reason I have come here. I am truly looking for someone." He settled in as he began his part of the tale.

"You see, some time ago, a vampire came to us from Spain, Ricardo De Flores. He came to us for sanctuary, he said. He was made by the same wild coven that made Gabriela and me. He proclaimed he was seeking a more peaceful life. He was questioned, tested over and over by the Council and after some time they became convinced he was in earnest. He took the Blood Oath and joined us as a member of the Catacombs.

"He was an adept student, doing well in the sciences. He worked with the Master Keeper of the Infinity Diaries to categorize and authenticate information. Everyone was quite pleased with his performance. He was a solitary chap, but that was not thought of as strange. Coming from such a wild place, we knew he needed seclusion and peace to settle his past.

"Excuse me." Both the men turned to Sarah as she spoke. She had been silent for most of their conversation, but now, her curiosity got the better of her. "Can you explain the Infinity Diaries?"

Richard spoke. "The Diaries are accounts of every human and Immortal that has ever lived or died. They account the re-incarnation of every soul. They were begun shortly after Queen Akira and King Khansu arrived on earth as a part of their research into human life. The Diaries have evolved over the years as knowledge and research techniques in the Catacombs have developed. They are ancient, yet far from complete.

"The Diaries are secret and sacred to our kind. Whoever holds them holds the key to knowledge of the world past and the world to come and that knowledge gives the holder great power. Time and events are not set in stone. If the proposed future is known, it can be manipulated. If the Master Keeper was unscrupulous, he could command the world.

"Because trust in newcomers to the Catacombs is built slowly over time and De Flores was new to our society, it was centuries before he held an important position. One day he did not appear to attend to his appointed duties. He had been prompt and industrious so the Master wondered at his absence. Another day and then a third. The Master sent for him and was told his chamber was empty except for one of the Diaries. When it was brought to him, it was found a soul chart was missing, stolen from the ancient holy records. After a great deal of research, it was discovered that the soul chart was of Elizabeth Wyatt's lives and deaths and re-incarnations. I tracked him through dimensions and centuries until I found his trail led here to Chicago, to Sarah."

Her eyes were wide in fright, the pupils dilated even in the dim light. Her skin felt cold and clammy. When she spoke her voice was a hoarse whisper. "The crimson roses on my pillow. A strange vampire has been in my room."

Aris rose quickly, moving to her side. "Do not be afraid. We are here. No one can harm you while we are here. You have my word."

"A crimson rose?" Richard leaned toward her, then backed quickly away. He didn't want to frighten Sarah any further. Aris explained the phantom florist to his friend. It took a moment for Sarah to regain her composure. She sat quietly trying to decide if it was fright or anger at the thought of a strange vampire creeping into her home.

#

"So who's the woman who answered your phone?"

Sarah could hear the curiosity in Colleen's voice even through the receiver of the phone. She wasn't really lying as she answered. "It's one of Carlos' relatives visiting for a few weeks. Carlos didn't have a place to put her up so she's staying here."

Another one of the undead in her life. When would it stop? Did she really want it to stop? The excitement of a life that was totally impossible and gravely dangerous generated a feverish exhilaration she didn't know she had in her. What was becoming of the old play-it-safe Sarah, the woman who got up in the morning, did her job and went to bed early at night? She was slowly disappearing into a world that was unfathomable and mystifying. She was now sharing her apartment with a female vampire, feeling perfectly safe and comfortable.

"So who is she? What's she like?"

"Her name is Gabriela Rivera. She's about his age and she's lovely."

"How long is she going to be staying with you?"

"Oh, I don't know." Sarah was noncommittal as she spoke. "For a few weeks. It's no bother at all and I'm enjoying having the company."

"Yeah? Well the girls will have to get together to welcome her."

"That would be nice, C."

"Got another call, got to go."

#

She had been so initially frightened at the thought of an unknown vampire in her apartment that Sarah didn't even consider when Richard brought Gabriela to Chicago she was inviting another one to move in with her. Immediately responding to the need of his chosen brother to keep his loved one safe, Richard contacted his mate and confidante to help them. He took charge of the situation while Sarah tried to collect herself still sitting in shock at the table in The Bistro. Through a fog she heard him say to book a flight on the next plane.

Aris stayed with her all night and the next day until Gabriela arrived from London. She arrived looking beautiful, unflustered and completely in control, another perfect Immortal. Her musical voice was soft, warm and encouraging. Sarah felt instantly and incomprehensibly secure with the tall, lean, golden brown beauty. She had effortlessly become a part of Sarah's daily existence, watching over her, making sure she was safe from the unknown intruder. Richard and Aris searched the city unable to locate any information about the Spanish fraud. Who was he really? What did he want with Sarah? Had he wanted to hurt her, he would have. What was the rose? Did it have meaning? Unanswered questions as the two Immortals scoured the city using all of their powers to find him.

Their search was to no avail. Each day they felt the bitterness of a stalemate. Sarah worked, ate and slept in a somnambulant state nearly all of the time, unable to truly accept the world she now lived in. For the most part she expected to wake from one of her lucid dreams to find her life just as mundane as it always had been, safe, dull, normal, whatever that meant. Yet every morning there was Gabriela, smiling with a cup of hot coffee, waiting as Sarah stumbled into the kitchen.

"Your friend, Maggie, makes me laugh. Are all Americans so light hearted?" Listening very closely, Sarah began to detect a slight British accent sprinkling itself gently through Gabriela's Spanish-softened English.

Sarah wrapped her robe around her legs as she sat on the sofa next to the dark beauty, sipping from the mug she held in her hand. She smiled. "No, Maggie is special. I really haven't ever met anyone quite like her. She does appear to always be happy."

"Such a rare trait for a human. Your kind seems to worry incessantly about situations that have not yet occurred."

Sarah was pensive. "Yes, I suppose you're right. We do have a lot of unnecessary fears." She sipped her coffee wondering why it always tasted better when Gabriela brewed it for her.

"Will we be going to your office today?" The Immortal had been accompanying Sarah everywhere she went when either Aris or Richard weren't with her. They watched her day and night, making sure she was in no danger from the phantom.

"No, I don't have any clients today. I have an appointment myself to see my therapist."

"Sarah, please explain the human need for therapists. You are not without close friends; why do you see someone outside your circle for your problems?"

"It isn't that I don't have friends, a psychologist has specialized training to guide their client into their own sub-conscious. A friend can listen and empathize, however they really rarely have the insight of a trained therapist. And Bonnie is a hypnotherapist as well. She puts me in direct contact with my deepest self. Answers seem to come more quickly with hypnosis."

"I see," she laughed and it sounded as light as the tune played from a child's music box. "Perhaps I should pursue a time with Bonnie. It sounds very interesting."

"It certainly has been for me." She took her last sip of coffee and placed the empty mug on the table next to the sofa. "Gabriela, would you mind telling me more about the Catacombs? The Infinity Diaries intrigue me."

"The Infinity Diaries are the tales of every human and Immortal soul that has ever lived or will be reincarnated. Each story begins at the inception of the soul and grows as the soul moves from life to life. Each incarnation is recorded, start to finish. It is the soul's journey throughout its time on earth. You are included in the diaries just as every other human is included."

"So reincarnation is in fact true?"

"Why do you sound so shocked, Sarah? Is it not the basis for your work?"

Sarah grinned sheepishly. "Yes, but it isn't something that can be proved. I just believed it made sense. May I ask another question?"

"Yes, of course."

Sarah did her best to appear nonchalant, "Well, it's about the relationships between male and female Immortals?"

"What would you like to know?"

She cleared her throat, "Well, are your marriages the same as for humans?"

"We do not call them marriages. They are different in many ways from the mating of humans. There is a deeper bond as we all share the venom of Akira, a sameness that runs inside all of us. We are more sensitive to the desires of one another. There is no jealousy, no anger, no misunderstandings because of it. We do not bare children so our households are just two, the male and the female.

We work, we play, we socialize. We create bonds that you would call friendships. Our mutual existence is rich and rewarding."

Sarah felt the color rise in her cheeks. "Umm, you don't reproduce you say." How the hell does a person ask a vampire how they have sex? She wasn't quite sure but she had to know. The feelings stirring inside her for Aris pushed her forward. "But you do share physical intimacy?"

"Oh yes. We experience human desire and release yet it is a great deal more. The venom speaks through our coupling. It flows between us, our life essence becomes one. The intensity is so great a fragile human being could never survive the exchange of the mating venom. It is truly impossible to describe in language the ecstasy, the bliss of the joining."

"I guess that gives me the answer," she thought. *"There's only one way to be with Aris. I just can't think about that right now."*

She spoke as she stood, taking her empty cup to the kitchen. "I'd better get dressed if I don't want to be late for my appointment with Bonnie." She turned to face her new friend. "Will you ride along with me?"

"Yes Sarah, one of us will be with you until this situation is resolved. Do not worry. You are safe."

"Safe," she thought. *"But am I safe from my own desire?"* Hurrying to her bedroom, she put the question from her mind as she began dressing.

#

Gabriela sat in the lobby glancing through a magazine as Bonnie took Sarah back in time.

SARAH HAGAN, transcript, session 5

The rushes beneath my feet let off a lovely, fresh scent as my riding boots bore down on them and my long blue velvet riding skirt skimmed them. As I hurried through the great corridor to meet my cousin,

Thomas, I drew warm gloves onto my chilled hands to shield them from the frost of the dawning day. The heavy fog was just beginning to lift and the sun to make its first appearance as I made my way down the palace steps toward the handsome young man who waited without complaint in the cold. His powerful black stallion, not nearly so patient, pawed the ground and snorted great puffs of steam from his flaring nostrils.

"Thomas, how handsome you look. Have you set that silver feather in your cap to catch some unsuspecting maiden?"

He laughed as he answered, "no, sweet Elizabeth, to charm no one save you."

"Dear cousin, I am thusly charmed." I returned his affectionate banter as my groomsman assisted me in mounting my perfect white hunter. The saddle trimmings captured the blue of my riding clothes exactly. "And what of this man I am to meet today? Who is he?" I asked because it was expected. I felt no interest in any man since losing Diego and coming to court except perhaps the tall, blond Adonis appearing out of nowhere at the royal banquet.

We walked our animals slowly while Thomas held the reins in a tight hand, his stallion pulling at the bit, ripe for a swift run. "A friend and a favorite of the King."

"But his name?"

"Aris."

I was puzzled. "Aris? That is all?"

"He came to us from a foreign court and that is the singular way he wishes to be called."

"So Thomas, tell me of him." Not truly caring, I feigned interest to please my cousin.

"He is courageous and a man of honor."

"Of course or he would not be in service to the King, but is he tall and of fair countenance?"

Chuckling my companion answered, "Yes sweet Bess, he is tall and very handsome although somewhat reserved with the ladies." He hesitated *but a moment. "Or so it seems."*

Sincerely intrigued, after a moment I spoke. "Tell me more."

"Rumor in the court has it that several of Lady Anne's maids-in-waiting have approached him yet he has responded not at all. No one knows why as there is no doubt of his virility. He is a champion of the joust and has won many great battles in foreign lands."

"How rare for a courtier to not take advantage of every opportunity for a liaison. I do look forward to meeting him."

"The time is now. He approaches."

I stifled a gasp as he swung from his horse and took the bridles from our hands. Standing before me was the golden god who captured my attention at the King's banquet. Powerfully built yet lithe with a strong jaw and fascinating blue eyes, his golden curls tousled beneath his Imperial cap, the soft tuft of hair on his chin begged to be kissed. Surely any woman would succumb to his potent charm.

A groomsman handed each of us a stirrup cup to ease the chill. He bowed to me. "Mistress Elizabeth." Then to my cousin. "Thomas."

And that is how I met him. Aris.

Sarah smiled as memories flooded her mind.

The courtship began. It was glorious. Long walks along the frozen Thames. Mulled wine beside the fire. Banquets. Hunts. Masques. And always as if I were the only maid in the realm. How could one not grow to love such a man? The ache in my heart left by the loss of my dark gypsy was slowly, meticulously healed by the attention and caring of this beautiful knight of King Henry's.

My cousin had told me true of the rebuked attentions of the other maids. There were stares full of jealousy and words of scorn spoken secretly behind my back. I knew yet I cared not. His presence brought me joy in a way I never dreamed possible.

Then one afternoon as I walked in the snow-kissed garden dressed warmly against the winter's chill, he appeared. He walked beside me silently for some moments. Taking my hand, he turned to face me. It was then he pledged his love and devotion. My heart soared as a great bird, its wings taking it higher and higher toward the warmth of the sun. I responded in kind, unable to restrain the declaration of my undying adoration. He gazed into my eyes as he asked me to share my life with him, to become his true wife. Tears poured down my cheeks as I uttered the only word that I could speak. "Yes."

He kissed away my tears of joy and held me gently. We were silent for some time, wrapped in our love and each other's arms. Soft white snowflakes began to fall gently, adding to the scattered powder on the ground. It was only then that he led me into the palace, our moment of solitary joy ending as we joined the courtiers. A secret smile filled my heart as I thought of my life to come with this gentle man.

CHAPTER 25

Gabriela and Richard had taken the evening to be alone in their hotel so it was Aris who watched from the shadows across the street from Sarah's apartment. She was dressed beautifully in evening clothes as the taxi pulled to the curb. He knew she was meeting a man and his un-beating heart ached in his chest. The pain tore through him as he hurried down the sidewalk. The evening traffic moved at a snail's pace, making it easy for him to keep the car in sight. His two vows, to keep her safe from the phantom vampire and to never intrude in her human life, battled within him. He would watch her only until she reached her destination. Unable to endure seeing her with another man, a human man, he would turn away as she stepped from the cab. He would not spy on her as she joined his rival. But was it truly a rival?

She had not seen fit to tell him of the man. He took that as in his favor. Perhaps it was of no importance, simply a friend, a colleague with whom she shared time. Yet, if it was of no importance, why did she not tell him? Why did she keep their meetings secret?

His human nature roared inside of him. His desire to set upon the other male, rip him to shreds, take him out of her life, fought constantly with his deeper integrity. Her choice would be her own. If he lost her, it would be his destiny to be alone throughout eternity. Perhaps that was his final judgment, his personal hell for being what he was. Could he withstand the loss of her? He was comforted knowing that through his great love for her, he could withstand anything this world put before him. He hurried on down the street, her silent protector.

#

DeMarco stood just outside the doors of the opera house so handsome and dignified in his evening clothes. Sarah exited the taxi and waved to him. Once again, he was there, waiting when she arrived.

"You look beautiful, Sarah." His eyes glistened as he watched her walk beside him. Heads turned as they entered the building. She knew they were a striking couple. "We have plenty of time before the house lights go down. Would you care for a glass of wine?"

"Yes, that would be nice." He slid her coat from her shoulders and took it to the coat check. She waited for him apart from the crowd milling around the lobby, watching all the women try not to be too blatant with their appreciative stares. He really was amazing to look at. *"Such a gentleman,"* she thought. She hoped that would remain true when she told him she was seeing someone else as well. She could tell by the way he looked at her and touched her he was ready to take their relationship to the next level. She enjoyed his company enormously and found him more than physically desirable, yet she was held back by her deep attachment to Aris. She felt DeMarco had a right to know.

He bought their drinks as she found a quiet place near an exit door for them to sit.

"Have you seen *Madam Butterfly* before?" His voice was soft and as she leaned closer to hear him more clearly, his fragrance floated on the air. It was strangely familiar to her, yet she couldn't quite place it.

"No, I haven't, but I've wanted to for a long time." She decided it was a good moment to talk. They had the whole opera together for him to digest her news before they separated for the evening. She hoped it would be time for him to accept the situation. She didn't want to lose him from her life, but she knew she had to be honest with him. If she thought about it too much, she wouldn't tell him.

"DeMarco," she began. "I feel I need to tell you that I am also seeing someone else. It's someone I've known for a long time and I have feelings for him." His jaw stiffened as he turned toward her giving her his full attention.

"Yes?"

She could see he wasn't going to give her any help with her confession so, a bit disconcerted, she plunged ahead. "Of course you and the time we spend together are also important to me. Very important. You have brought a whole new element into my life and I'm very grateful. I just need a little more time before we move forward any further."

Her deeper thoughts were along a much different line. "*Am I crazy? I haven't had sex in at least a hundred years and this hunk is sitting here right in front of me like candy in a candy store.*" She was aware Colleen would never let her forget it if she knew.

His face froze and he was silent as she told him of his rival. She wished she could read his mind. When he finally spoke, it was with a forced smile. "Sarah, I am rather old fashioned myself. Please, don't worry. There is plenty of time for us to get to know one another more fully and I am happy simply sharing time with you." He touched her hand lightly. "You don't mind a kiss once in a while, do you?"

Blushing, she cast her gaze at the floor. He lifted her chin and looking into her blue, confused eyes, kissed her gently just as the house lights flashed signaling the patrons the opera was about to begin. Taking her elbow, he helped her to stand. She was glad he did, because her knees were weak at the feel of his thick, silky lips on hers.

As they moved into the theatre, his thoughts were in a completely different vein than their conversation had been. "*I will have her. She will not be taken from me by another. She is mine.*"

CHAPTER 26

"So what's up with the men in your life?" As they sat on Sarah's couch, Colleen unconsciously rubbed the pregnancy bulge that was now obvious through her sweatshirt.

"What do you mean 'what's up'?"

"Come on kid, don't be coy with me." She looked at her friend, disbelief registering in her eyes. "Don't tell me, you're still the only divorced, semi-virgin in town. Don't you know it's illegal to be seeing two such gorgeous men and not getting any action?"

"C, it isn't about action, it's about commitment."

"Honestly hon, I don't know how I can be best friends with such a freak. What in the hell is wrong with you?" She spoke through her laughter, but Colleen's question was sincere. Sometimes she just couldn't figure out how Sarah's brain really worked.

"First of all, I'm not a freak." She paused a moment as she thought then answered. "Well, maybe I am, just a little. I just want to be sure before I sleep with DeMarco that it isn't something I'll be sorry for? I don't want to step into something that may hurt him later on. Or hurt me for that matter."

"DeMarco? What the hell about Carlos? He'd be all over you in a second if you gave him the slightest indication you were willing.

I can't believe you two haven't done it yet." She shook her head in mock sorrow. "That poor guy."

"Come on, C. He and I have talked about it. He knows it's something I don't take lightly. He's also young and been through a lot. I'm not even sure how I feel or if it could work anyway. And maybe it's just because I haven't been too active lately. It's sort of come to mean something more to me than it does to most people." She thought, *"And as a human, I'm not quite willing to be ripped limb from limb for an orgasm with Aris."* She giggled nervously at the thought of making love to him.

"I don't think it's funny. I honestly think you need to talk to your therapist about this kiddo. There is definitely something amiss in your brain to walk away from goodies like that." She grabbed Sarah's hands to pull her off the sofa. "Come on Virgin Queen, let's get a move on or we'll be late for the movie."

Sarah called out to Gabriela who was reading in the guest room. "We're leaving Gaby. Are you sure you don't want to go?"

Responding, the dark beauty walked into the room. "You know, I changed my mind. I think I will join you after all." Gabriela winked at Sarah as she grabbed her coat from the closet and the two women and one Immortal made their way down the hall to the elevator.

#

Rain was pounding the windows of Bonnie's office as the two friends sat in comfortable chairs facing one another.

"Bonnie, do you think there's something wrong with me? I mean about sex?"

"Please explain that unexpected bomb a little further."

"Well, Colleen and I were talking and she pretty much told me she thinks I'm crazy because I won't have sex with DeMarco because I don't feel ready." Sarah didn't want to bring Aris into the equation because her reasons for not jumping his bones were completely different--her life and the survival of her body, for example.

"Humm." Bonnie was thoughtful before she spoke. "I don't think you're crazy, Sarah. I think you're old fashioned about this, but you've always been like that. It's the way you were brought up and it's just never changed. As long as I've known you, your sex life has been something you've kept to yourself except during your divorce from Jeff. Even then, you weren't too verbal about the personal things, just your dissatisfaction with his attentions. I must admit, it's a whole lot different from most women your age and in your present circumstances, but crazy? No. It's just a part of your basic character. You're also trying to prevent your heart from being hurt again."

"Thank goodness. I was beginning to worry. I just don't want to confuse lust with love and that's an easy thing to do, isn't it?"

"Yes it is, obviously. That's why there are so many divorces. But today, a whole lot of people are happy to just satisfy their lust without the whole love/commitment thing. Do you think that's a wrong way to look at it, Sarah?"

"No. I think what people do in their bedrooms is up to them. And it isn't that I don't have the desire." She thought about her dreams and visions. "Yes, I definitely have the desire. There's just something that holds me back, makes me feel it must be for something deeper."

"Does it bother you that you feel like that?"

"Honestly, no. It bothers the hell out of Colleen though." She laughed.

"Well, this is your session, not hers. Why don't we put you under and see if we can come up with anything from Elizabeth that might give us some insight into this other than your own Puritanical background." They both chuckled as Sarah moved to the recliner.

SARAH HAGAN, transcript, session 6

His face was flushed against the chill and from his hurried steps through the corridor to my rooms. "Wolsey said yes, he will approach Queen Katherine." Genuine mirth sparkled in his bright blue eyes as he told me the news. He lifted me from the floor, spinning me in a gentle circle. "You are to be my bride."

"Aris, how soon?" Desire welled within me to be held, to be loved by this man. To consummate our union. To be one with him.

"Soon, my love." He moved us nearer to the fire to warm his hands and still be close to me. "Meanwhile, I must be gone from the palace for a few weeks."

My face fell as an emptiness filled my heart at the thought of not having him near. "A few weeks? But where do you go, my love? How will I survive without you for even a few hours?"

"I must go on a King's mission, Elizabeth. I am unable to tell even you whence it will take me. But know this, there is no danger to me and when I return, we will be wed. That I promise you. With Wolsey's help, there will be no interference from the King. The Queen is greatly influenced by the Cardinal. She will see fit to give her permission and all will be as it should be."

I did my best to cover my ache at the thought of his being away. I chose not to tarnish his wonderful news with thoughts of his absence from me.

The next week was filled with love and anticipation, yet sorrow and regret surrounded me at the consideration of his imminent departure. When the day came for him to leave court, I followed him to the great doors of the palace. I watched, fighting tears as he rode away. He turned, throwing a kiss to me and I thought I would die without him. Never did I think there could be such depth of feeling about another. I began to understand in my heart the fire of true love. All I had felt before was infatuation, sensual appetite, carnal passion. My desire for the gypsy had been nothing more than that, desire. But to my simple maid's mind, it was love. As a woman who now lived for a man, I understood for the first time that true love was not just about the desires of the body but of the mind and the heart. My love for Aris was never ending. Nothing could ever separate my heart from his. There was no other love for me in this life or the next.

Bonnie smiled as she thought, "And there dear friend, we have our answer without even trying. True love or nothing. Most certainly a double-edged sword."

I waited impatiently. Days turned into one week, two. I attended Queen Katherine and visited Anne's rooms whenever she called for me. I watched her grow more nervous. She grew thinner and more belligerent with her ladies and her court. I could see the toll her part took upon her as she did her all to keep the King wrapped around her finger. One afternoon I heard her tell Smeaton she must rid the palace of the Queen. As long as Katherine queened it over the court, Anne could never have the full attention of Henry. Yet as I watched them together, it appeared the King was besotted with his mistress. I could see her become short in her dealings with him and wondered to what lengths she would go to find her way into the royal crown of the Queen of England.

It was late on a cloudy afternoon as I walked the royal labyrinth alone when my past intruded into my present. Stepping from behind a tall bush, Diego stood before me, his clothes rumpled and his beard so thick it took a moment for me to recognize him. I stood frozen on the path.

When he spoke, his voice was hoarse with emotion, his eyes blazing with love and much more than love - desire. "I have come for you, Elizabeth. I will take you from this place and we will be together once again."

Shocked, unable to speak, I stood rooted to the spot, my mind racing, trying to comprehend what was happening. How did he find me? What could I possibly say to him to make him understand that we were finished, that I loved another?

He approached me, taking me in his arms. My body stiffened and I turned my face away from his seeking lips. "What is wrong Elizabeth? Why do you turn away? It has been an arduous task to find you, to come to rescue you." He held me at arm's length, staring into my eyes. I couldn't meet his gaze and looked to the ground. Placing his hand beneath my chin, he lifted my face.

Looking deeply into his eyes, I spoke. "Diego, I never thought to see you again." I pulled away from his grip, stepping out of the range of his embrace.

"And so you forgot me? What of your pledge of love?" His tone was no longer soft, sweet. It was hard and demanding. "Have you forgotten the blissful moments we shared? The promises we made?"

"Diego, those promises were made by two different people. I live a new life now. Please understand. The promises were true in the moment, but the moment is passed. I have made new vows."

"New vows? What is meant by those words, 'new vows'?"

I hesitated, not wanting to hurt him, yet knowing he must be told the truth. Finally, I spoke. "There is another."

"Another?" He did not move, but stood frozen, blocking my path. His voice was flat, without emotion. "What other?"

"I was sent to court against my will. I fought it but to no avail. Finally, after many long nights and days of tears, I was able to put the past behind me. "

"Why did you not run away; why did you not return to me? What other man is in your life? What new vows have you made?"

"Diego, it was impossible. I mourned you and lived in sorrow for a very long time, but slowly I adapted to my new life. It satisfied me. I found contentment."

"You found contentment?" His voice grew louder as he spoke. "You found happiness without me while I suffered my loss and searched for the woman who had proclaimed her love for me."

"My proclamation was not false. My love was true, but it was the love of a girl. I was not yet a woman when we met, when you took me and made me yours. I have grown into a woman. Diego, I have found a woman's love."

Dark eyes flashing, he struck me in the face with such force, I fell to the ground. He shouted at me as I lay upon the cold earth. "A woman's love? What do you know of a woman's love? You have been seduced into the life of a courtier." Realizing what he had done in a fit of anger, he reached to pull me to my feet. I ignored his outstretched hand and rose from the ground without his assistance. I stood several feet from him. . Without the least hesitation he approached me, his arms open to embrace me.

"Do not come near me, Diego. I will call for the guards that surround the labyrinth."

"Please, Elizabeth. I adore you. I have thought of nothing but you since you were taken away from me. I must have you for mine." I stepped farther away from him. My adding to the distance between us fueled the rage he barely had under control.

He snarled as he reached for me, the look on his face one I had never seen before. "Enough! You are mine and you will come with me now." As I turned to run, he lunged for me, sending both of us into a pile on the ground. "No, I will take you here. You will forget any other man that has come into your life. You are mine." I fought him as he tugged on my skirts. I felt his rough hands bruising my thighs.

"Let me go, let me go." My teeth clenched as I used all my strength to push him from on top of me. Again he slapped me, harder than before.

"Guard! Guard!" I shouted with the full force of my lungs. We could hear the sounds of the soldiers as they ran through the labyrinth toward my call.

He jumped to his feet, moving to make his escape. He turned just before he disappeared into the thick brush of the tall hedge. He looked at me one last time. "You have not seen the last of me, Elizabeth. Rest assured of that." And he was gone. By the time the guards reached me, I had composed myself. I told them I slipped and fell. I told them I thought

I injured myself, but realized I had not. I asked them to accompany me to the palace and, once there, I hurried to my room.

There was fear in my heart and I vowed to stay in the palace until Aris returned. I knew he was my protector. He would keep me safe. But how could I tell him of my past? Would he still accept me knowing I had belonged to another? I could only pray. I waited restless and uneasy for his return.

Early one morning just a few days after the incident with Diego, I was summoned to the palace of Cardinal Wolsey. I went with joy in my heart. Queen Katherine must have given her blessing on our betrothal and the Cardinal was the man chosen to give me the wonderful news. When I arrived, I was shown into his private rooms.

He sat in a great carved chair in front of the fireplace, his red satin robes sprawling around his enormous hulk. He raised his hand so I might kiss his ring. I curtsied, my lips brushing the cold of the jewels and the gold. As I rose I saw his eyes. They were dark and ominous. All was not well in his bringing me to his chambers. My heart began to race in my chest.

"Lady Elizabeth, I regret to tell you that Queen Katherine has seen fit to refuse your petition for marriage."

I drew in my breath sharply as I fought back the tears that stung my eyes. I spoke without forethought. "Your Grace, how can this be? For what reason would she deny us this request?"

His tone was stern. "My Lady, you question the decision of your Queen?"

More able to control my voice, I spoke. "I do not question, your Grace. I simply do not understand. Neither my suitor nor I am of great value to the Queen. We would both remain in her service. May I not know the reason for my heartbreak."

"The reason, my Lady, is that we have found a more suitable match."

My head grew light as I reached for the arm of his chair to steady myself. "A more suitable match, your Grace? Who would be more suitable than a Knight and a maid?"

"Again you question." A deep scowl creased his brow as he rose, brushing my hand away from the chair. I swayed, willing myself to stay on my feet. "You will sail tomorrow for Spain and your immediate marriage. You will go to your chambers now to prepare for the voyage and you will see no one, tell no one of this decision. No one, do you hear? This is the Queen's wish and so my command. Be gone."

As I staggered toward the door, it opened and the Cardinal's guard marched into the room. They surrounded me as if I were a prisoner, accompanying me to my rooms where I was locked behind the huge wooden door to sob and mourn my impending fate, alone and without recourse. There was nowhere to turn. The single door was the only way from my rooms. It was locked and flanked by soldiers. If only there was a way I could reach the Queen, yet I knew it was hopeless. Wolsey had made certain of my capture and departure. How could I live a life without my love? I could not. I would not. I would throw myself into the sea rather than be touched by another man. As I gathered my things for my hasty departure, I made my decision. I would never reach Spain, never be possessed by another. I pledged my life to my love and was determined to end it rather than betray him. I packed but a few items into my trunks. There is little that is needed at the bottom of the sea.

#

Sarah lay in the recliner, silent, eyes shut against the twilight as it turned the sky as gray as her mood. So this was how it had happened. This was how they were separated.

"Sarah." Bonnie's soft voice called from somewhere outside herself, calling her back into the moment, into a reality that carried with it new insights. "Sarah, come back to real time."

"I am Bonnie. I'm here." She opened her eyes as a huge sigh escaped her lips. "That was a really hard one, wasn't it?"

"Do you want to talk about it now?"

She swung her legs over the chair as she rubbed her eyes. Glancing at her watch, she shook her head. "No, not really. We can cover it next time. Besides, DeMarco is meeting me for dinner and I don't want to keep him waiting."

"I'm sure he won't mind if you need a moment to clear your mind."

"No, really, I'm fine. Just a little shocked. It isn't what I expected."

"I suppose not. Well, remember, I'm just a phone call away."

Sarah pulled her coat over her sweater then hugged Bonnie. "I'll call you tomorrow and we'll make a gym date. Really hon, I'm okay. Just a little residual tiredness, that's all."

Bonnie kissed her cheek as Sarah hurried past her to meet her dinner companion.

#

Candlelight sparkled in his dark eyes as DeMarco asked the waiter for the check. He turned to face her. His words were casual but his tone was serious, more serious than she had ever heard from him.

"Sarah," he reached across the table to take her hands in his. "When we were at the opera it was you who needed to speak and now it is I."

She tilted her head in question as he continued. "First, I have fallen in love with you. This must come as no surprise. I know our relationship is new, yet I feel I know you so well. You are everything I have ever wanted in a woman. And more. Your beauty, your intelligence, the way you live your life all make you someone to openly adore."

"DeMarco."

"No, please let me go on. I made this decision after our evening at the opera when I realized I might lose you before you know my feelings. My desire is to win your affection, to be the only one in your life. He stopped talking as he turned her hands in his to kiss her palms one at a time. "You told me there is someone else that you care for and I appreciate your honesty, but I am determined to win you. I will court you until you recognize that I am the only one for you. And when you do choose me, my very existence will be centered on making you happy. I can give you all the material desires you might have and more love than you know is possible." He sat silently, waiting for her response.

"DeMarco, I'm a bit overwhelmed." She chose her words carefully, slowly. "You're right, our relationship is very new. We are just getting to know one another and what I have come to know about you is all good. I'm grateful and happy to have you in my life and I'm sincerely honored that you expressed your feelings to me so openly. I must admit I definitely have feelings that are drawing me to you." She wondered how her voice could be so calm when her heart was racing in her chest.

"I felt I must declare myself because I am traveling once again to Italy. It was important to me that you understand how I feel since I leave soon and will be out of the country for a few weeks."

"When will you leave?" There was disappointment in her voice.

"In just a few days. However, when I return, it is my hope that we will be spending a great deal more time together."

"I will miss you. I enjoy every moment we spend together and I'll look forward to many, many more when you are back in the states."

He sensed her sadness at his leaving and was silently pleased. She had no idea how determined he was to have her. She had no idea what he was willing to do to make her his alone. She had no idea why. He laid his credit card on the check as he answered, "That is all I ask, Sarah. Just one more moment. Time and again, just one more moment."

#

She lay in her bed, her head throbbing. It had been a day she never wanted to re-live. Suicide. My God, did she really commit suicide? She supposed her next session with Bonnie would reveal the answer to that. And DeMarco? Could she love him? He had been a new ray of sunshine in her hope for a human love. But could she allow herself to fall in love with him? She was drawn to him, excited by him, yet something kept her from running into his arms. Questions. Always questions. She wondered again if she should tell Aris about DeMarco. Her feelings for the Italian doctor were becoming deeper, more demanding. She felt Aris needed to know, but what would that do to her relationship with the vampire?

She knew she cared for Aris. She laughed at herself. Such a shallow word for her feelings for him. She so very much more than cared for Aris, but the price she would have to pay to be with him was enormous. How could she give up her life, her friends, her family. A small voice inside her head kept repeating, *"The only thing you will have to give up is your human life."* Her human life, her human past. All the people she had ever known and loved. The voice answered, *"No one will ever know. To everyone, all will be the same. Only the Immortals will know what you have become."* She pulled the pillow over her head to silence the murmur. And then it became a shout. *"What will your life be without him?"*

"What will become of my life at all? Without him, there is emptiness. With him there is death. Either way, I am doomed."

"I'll think of this in the light of day," she chanted over and over to still the voice until at last, she drifted into a troubled and restless sleep.

#

Her dream took her once again to Henry's court in England. It was the day of a royal joust. As one of the Queen's maidens, she shared the royal box. But she realized she was dressed in a twenty-first century business suit and her hands were tied behind her. She struggled with her bonds to no avail. Queen Katherine laughed at her as she strived to free herself.

"Quiet, Sarah. Desist from fighting. You will be the prize to the winner no matter what you do."

Even in the dream she was shocked. She was 'Sarah' dressed much as she dressed to go to her office in current times, yet here she stood, in sixteenth century England as a trophy for the games. Her subconscious quieted and allowed the vision to continue.

A loud fanfare sounded and two contenders entered the arena, both dressed in silver armor riding enormous white stallions. One of the mounts stood quietly waiting while the other pulled at the reins, stomping his feet and pawing the air.

They both circled the arena, both stopping before the Queen to ask her blessing and her favor. Her blessing she granted to them. Her favor? It was handed to a maiden who tied it around Sarah's throat. It was soft and pink and smelled like lavender flowers.

"Show your faces," demanded the Queen.

Sarah lost her breath as the two knights removed their helmets. Aris and DeMarco revealed themselves. It seemed there was no rest from her confusion. Even in her dreams, it was a contest between the two, the man and the vampire.

Another fanfare and the two riders replaced their helmets and rode to opposite sides of the arena. The Queen stood, dropping the gauntlet and the joust began. The giant mounts pounded toward one another carrying the tremendous weight of the men and their armor. There was a loud crash as one of the riders was dismounted and lay unmoving in the dirt. The victor disappeared from the scene as one can disappear only in a dream.

When the horsemaster came to remove the helmet from the fallen knight, it was neither Aris nor DeMarco. She gasped as she saw Diego, her gypsy lover dead in the dirt.

When she woke in the morning, her pillow was still wet with her tears of frustration and sorrow.

CHAPTER 27

The four companions sat in Sarah's living room. Three Immortals and one human bonded in a way that had made them friends. They had just gathered and settled in for a quiet evening. Richard asked that they meet to share his last communication from the Catacombs.

Aris rested his hand on Sarah's shoulder as Richard began to speak. "I have good news from Sebastian. De Flores is in Spain. He is being watched by Immortals now. He has joined his coven once again. His whole subterfuge with us in the Catacombs seems to be for no fathomable reason at all. The only evidence we have of his even being in the U.S. are the roses on your pillow, Sarah, and that really isn't positive."

"But Richard, no one knows what in the world he wanted of Sarah? Did anyone find the reason he took her name from the Infinity Diaries?" Gabriela was puzzled and it was apparent in the tone of her voice.

"No, the Master Keeper was able to recreate her soul chart to complete the sequence for her, however, no one is any the wiser as to why it was taken in the first place."

Sarah trembled. Aris reached for the afghan lying over the arm of the sofa and covered her tenderly.

"It appears he is finished here and she is perfectly safe. The Immortal spies report from Spain that no other coven members are missing. It seems they are now rallying around De Flores as their leader. He is the only one of them to have traveled so far or had such an adventure. They admire his courage and wit to have made such a journey so they have proclaimed him their first King. From what is reported, they are no more developed than they were when Gabriela and I made our escape so many centuries ago. They have had no government and no leader until now."

It was Gabriela's turn to shiver. "They were murderers then and are still in spite of government, King and all." Richard reached to take her hand.

"Butchers." She interlaced her fingers with those of her mate.

"Richard?" Sarah questioned her friend. "What makes the Spanish vampires so different than those of the Catacombs? Aren't you all blood drinkers?"

"Yes, Sarah, both covens drink blood and we all are able to live as human or vampire. It is there the similarities end. The Immortals of the Catacombs are refined. We were made by Queen Akira and have her pure venom in our veins. Those of us who make others pass on that purity. We of the Catacombs are intellectuals. The Spanish coven came to being when an ancient, evil enchantress discovered the powers of the Immortals. She searched until she found a young changling who she wooed until he loved her. She convinced him to change her. She came into everlasting life a wicked and cruel witch. She used her Immortal powers to create a species of evil blood drinkers who are without conscience. They kill for the blood lust, not to survive. They find pleasure in the fear and pain of their victims.

"They have never been able to touch us. They are fearful of the Immortals and we most assuredly will never go to Spain." He stood as if to shake off the heavy feeling their conversation about the Spanish vampires had left them all experiencing. "Come, my friends, let us walk in the early spring air. It will refresh us and cleanse the vile taste of those monsters from our mouths."

"Excellent idea." Aris rose, reaching into the closet to find his jacket and Sarah's trench coat. As he helped her into it, she finally accepted the grave danger to which she had been exposed and the commitment of the Immortals to protect her. In the world she was discovering, it seemed to her it might not be such a bad idea to be invincible.

CHAPTER 28

"I can't believe you guys actually did this." Colleen held back tears of happiness as her friends led her into the large private room in the back of The Bistro. It was decorated with everything baby. Pink and blue crepe paper hung everywhere and pink and blue balloons were suspended from what appeared to be every inch of the ceiling. The couple was still in the dark about the sex of their unborn child so Bonnie and Sarah made sure both sexes were equally represented.

Tables were set; gifts were piled on a large sofa near the door. Women of every age, shape and size filled the chairs and applauded when she entered. Both the parole board and the police station were duly represented. Not one invitation sent was refused. Colleen and Bob were both loved by their co-workers and they all shared the couple's joy over this pregnancy.

"You can't have a baby without a shower." Sarah kissed her best friend on the cheek as she showed her to the place of honor in the center of the front table. Maggie waited for them to be settled before she stood, tapping loudly on a water glass to get everyone's attention.

"Good afternoon ladies. Thank you all for coming today to welcome little Bob Junior or Collette into the world. The order of the day is lunch, massive quantities of blue and pink cake and the opening of the gifts surrounded by the sipping of wine with lots of laughter throughout. And now, bon appetit."

The waiters brought in the plates as happy chatter filled the room.

CHAPTER 29

Aris and Sarah sat on her little balcony, silently watching the early spring twilight as it changed from dusk to dark. It still wasn't quite warm enough to sit outside in shirt sleeves so he wore a jacket · and she was wrapped in a blanket. She sipped a warm cup of tea as the stars began to make themselves known in the darkening sky. Her decision to tell Aris about DeMarco plagued her and her heart pounded in her chest.

"There never will be a good time so now might as well be it," she thought.

"Aris?"

"Your voice sounds very serious, Sarah. What is it?"

She stammered as she answered. "I don't quite know how to say this or if I even need to say it." Unsure as how to continue she paused, hoping he would speak to ease the discomfort of the moment.

His only reply was a single word, "Yes?"

She was reminded of DeMarco when she told him about Aris and she remembered DeMarcos's single word reply. It had been the same. She wondered if it was a universal male-thing to not help the female at all when in the midst of what could become a strained conversation. Continuing on, her sentences were short, clipped and to the point. "I've met a new friend and I've been seeing him for some time now. He told me he wants to be more than friends and I feel an attraction to him that I can't explain. We haven't taken the next step and I don't know if we will or not. I don't know why I even feel like I need to tell you, but I do." She realized her words sounded as if they were spoken by a computer generated voice at the end of a phone line. She leaned toward him, taking his hands in hers. "I guess it's because you're one of my dearest friends and it feels dishonest to have someone in my life that you don't know about."

Staring into her eyes his voice was soft, controlled, as he spoke. "I have known about him for some time." He leaned her back in her chair and released her hands.

A look of astonishment covered her face. "But, you never mentioned it."

"No, I never did." His face turned to stone, his voice a monotone. It took all of his Immortal power to control his jealous rage. He felt no competition from the outsider as long as Sarah didn't speak of him; he was just a new colleague. The fact that she had been driven to tell him was the first sign this man was an opponent. He longed to roar from his soul, to break things. To hold her. To take her in his arms, to make her his own. Visions of ripping his rival to shreds filled his frantic mind. "I never did mention it." With Immortal self-control, he held himself back. He could not influence her decision to become like him, to become a blood drinker. "*It must be her choice and hers alone.*"

He leaned toward her, holding her hands again as he spoke out loud. "Those who are in your life are none of my affair. Sarah, any time I spend with you is a treasure. As long as you are safe, what you do when I am not with you is your business and yours alone."

"Aris, I. . ."

"No, no more conversation about my rival. You have no reason to feel guilty." He laughed to lighten the moment. "I would say let the best man win, however, that would put me out of the running, would it not?"

A tentative smile crossed her lips.

"I told you long ago, I am prepared to wait. That has not changed at all." He spoke calmly while inside the venom in his veins boiled. He fought silently to hold the beast within him at bay. If he followed his instinct, he would crush her to him. He would devour her. He would change her. He would create his mate and there would be no other rival. With great effort, his alien side claimed power over him. The philosopher created by his centuries of existence quieted the human monster of jealousy. He calmed, acknowledging, once again, the choice must be hers.

A sense of relief flooded her at his response to her statement. She had anticipated more of an argument, yet here he was, a vampire and a gentleman.

He paused a moment before he spoke again and when he did, she noticed a great change in his demeanor. "Apart from all of that, I, too, have news."

Sarah leaned more closely toward him.

"What news, Aris?"

He hoped she would understand his reason for telling her about his talk with Richard. It was two-fold, partially because he shared just about everything with her and partially so she would feel free to see whomever she wished to see without it driving him mad. If he wasn't there to watch, he could ignore the fact there was someone else in her life. She needed to choose him, Aris, of her own accord.

"Richard spoke to me today about Sebastian."

"Yes?"

"Of course, Sebastian had to be told the whole story of the

intruder and in the telling, he came to find out I am alive and incarnate."

Sarah's heart began to race.

"Yes?"

"Well, they both seem to think it might be a sound idea for me to return to the Catacombs to beg forgiveness. Sebastian believes it will be given and I will be welcomed back. He worries about the Spanish coven and knows I am the only Immortal with experience as a warrior. Information from our spies has led him to believe a conflict is coming and he wants me to return to lead the campaign. He told Richard Akira has longed for my company these past centuries. She cares for all her children, but I was one of her special ones. Richard agrees with Sebastian." He grew silent as the sky darkened and more stars became visible.

"Sarah, there is a longing for my own kind. Being here with Richard and Gabriela has made me see that. I know I am able to live in a human world and I find your time fascinating. Yet each day I crave the company of the Immortals, of the creator of my kind. Can you understand that?"

She understood his need to be with his family. Even before she told him about DeMarco, she wondered how long it would take before he wanted to go back to London once Richard and Gabriela were in his life again. She more than understood. Imagining what it would be like to be separated from her family, her friends, was something that caused her a great deal of pain. But to lose him? What would become of their relationship if he left? Would he survive the inquiries of the High Council? And how would DeMarco fit into the equation if Aris was gone?

At last, she answered his question. "Of course I understand."

"I have made no decisions. There is no certainty they will allow me to continue and I am without desire to end my existence now that I have found you. Yet I am sure my love for you will be one saving grace in my plea. That and the additional fact they need a warrior in the face of a possible war with the Spanish coven. I am the only one of the Catacombs who has ever been at war. They will need my experience and leadership." He paused a moment before he continued. "However, if you wish me not to go, all you need do is to say it."

It distressed him to tell her he might leave. He hoped she would ask him to stay. He wished she would tell him no human could mean as much to her as he did. He waited for her reply.

She sat without speaking as the silence surrounded them, deep as the space that held the now twinkling stars above them. In spite of her sense of losing something much greater than herself, when she finally spoke it was from her heart. "I understand, Aris. I honestly do. Maybe it will be good for us to be apart for a while." She choked back the tears that fought to spring from her eyes. "I will miss you dearly."

"Sarah, I will not leave here until Sebastian has had a private conversation with Akira. He feels he will be able to convince her without giving away too much about my present life. When we are greatly assured of an acquittal, I will travel to London. While I am gone, if I do go, you will be able to live your human life without my intrusion." Stepping aside for a while would give Sarah complete freedom to spend time with the human without guilt. As desperately as he desired her, he didn't want to use his Immortal influence to manipulate her.

"Aris, I've never thought of you as an intrusion."

"Those were the words you used when you thought I was the one to leave roses on your pillow."

"You must believe me, you are a welcome part of my life, someone I will dearly miss if you are to leave. But I do understand your need and I respect you for your courage to embrace it. Of course, I want you to do as you feel you must. Just know I will miss you and wait for your return." She said no more but her mind kept going back to that century so long ago when, in her regression, he left her to go to the Catacombs. It ended in misery and death, but that was a different time and a different life. *"I won't think about that right now,"* she thought. She rose as she spoke, "Let's go inside. I'm getting cold."

Gathering the blanket close around her to shield herself from the chill she went inside, then slid the door silently closed.

#

She shut her journal for the night, placing it and her pen in the night stand drawer. Her thoughts had been pushing her from one hemisphere to another, one century to another all evening. Journaling hadn't been much better. Her session with Bonnie clouded her every thought. Suicide? If she committed suicide then, how would she get on without Aris now? He meant so much to her. Never had she felt more safe, more protected than she did with him. That was one fact she was sure of. She would feel empty without him if he left for the Catacombs. Another fact. She didn't want to influence his decision, it must be his own. He said he would stay with her, to be only her friend, if she just asked him but in her heart, she knew he needed his own kind just as she would need hers if she were to go to the Catacombs.

Go to the Catacombs? Not probable, hardly even within the realm of possibility. However, the Immortals didn't bite humans any more. That was a fact. Her existence had been so simple, so easy. Then Carlos walked into it and brought Aris with him. It had been upside down ever since. Would she change it? Not on her life.

And woven through and around her thoughts of the vampire was an unquestionable desire for the human male who had come into her life.

Her thoughts raced on until they were silenced by the dark cloak of sleep.

#

Her dream self was Elizabeth Wyatt and her dream time was sixteenth century England. Gazing at the tapestry on the wall of the chamber, she knew where she was at once. Candle sconces held glimmering lights that shined and shimmered on the silk threads depicting the hunt. Heavy, deep green bed curtains hung on the four huge posters, one at each corner of the down mattress. It was his chamber. Her beloved. Her Aris.

Standing nude in front of the tall, narrow window, the moon slicing through the dark sky and the stars, his back was turned toward her. His golden hair shimmered as a sharp wind cut under the glass causing the candle flames to gutter, then revive.

She rose from the bed, her chemise soft against her skin as she lifted it over her head. Quietly she crossed the room. Wrapping her arms around him, she pressed her warm full breasts against his back. He shivered. His desire rose as he felt their softness brush his hard muscles. Turning, he carried her back to the bed.

He laid her in the pool of satin made by her long blond hair. Lifting one thick curl, using it like a paint brush, he began to trace the contours of her body. He outlined the mound-like shape of each white breast; he traced the deeper pink full moon in each center. Lowering his head, his tongue traced soft trails behind the curl. She gasped as he took her sweet nipple between his lips. It grew hard as if to greet him and entreat him to continue.

He wrapped the waist-length velvety tendril around his throat as he began to kiss hers, sliding the tip of his satiny tongue slowly from her collarbone to her ear.

Her breath came in gasps as she attempted to wrap her legs around his powerful hips. He moved away only far enough to keep her from encircling him. Her taste reminded him of honey melted by the sun. Arching her back, she lifted her throat to him. His words were murmured in time to her pulsing heart.

"No, my sweeting, no," yet still he teased her with his warm breath caressing her ear. "This is not the moment. We must wait."

"Please," she moaned, as his lips traced the edge of her jaw.

"I must not."

"Please," she cried out, tears in her eyes, the pain of desire making her voice thick and deep. "Please, draw just a taste of my blood. Please."

He could refuse her no longer. Slowly his teeth penetrated her pristine skin. She groaned as she felt him draw gently on her vein. As blood trickled from the tiny wound drop by drop into his waiting mouth, she exploded in spasms that wracked her body with a pleasure undreamed. Licking the final crimson drop, he kissed her, touching the very tip of his tongue to hers.

"Taste my darling. Taste the elixir of your life."

Sarah's eyes flew open. She bolted upright in her bed and grabbed her throat. There was no wound, no trickle of blood. Only an unanswered yearning.

CHAPTER 30

The four friends chatted about their afternoon spent strolling in Millennium Park as they sat in Sarah's living room gathered around the coffee table. They seemed very similar except for one rather large difference, only one of them needed to breathe. She was forever astounded each time she became fully aware they were not living beings such as she was. It was becoming more and more easy to forget they were not all exactly the same.

She heard Richard's voice cut into her thoughts. "Aris, Sebastian would like to come to visit you. He will make certain it is a private trip. He simply wishes to see you once again. He knows you are the only one who can help us if war should come to the Catacombs and he believes it is imminent. Our spies tell of a training camp in the Spanish coven and battle weapons being forged." Holding her hand in his, Richard traced patterns in the soft lines of Gabriela's palm. He wasn't sure how his friend would react to his request. Sarah sat quietly next to Aris watching his eyes. She saw the corners tighten and wrinkle as he winced.

"He cannot come here without Akira knowing, Richard. War or not, I am not ready to go before the Council. I am not ready for a verdict."

"He will come without anyone knowing he is here. He will stay but a day or two. Please see him. He is your brother just as I am. Knowing you are here brings Gabriela and me great joy. Knowing Sarah," he smiled at her, "also fills our hearts. Sebastian and I both stood by you in your deepest sorrow, understood the lengths you would go to avenge the death of your beloved. He would like to speak with you. When he sees the love in your eyes, the deep connection of your soul's path with Sarah's, he will convince Akira to see you, to champion you with the Council."

"Aris, we will all stand for you." Gabriela spoke softly. "You need your own kind; we all need you to be a part of us once more." Not wanting to leave Sarah feeling inadequate, she turned to her blond friend and added, "You and your protection have become very important to us, Sarah. We would wish to have you travel with us. I would stay above ground with you while Richard and Aris meet with the Council."

Silent for a moment, Sarah was pensive before she answered. Then she smiled, "There is a possibility; let's wait to see what happens if Sebastian visits here."

Black eyes questioning, Aris turned to look at her. Did he dare hope she might one day decide to share his eternal life? But his Immortal existence would go on only if the Council chose to allow him to continue. It was too soon. He had only just returned to her. He could not face the Council, the possibility of extinction, when he had waited so long just to touch her, to hold her, to taste her, to be her protector.

"No Richard, I am not yet ready to see any other of our family just yet. I need more time. Please, indulge me in this."

"We will all abide by your wishes. Just know we all hope for your homecoming soon."

Sarah gripped the hand of the dark Immortal sitting next to her and prayed for a little more human time with him.

\#

Her usual booth at Saul's Deli was occupied so the waitress seated them near the kitchen. The sounds of the cooks and dishwashers drifted out of the double doors as the servers moved quickly to feed the hungry diners. Breakfast was always a noisy, busy affair in the neighborhood restaurant.

"I spoke with Richard this morning." Aris said with reticence. Sarah chewed her rye toast slowly, waiting for him to continue.

"He spoke to Sebastian. It seems De Flores has taken a woman. One of his coven has been chosen to be his consort. Our spy says she is quite beautiful and even more evil. Akira is sending re-enforcements to watch them, to make sure they stay under control. Of course the evil ones will never know we are in their country. We are not there as an act of aggression, only to keep our coven safe from their greed and our Immortal culture safe from discovery by the humans."

"Is Sebastian coming here to see you?"

"No, not just yet." He seemed uncomfortable speaking about his lost friend as he stirred the untouched deep brown liquid in his coffee cup. She ate silently as they both had their own private thoughts.

After several minutes without conversation, he spoke. "You'll be glad to hear I received a call from John Marshal. He would like to showcase my work at the next gallery presentation. He feels my shady background, mixed with my ability to do fine Impressionistic work, makes a good combination to bring the media into the picture. He's invited a few journalists from several art magazines and received an acceptance from *Impressionism Today*. He's quite over the moon about it."

"Aris, that's great. Wouldn't it be great if your art became popular? It just doesn't seem quite right for you to go from being the aid of kings to throwing boxes around at a market." She smiled as she spoke.

He took her hand. "Sarah, my life is perfect as long as you are in it. However," he laughed, "I wouldn't mind moving up a step or two in your world."

#

Sarah finished answering the last of her emails and placed her laptop on the coffee table. It was late and she was tired. It had been a long day with client sessions backed one into the next. When she finally arrived home, dinner had been a carton of yogurt and an apple before she sat down to work on her computer. She yawned and stretched as she thought of DeMarco's last communication.

He wrote almost every day. His emails were neither long nor intimate, however, she looked forward to receiving them. She missed him. Their conversations were always so lively. Her relationship with him was peaceful, non-threatening. There were no deep, dark secrets to be kept from her friends and family.

She made sure the front door was locked, turned off the lights and crawled into bed. In her subconscious the two men in her life, Aris and DeMarco, morphed into one another over and over until she drifted to sleep.

She had been sleeping only a few hours when the ringing phone woke her. Sarah's heart pounded in her chest. She glanced at the clock as she reached for the receiver. Midnight. Her voice sounded gravely as she spoke from a deep sleep. "Hello?"

"Sarah, it's Bob. It's a girl. A beautiful six-pound-four ounce girl. They're both doing perfectly well and Colleen's resting, but she wanted me to call you right away."

"I'm so happy for you. So little Collette has arrived. I can't wait to see her. Tell C I'll stop by the hospital first chance I get tomorrow." She sat in the middle of the bed rubbing her eyes, a huge smile on her face.

"I know she can't wait for you to see her. She's just amazing. I can't believe how tiny she is. Her little fingers and toes look like they belong on a fairy. And she's my daughter. I have two women to love now." The joy in his voice came through the telephone and wrapped Sarah in tender arms. "They're both sleeping now and my cellphone didn't work in the hospital so I had to step outside. I'm going to get back to them." She felt his urgency to be close to his new family.

"Give her my love and tell her I'll see her tomorrow." Tiny tears of happiness for her dear friends trickled down Sarah's cheeks as she went to her kitchen to fix a late night cup of tea.

#

Sarah sipped coffee while Aris played with an unopened bottle of water as they sat in the noisy hospital cafeteria. The sounds of voices, dishes and trays blended together to create a symphony of clatter. "They look so happy, don't they?"

"Yes, they do. Having children seems to complete some need in humans though I don't quite understand it. I have not been exposed to many true families in my existence. My human life ended so early. All of my Immortal existence has been on battle fields or in royal courts and those certainly did not promote any facet of loving kinship. Immortals are unable to breed children so my experience is very limited yet I must admit holding that small being in my arms brought out a fierce protective emotion that was quite new, similar yet different than the one I feel for you."

Sarah said, "I remember, you told me that in your world, a male and female constitute a family. You don't have children."

"That is correct, we are genetically unable to reproduce and so we feel no drive to create others in our own images. We live for eternity; we simply always are. Your kind dies and so it appears you need to leave a part of yourselves behind in your attempt at a more human form of immortality."

"I hadn't thought of it that way. I guess you're right. There is sort of a biological drive that almost demands to be met." She laughed. "The propagation of the species."

"Do you have that drive, Sarah, that basic need to leave something of yourself behind?"

Sarah was thoughtful before she answered. "When I was younger, I suppose I did. It's something we humans can't avoid. It's kind of a mammal thing, I suppose. But for the last few years it's not been anything that's been too compelling. I still think about it occasionally, but I believe it's something that is pretty individual as a woman passes from her twenties. Some continue to feel a demand to have a child, others don't. I have my work and sometimes my clients are more like my children than I would like." She laughed.

"So Sarah, you would be content for a family to contain just two?"

She wrinkled her forehead as she sincerely contemplated his question for a few moments before she answered. "I suppose it would matter who the other half would be, wouldn't it?"

She hadn't said yes, but she hadn't said no. There was still a chance that he could be enough for her. He smiled, "Yes, it would, wouldn't it?"

CHAPTER 31

Sarah closed the door quietly after making sure the baby monitor was turned on. Collette looked so sweet, her little hands balled into soft fists and her dark curls circling her head like a halo of night sky. She was a bit nervous taking care of the infant, but she knew Colleen and Bob had complete faith in her so she took a deep breath and accepted the challenge when they asked her to babysit. It was their first date night in months. Besides, she had Bonnie for back up.

She curled up on the sofa next to her friend. "Want a refill on your wine? You didn't even drink half a glass."

"No Bon, I think I'll skip it and change to water. With the responsibility for that little critter in there, I don't want anything to cloud my judgment."

"You're right. I'll grab a mineral water out of the fridge." She returned from the kitchen with a frosty bottle and two glasses. "So, you still have your roommate. It's really turned into a long term thing, hasn't it?"

"Sort of, I guess, although I really like Gabriela. It's been a lot of fun having her stay with me."

"The few times we've all been together, she's seemed really nice.

She sure is gorgeous. Sometimes when she sits very still, she looks like a mannequin in a department store."

Sarah cleared her throat. "Oh, I hadn't noticed." She sipped her water. "But you're right, she is very beautiful."

"I see some sort of resemblance between her and Carlos although I can't quite pinpoint it. Maybe because they are both so golden and have that thick black hair and shining black eyes. Although it seems something more that I can't quite grasp."

"Well, they're cousins a few times removed. Maybe it's just genetic." Sarah hurried to change the subject from their otherworldly resemblance. "She's planning on leaving soon. I'll miss her." She told the truth. She had grown accustomed to having the beautiful Immortal live with her and she enjoyed the company. She had learned so much more about the Catacombs from a female perspective having her as a roommate. She felt safe as long as Gaby was nearby, although there had been no threat in any way since De Flores returned to Spain. She would never understand what the vampire had wanted with her. She put it out of her mind as Bonnie spoke.

"When is she leaving?"

"In a week or so."

"Is she going back to Mexico City?"

"No Bonnie, she is going to England to see some family she has in London."

"Must be nice to be so free, don't you think?"

"Yes Bon, I'm beginning to think that kind of freedom might be very nice."

CHAPTER 32

It was the first time Sarah had invited DeMarco to her home. After his return from Italy, she decided to welcome him back with a meal she prepared. She cooked most of the day and the authentic Italian dinner she created for him impressed him no end. It made him happy to know he had won her enough that she had gone out of her way to please him.

"What a delicious meal," he stood to help her clear the table. "The next time we eat dinner here, I will cook for you. I am quite the expert in the kitchen."

"If it's spaghetti, you'll probably put me to shame." She rinsed the dishes, placing them carefully in the dishwasher.

Standing behind her, he handed her the last of the silverware. "No, you did a beautiful job. The sauce is the beginning and the end of an Italian meal and your's was impeccable. Everything you do is flawless."

Turning to face him, she dried her hands as she smiled into his eyes. Slowly, tentatively he grasped her shoulders waiting to see if she was receptive to his embrace. Her body relaxed. She stepped closer, laying her hands on his broad chest.

His mouth was undemanding as he kissed her with small sweet

kisses. His gentle touch kindled a new yearning for more of him. As she wrapped her arms around his powerful shoulders she felt his muscles tense, his lips part. As he caressed her lips with the tip of his tongue, she gasped at the intense heat that flared within her.

A fire began to rage. It was raw and demanding and there was something strangely familiar about it. As their kiss grew more passionate, she knew she was losing control. Pressing her body into his, she felt his arousal strong against her. As she twined her fingers into his thick black hair, a faint groan escaped her throat.

It was as if the sound incited him beyond control. With a deep soft growl he lifted her into his arms. He made his way toward the bedroom, his eyes glazed, blazing with desire.

As he crossed the threshold, he stopped, a voice in his head shouting it was not yet time. He must wait. His rational mind clawed its way out of his need. Standing stock still, he spoke through his rasping breath. "No, not now. It isn't time. I want you desperately, but it isn't time." His hands were shaking as he put her feet on the floor and led her back into the living room. He intertwined his fingers with hers as he opened the front door.

"I'm leaving you now, sweet Sarah. Sleep well and I will phone you tomorrow." He stepped into the hall. He released her hand and leaned across the threshold, kissing her on both her cheeks. "Thank you for a wonderful dinner."

Her knees were weak and her face still flushed as she watched him walk down the hall to the elevator. She couldn't see his face as he bit his lip until a tiny drop of dark liquid appeared. He licked it away with his tongue as he pressed the down button.

CHAPTER 33

SARAH HAGAN, transcript, session 7

Wolsey's uniformed men saw me to the waiting ship. As they marched me up the gangplank to board, I saw a man who looked like Diego on the crowded wharf below, but when I turned to get a better look, I lost sight of him. I became even more frightened when I was handed off to the captain who locked me securely in my cabin. Beating on the door, I demanded release but to no avail. I could hear men's voices outside the solitary bolted exit to the small room. I was under lock and key as well as guard. There was no discernable escape from my fate. Curling up on the small, tidy bed, I cried myself into a fit-full sleep.

I have no idea how long I hid in the darkness of unconsciousness. My dreams had been of Aris, riding to the hunt on cold frosty mornings, evenings before the fire in my chamber, our lips touching softly. The desire I felt for him. His tender restraint telling me of his great love, his pledge to make me his wife before he possessed me. How I regretted that pledge even in my sleep. How I wished we had become one in this life. And now, it was too late. My fate was sealed.

Loud pounding on the door awakened me and I sat quickly on the side of the bed. My head swirled in the darkness of the room. "My lady, a squall approaches. The sea will become rough and the boat unsteady.

Take to your bed and remain there until we have safely maneuvered through it."

I opened the only small round window in the cabin and looked into the ominous night sky. Dark clouds whirled overhead, twisting and coiling like huge, deadly snakes. Brilliant bolts of lightning exploded from them, forked tongues reaching to strike death into any they might touch. Crashing explosions of thunder set a ringing in my ears that brought pain so intense I covered them with my hands to muffle the shattering blasts. Curling once again on the small bed, I drew the cover over my shaking body. Fear gripped me and I felt its sharp relentless talons dig into my broken heart.

The ship was large, laden with cargo yet it was tossed as if it were salt in the wind. I was tumbled from my bed onto the wooden planks of the floor. The deck heaved and floundered as a horse not yet broken to its saddle. Crawling, I made way toward the false safety of the cot.

Without warning, a terrifying explosion shook the vessel. First one, then another and another. The smell of gunpowder, sulpher and fire filled my nostrils. Thick black smoke choked me as I clawed at my throat, gasping for air.

The door was ripped open. Flames silhouetted the form of a huge, torn and bleeding man reaching for me. I screamed as I scrambled to the far side of the pitching cabin. "No fear of me. I come here to save you. The ship is going down. Make your way with haste to one of the waiting boats. It is your only hope." He reached for me, lifting me into his arms, carrying me as he would a child onto the deck into the open air.

Rain and hail pummeled the bleeding, dying men who were scattered in every direction. The mast lay broken across the deck, men crushed beneath its enormous weight. The great ship was ripped in two. Fires burned everywhere I looked, somehow consuming the soaking wood like kindling. When, at last, the flames were drowned by the raging tempest, the sound of the hot wood hissing in its' death rattle added to the roar of the storm. The sailor deposited me into a small boat suspended by ropes hanging next to the bow. He began to lower it into the swirling black water when another explosion rocked all that remained of the only world left to me. The shock sent him flying to the other side of the ship, and blew me out of the skiff into the churning water. My blood froze in my veins as I hit the convulsive, angry waves. My arms and legs grew numb as I fought a battle for my life.

In no more than a moment, I knew to whom the victory would be given. "Aris, my only beloved," was my final cry as the raging sea filled my lungs with a watery death. I sank into the darkness, my last memory his face before me. And then eternal peace.

#

Sarah lay in the recliner with her eyes closed. She could hear Bonnie's breath, the therapist's hand resting reassuringly on her friends arm. "I'm here Sarah. Breathe deeply and just relax. Everything is fine. You're safe here with me in my office."

Thoughts raced through Sarah's mind. "Safe? How safe can I be with the image of my own death rattling my brain? How safe can I be when I realize that I don't want to live without the Immortal that returned to my life from a place where fables walk the earth? How safe can I be as my heart lay open, tempted by eternal love?"

#

She curled in the corner of her sofa. A light spring rain shower fell from intermittent cumulus clouds. Occasional narrow shafts of sunlight lit the shimmering drops creating rainbows against the glass of the sliding patio doors. The sound of the drops, so soft, so tender, unlike the terrorizing tempest of her vision. She had been sitting in one spot for what seemed like hours. To see one's own death, to hear her own final cry of his name. Would that be the cry she heard as she breathed her last human breath in the depths of the Catacombs? Did she have that kind of courage? Did she cherish him enough to give her life for love? He asked her once. She asked herself time and again. The answer seemed just out of her reach but she feared it as much as she struggled toward it. The voice in her head spoke only one word. "Aris."

CHAPTER 34

She opened the door to her office to find pale sunbeams shining around dried drops of rain dotting the large window. The sun seemed to spotlight a small branch resting in the middle of her desk. As she approached, she saw it was a gnarled bramble full of wicked sharp thorns. "What in the world is Maggie doing now?" She laughed as she picked it up, tossing it thoughtlessly into her garbage can.

Settling into her chair, she kicked off her shoes. She always arrived early before her first appointment to read the records of past sessions with the clients she would be seeing that day. She waited for Maggie to appear with her large coffee loaded with her one vice-several sugars stirred into it to make it as sweet as a doughnut. She hit the snooze button once too often this morning and missed her breakfast at Saul's. Her stomach growled its annoyance. She patted it tenderly, "You're just going to have to wait until lunch, little buddy. We have no time for food this morning." A long disgruntled grumble was her only answer.

She heard the outer door of the office open just as her phone rang. Reaching for it she slid into her shoes in case it was an early client who had just arrived.

"Just me, boss." Maggie's voice carried from the outer office as Sarah spoke into the receiver.

A deep accented voice responded to her greeting. "Good morning, Sarah, it is DeMarco." He waited.

"DeMarco, I'm so glad you called. About last night?"

"A delicious meal and delightful company. That is what I remember about last night."

She sighed in relief. She had been worried their turbulent moment of passion might interrupt their friendship. Even with her deep feelings for Aris, her time with the Italian doctor meant a great deal to her.

"No more thoughts about it. Now, when may I prepare dinner for you?"

"Let's make a date." She had no sooner spoken when Maggie leaned her head around the door motioning to Sarah there was a client in the waiting room. "DeMarco, I have to go, my client is here. I'll speak with you later."

"I'll phone you soon. Ciao, Sarah."

"Ciao, DeMarco." She smiled. Her charming friend had smoothed out an uncomfortable moment with his usual diplomacy.

#

Saturday mornings at Saul's were a madhouse. They waited for a table for almost half an hour and Sarah was chomping at the bit to really talk to Bonnie. She was confused by her own feelings and actions. She really hoped Bonnie could give her some insight as her friend as well as her therapist. What in the world was she doing having DeMarco to her house again? She knew she wasn't ready to have an intimate relationship with him. Even if Aris had not been in the picture, she didn't know enough about DeMarco to be emotionally vulnerable to him and sex with him would certainly put her in that position.

Finally when they were settled, their orders placed, their coffee on the table steaming hot in front of them, she felt able to begin the conversation.

"Bon, I've got some questions here so put on your therapy hat, okay?" She chuckled as she watched Bonnie's expression change, becoming serious and quizzical.

"Yes?"

"Well, it's kind of embarrassing. DeMarco and I."

Bonnie leaned closer, "Yes?"

"He came to my house for dinner the other night."

"Go on," she urged quietly.

"We got pretty carried away and almost did the deed and I'm kind of scared. I don't want to be hurt again. We don't even live in the same country. He says he has feelings for me, but I'm not sure of mine for him. I'm feeling pretty confused and honestly don't know where this could go anyway."

"Yes?"

"I invited him over again and I'm not sure why."

"Are you sure you don't care for him?" Bonnie waited for her to answer. Sarah knew she would continue to wait for as long as it took to get a response.

"I'm not sure, but my heart just about jumped out of my chest when he kissed me."

"Yes?" The old therapy trick of agreement, then silence, always seemed to work even when it was used on another therapist.

"Okay, maybe I do have some kind of thing for him, but I don't know what it is."

"Sarah, DeMarco and that mindless attorney you dated for a while are the only two men you've been associated closely with except Carlos since your divorce. You and Carlos have become incredibly close friends but nothing more, or so you say. Is it any wonder you're stirred by some exotic, handsome Italian who tells you how much he wants you? Come on woman. It doesn't take a rocket scientist to understand that."

"So you think it's just hormones, nothing more?"

"Nothing more than hormones? What is wrong with your brain this morning? Hormones are some of the most powerful drivers of human action. He's gorgeous, he's here, he wants you. You'd have to be dead not to respond in some way."

"Yeah, I guess you're right." Silently her thoughts raged. *"Life, death, immortality. So many choices, so little time."* Her indecision was becoming tiresome even to her.

#

Sarah held the baby on her lap while Colleen and Bob set the table for dinner. Her heart melted as Collette's tiny fingers curled around her thumb, holding onto her hand. Her baby eyes held such innocence. Sarah was amazed at the feelings that surfaced looking at the miracle she held in her arms. A new life. So dependent. Sarah was filled with nearly overwhelming emotions.

She felt protective, nurturing. This miniature person was totally vulnerable to everything that surrounded her, so helpless. It almost frightened Sarah to think of having the responsibility of raising a child, teaching it, giving it a solid foundation for life.

As a therapist she understood that parents, without even realizing it, can color a child's entire future simply by thoughtless words spoken in a moment of anger or fatigue. Time and again she had listened to her adult clients with tears in their eyes and holes in their psyches speak about incidences that occurred in the toddler stages of their development; incidences that still pounded them into the ground even as full grown adults. Insecurity, obesity, a lost sense of self. It is a rare parent that wants to instill such sorrow in their child, yet a common occurrence in families simply through careless statements a child may never forget. A parent is a god to a child. Their pronouncements are taken as ultimate truth in the tiny world of an innocent. *"How can you possibly know if you have what it takes to be a good parent?"* she thought. *"Would I be a good parent?"*

"Hey, little girl, ready to go to bed?" Lost in her thoughts, Sarah was startled as Bob came close, reaching out his arms for his daughter. His eyes lit up at the sight of her and his voice took on a soft sweetness that Sarah had never heard before, not even when he spoke to his wife. He lifted her tenderly and cradled her in his huge arms. Nothing could harm her while this man was near. She smiled as he carried the small bundle from the room. Even his walk was different, special, as he carried his daughter. Slow, small steps, his feet placed gingerly so as not to disturb her sleep. She was a very lucky child to be born to these two caring people.

"Dinner's on the table. Come on, Auntie Sarah. Let's chow down." Colleen made a quick stop in the baby's room to tuck her in and make sure the baby monitor was working before she settled into her chair.

"Wow, this looks great." Sarah placed her napkin on her lap as her best friend spooned steaming vegetables on her plate. "You sure have come a long way from ordering in."

"Yeah, well now that I'm not working like a dog, I have the time to cook." She kissed her husband on the top of his head. "As well as a reason. I want this guy healthy."

Sarah watched the couple as the three friends ate a relaxed meal together. Bob and Colleen were so completely comfortable with each other. Their movements seemed to meld into a perfect dance. There was obvious love and so much more: respect, real companionship, friendship. They communicated with their eyes without words. Would she ever know such comfort as they shared? She knew Aris had been the answer to this question even before it was formed. But what of the humanity she would have to sacrifice to consummate her love? With DeMarco in her life, it seemed she might have other choices.

CHAPTER 35

The lights in the restaurant were soft and romantic. As the waiter cleared the plates from the table, DeMarco asked for a brandy while Sarah sipped the last of her second glass of wine. Their conversation had been light, friendly. They spoke of his travel, the lovely weather, their mutual work, all things mundane and none of any great importance. However, she could tell from the look in his eyes that was about to change.

Reaching across the table, he took her hands in his as was his habit. "Sarah, I told you I would not put demands upon you or our relationship and I hold true to my promise. I would not even bring this up if the limbo of not knowing your feelings for me were not driving me to distraction. I have trouble concentrating on my work; thoughts of you intrude in my every moment. You told me there was another man in your life yet I hope there is the possibility one day to have an exclusive relationship with you."

She looked at his handsome face, his eyes glowing in the . candlelight. How could she walk away from this exquisite man?

"Please. I am willing to accept any decision you make, but I must know. Is it possible for there to be a deeper relationship between us in the future?"

She knew she owed him an answer. He was a kind, generous and gentle man. She could no longer leave him in torment while she wrestled with her fear of letting go and falling in love. Her respect for him forced her to face the reality of her relationships with Aris and DeMarco. Regardless of the answer to the life or death enigma she faced if she chose Aris, she knew she had feelings for both of them.

She stared into the candlelight for a long moment before she met his eyes. "I can't lie to you, DeMarco. I don't know what I feel."

"Very well, Sarah. I will give you time." Placing his napkin on the table, he reached into his pocket to withdraw his wallet. His voice was cool, collected, without passion. "Take all of it that you need. Just know that I am in love with you and have been since I first saw you, which seems to me an eternity ago. I will not push you or tempt you. Your decision is your own."

She sat in silence. *"What did you expect?"* The small voice of reason spoke to her shock. *"This man just offered you his heart and you refused it. Did you think he was the type of man to beg?"* At least this was one question that had an immediate answer. No, of course not. In spite of his declaration, he was a man with great pride. He didn't need her, he wanted her. He was a man obviously accustomed to getting exactly what he wanted. Without her he was precisely the same as he was before he met her. Complete.

"I will return to Italy tomorrow. I will return to my family until you decide what you want. When you know, phone me. I will be waiting to hear from you, however, I believe I already know the answer even though you do not." He signed the check, then stood.

She placed her napkin in the vacant space on the table in front of her. He was distant as he helped her from her chair and guided her to the door of the restaurant.

CHAPTER 36

They sat on Sarah's living room floor, piles of canvas of every size surrounding them. One by one Aris revealed to her the work that had been consuming him for the last few weeks. One miracle after another was presented to her. Colors and shapes exploded from each canvas, each painting more powerful than the one before. She expected his work to be exceptional, but now realized he was a master of his art.

"These are all unbelievable. Each brush stroke has a voice."

He laughed out loud as he leaned toward her to kiss her lightly on the lips. She ached for more. "I am so happy you like them. I thought of the light coming from your eyes, your face, as I painted. You are my muse and inspiration."

"Yes, well that and your small, insignificant teacher, Monsieur Monet." She wondered at all his past life experiences as well as all he observed silently during the centuries he was without a body.

"My many teachers to be correct. When one is only consciousness, there is no limit to eavesdropping." He chuckled as he stacked the canvasses by size and shape. "I have watched many of the great masters at work in very close quarters. I have learned well."

"I'm so excited. Your show might be all it takes to launch your career and afford you the material security you so need."

"Yes, from the palaces of kings to my small apartment has been quite an adjustment, even for such as I am. It has been my destiny to move in the company of renowned men and women, some notorious and some truly great. It appears from all I have seen and learned that small day-to-day obstacles are so much more difficult to overcome than issues of state. Working people are so tied to just creating a life for themselves and their families they have little time for true introspection. Their lives are dictated by their basic human needs; finding food and shelter has been paramount since those first humans who lived in caves.

"Yet while many of those of great power have those basic needs met quite easily, they so often have no desire for self-reflection, believing their power gives them all that is necessary in their world. And so we have two sides to the same coin; different reasons yet the same outcome, life and death without depth of knowledge of oneself. One of your famous authors believed that the purpose of human life is joy, yet it is truly a rare commodity in the human world."

"Is there great joy in the Catacombs?"

"In the Catacombs? Often." He fought his intense desire to hold her in his arms and instead spoke from his heart. "For me, wherever you are, Sarah, there will always be joy."

CHAPTER 37

Sarah sat in the lobby of her apartment building curled into a ball, her cell phone pressed to her ear. Aris answered on the second ring, but it seemed to her to be forever before she heard his voice.

"Aris, it's happened again-only worse." He heard fright and something that sounded like anger in her voice.

"Sarah, calm down. I'm here." His soothing voice and assuring words relaxed her and she uncurled, sitting upright. "Now, what is it?"

"Someone or something has been in my apartment again."

"Slow down. Take a moment. Now take a deep breath." She complied. "Now, another one." He waited without speaking while she took a moment to breathe. "Where are you now?"

"I'm in the lobby of the building. Tom is here with me."

"Stay right there. I'm on my way. I'll get in touch with Richard and Gabriela to meet me there as soon as possible. Are you feeling a bit more settled?"

"Yes."

"Make sure Tom doesn't leave your sight and I'll be right there. If you need me, call my cell phone. You will be able to reach me any time you need to."

"Okay."

"Sarah, we will not let anything happen to you. You are safe."

"I know. I'm just sick to death of all this scary movie crap." She fought back angry tears.

"Hold on, I will see you very soon. Do not leave the lobby."

"I won't. Bye."

She watched the digital clock on the wall tick the seconds away. In record time, he hurried through the door. "I'm not leaving you alone again. Richard and Gabriela are on their way." He lifted her chin and it trembled in his hand. "What happened?"

She glanced at Tom who had busied himself with a stack of papers on his desk, ignoring the couple as best he could.

"Well, I came home from work and noticed the light on in my bedroom. I thought I had turned it off when I left for work this morning. I went into the bedroom and there was something on my pillow. I could see from across the room it was a gnarled bramble from some sort of thorn tree. Aris, the thorns were coated in something that looks like dried blood." Her voice was hoarse and deep as she fought a new wave of tears.

"I am here now. Just let it all go. Cry if you need to, I am here."

Composing herself, she continued. "No, I'm feeling better. I ran out of the apartment and came to the lobby. Then I remembered. A while ago there was a bramble on my desk at the office. I thought Maggie had left it there as some sort of joke. I got busy and forgot it and never mentioned it to her, but now I know it wasn't Maggie. She can't climb the outside of a building."

The sound of the revolving door caught their attention as Richard and Gabriela entered the lobby.

Aris told them of the re-emergence of the intruder. Gabriela sat with Sarah while he and Richard searched her apartment. There was no sign of anyone having been there except for the bramble. Richard stayed upstairs while Aris returned to the lobby to gather the women. Richard broke the bramble into small pieces. Taking the liner from the bathroom garbage can, he wrapped the broken branch securely so Sarah didn't have to look at it again. She was right; the thorns were covered with blood.

When they were all settled in the living room and she was reasonably calm, Aris questioned her about the first appearance on her desk.

"I honestly don't remember when it happened. It seemed so insignificant at the time, I just forgot it. What can all this mean?"

"I honestly have no idea, Sarah, but I plan to find out. Gabriela, will you stay with Sarah again until this is settled once and for all?"

"Of course I will. She will not leave my sight."

"Richard, will you telephone Sebastian? We need to know where De Flores is and what is going on in his coven."

"Yes, I will do that now." He stepped onto the balcony to speak in private. His concern was for Sarah. Whatever the outcome of his conversation, he wanted to make sure she wasn't further upset.

"Lie down. I will brew some tea." Gabriela stood, moving to the kitchen as she spoke.

Sarah began to shake as the shock of the experience began to wear off. She fought an hysterical laugh. Only she would feel safe in a house full of blood drinking vampires, more safe than she ever felt before in her life. She curled against Aris. Closing her eyes and feeling the warmth of him against her, she fell into a healing sleep.

#

She slowly woke to the sounds of soft voices. Her face was pressed against Aris' chest as he held her, cradled in his arms. Her slight movement caught his attention. He kissed her forehead tenderly. "Are you feeling better?"

"Yes. Did I sleep very long?"

"A few hours," Richard spoke from across the room.

"What's going on?" She sat up, stretching her arms over her head, stiff from sleeping on the couch. "Did you speak with Sebastian?"

"I did. It seems De Flores has just taken his consort as wife and the coven now has a Queen. They traveled in Europe. Some days in France, some in Portugal, a few in Switzerland. It seems they were visiting covens of their own kind, rallying them around the new self-proclaimed royal couple. Queen Mariska returned to Spain, but the spies lost sight of De Flores."

"The only reason they made contact with the other wild ones could be war." Aris rose and paced the floor. "These creatures do not socialize even among their own covens. They are isolated, untrusting of each other. To create a kingdom of these primitive killers would be impossible."

"I am not sure that is so, Aris." Even with the strain of the evening, Gabriela's voice was gentle, melodious. "I believe they understand there is strength in numbers despite their savage minds. When there are more than just a few, there must be a leader. None of them has ever attempted to lead until now as far as we know. This De Flores seems powerful. He has proven himself by leaving his own country and traveling across the sea. Perhaps that was his reason for seeking Sarah. She may have just been a random choice, a challenge. That we may never know. However, the fact remains that they now have a King and Queen. They have a community with a leader who is thinking, reasoning. That is very dangerous not only for the Catacombs, but for humanity. These are brutish butchers; their new Queen the most ruthless of them all."

"Why do you say that?" Sarah reached for Aris' hand without forethought. He sat beside her.

"The spies say she is evil incarnate." Richard's words were matter-of-fact, without emotion. "Sebastian searched the Diaries for both De Flores and Mariska. There was little to be found. It seems they both traveled from England sometime in the sixteenth century, but separately. De Flores arrived in Spain first. She followed close behind. They were both changed by the same coven that created Gabriela and me. For centuries they lived apart without any acknowledgement of one another. We do not know if they were acquainted in England but it appears not. She seemed to search for something, yet to this day no one knows what that was. Some treasure without price it seems. De Flores lived as a hermit, with the coven yet separately. Then he fled to England. There he joined the Catacombs. From there you know the story."

"Yes," Sarah's tone was muted as she remembered.

"He journeyed to the United States, but returned quickly to Spain. He took Mariska for his consort and recently for his Queen. And now, they look to make an alliance of all the evil vampires in Europe. Whatever their reason, it is for no good."

"But what can I possibly have to do with it all?"

"We do not know, Sarah. The Diaries have no mention of you being involved with these wretches, but the Diaries are not yet complete. The full story is a mystery to us now but one we will solve." Richard paced as he spoke.

"In the meantime, my love, Gabriela will stay with you once again. We will watch you every moment until we have answers. That I promise you."

Richard wrapped his arm around Gabriela's shoulder. "We are here to protect you, to keep you safe. You will not come to harm under the wing of the Immortals."

"I am so grateful, but I just don't understand why you would do this for a human."

"Human or Immortal, you are the soul-mate of our brother. Gabriela moved to stand by the woman's side. "Besides," she laughed. "You are the only human to know what we are and still want to be friends. You are a rare bird to be sure."

"It's easy to be your friend."

Gaby sat next to Sarah as she spoke. "It seems whoever the intruder is, they do not want to harm you, Sarah, or they would have already. They simply want to frighten you."

"Well, they've done a damn good job."

"We will not rest until we solve this puzzle." She turned to her mate, "Richard, what will we tell Sarah's friends is the reason I have not left for England? They expected me to travel."

Sarah smiled her first of the evening. "I have it. We'll tell them you really like living in America and want to stay here to work for a year. I'll tell them I'm sponsoring you for a work permit and you'll work part time in the office. It all makes sense and they all know how much I like having you here."

"A wonderful idea. Now Aris will stay with you while we return to the hotel to gather my things. I will live here with you until we have found the answers we seek."

Aris drew her into the crook of his arm once again and before the couple had left her apartment, she fell back to sleep.

CHAPTER 38

Sarah settled into what her friends called her "Scarlett O'Hara Syndrome" and refused to dwell on her fear. She enjoyed having Gabriela living with her once more. She felt safe and cared for.

They held to their story of the beautiful Immortal wanting to work in the states for a year and being Sarah's roommate. The two women settled into a routine that seemed satisfying to both of them. Whenever Gabriela and Richard went to "dinner" Aris stayed with Sarah. They made sure she was never left completely alone yet somehow she never felt her personal space was being violated.

Sarah's friends accepted Gabriela as Carlos' cousin. Her good humor and obvious care for Sarah made her a welcome companion whenever she chose to join in for group activities. Richard wasn't a part of the equation because Maggie had met him as a policeman and a short term visitor to Chicago. It seemed so long ago when he had come into her office in the guise of a detective looking for a criminal. She had no idea he was a vampire until she mentioned his name to Aris and he told her. So much had happened since that day. Richard and Gabriela were in her life. The close friendship that had developed between them. A new depth in her relationship with Aris. Sarah marveled at her double existence and the ease with which she lived it. She had always worked to simplify her life, yet somehow the complexity of her strange new world was not only comfortable, but welcome.

In the days that followed the bramble incident, Richard continued to communicate with Sebastian for news about the Spanish coven. As it grew in numbers, the Council of the Catacombs became more unsettled. Their spies weren't able to ascertain the true reason for De Flores' recruitment of new members, yet it was apparent to those who knew the facts, he was developing an army for his kingdom.

One evening as the four friends sat on Sarah's balcony enjoying the balmy evening air, Richard announced his intention to return to London for a few days. "I want to look at the Diaries myself. Perhaps I will find a link that has passed the eyes of the others. According to Sebastian, the Spanish coven is now almost as large as the Catacombs and they are making and stockpiling personal weapons as well as a weapon of mass destruction."

"Weapons?" Aris leaned closer. "They need neither weapons nor an army to kill humans. It is obvious they plan to battle the Immortals."

"That is why I feel so strongly about returning to England."

"Does he know any reason why they would attack us? We are peaceful and they know that."

"He does not know their true motive. We wonder if it does not have something to do with the Infinity Diaries. To possess them would put great power in the hands of the unscrupulous. Once De Flores learned of their existence, he began to band his people together. Sebastian is positive the two events are linked. We are told the royal pair are driven by their hunger for power. The spies have not yet been able to breach the inner circle of their government, however, they tell us there is now some sort of Council that sits with the King and Queen. Even with a governing body, the coven remains wild, without law or order. As more of them join the coven, there is greater unrest among them. They are uncivilized and unsocialized. They think nothing of murdering each other and there are no consequences for anything that they do.

"The Council fears their blatant killing will bring attention to our kind. While they live in the mountains and hunt away from the cities, they are relatively safe from discovery but as their numbers grow, they will be forced to hunt where prey is more plentiful."

Aris stood and gazed over the railing of the balcony deep in thought. When he spoke his voice was soft, obviously concerned. "If these weapons are to be used against the Catacombs, we are defenseless. We are a peaceful breed. We have never, in all the millennia our society has been in existence, known war."

Richard responded. "What you say is true. This is yet another reason I must return to London. I must meet with the Council to discuss the possibility of eventual attack. Sebastian says at this point they will not even consider the idea of an army. It is against all that we stand for. They must be made to understand these creatures are without rational minds, without conscience. I hope, because I was changed by them and lived with them, the Council will listen to me."

Aris placed his hand on his friend's shoulder. "Then go, but come back as quickly as you can. We wait for your return."

CHAPTER 39

The late afternoon sunshine illuminated one of Aris' paintings as it sat, showcased in the gallery window. Sarah squeezed his arm as they entered the door. His work filled the walls of the main gallery, which was already full of people milling about, sipping wine and discussing Aris' art.

John Marshall approached the couple, a huge smile on his face, his right hand extended toward Aris. "Great to see you both." He kissed Sarah's cheek softly.

"You too. Wow! I didn't expect such a turnout." Aris grinned as he spoke.

"Once we publicized your shady past, your work took on a whole new dimension." The gray-haired man laughed. "Come, let me introduce you to some of the collectors who have a real interest in your ability. I've heard nothing but positive feedback and I honestly think you're going to do very well with this collection."

He led them from group to group gathered around the various paintings hanging on the walls. All were of distant lands and times past and all had the haunting techniques of old masters. Sarah smiled as she watched the ladies. They marveled at the work, but seemed even more enthralled by the artist.

Aris was his usual handsome self with just a little bit of added old world charm. Sarah stood back a bit to watch him work his magic. It appeared she was not alone in being made breathless by his magnetism.

#

Sarah spotted Bob and Colleen soon after they entered the gallery. Bob carried the baby in his arms. "*What a beautiful family,*" she thought.

"Hey, this is quite a turnout." Bob's eyes searched the crowd. "Where's Carlos?"

Sarah kissed her friends on the cheek and the baby on the forehead before she answered. "He's doing an interview with the journalist from *Impressionism Today*. She seems really taken with his story."

"John Marshall had a great idea to bring his gang-banger-turns-artist past into the promotion. It makes Carlos even more intriguing." Colleen took hold of the baby as Bob guided them to the refreshments laid out in another room. "Man, this is really remarkable. Where'd all these people come from?" He filled a plate with cheese and crackers and offered the women something to drink. They both refused so he poured himself a small glass of wine.

They moved from painting to painting, listening to the patrons talk about the work. "Everyone seems to really like it." There was pride in Sarah's voice as she spoke. Bob and Colleen looked at each other with a knowing smile. It had been obvious for some time that their friends were in love and they were glad to see it was something they no longer held as a secret.

"Even I can see it's great and I don't know anything about art." Bob leaned closer to read the small slip of paper under one of the paintings. "Whoa. There are some pretty steep prices going on here."

"Yes, John felt they are really worth it. Besides this crowd wouldn't be nearly as receptive if the prices were lower." Sarah turned to Colleen. "Here, let me take the baby for a while. You two go look around. I'll just hang out here and eavesdrop." She changed her handbag to her left shoulder then nestled the baby into the crook of her right arm. The little girl looked like a miniature of Colleen with her dark spiky hair and long black lashes.

"If she wakes up, come get me. It's almost her feeding time." Colleen linked arms with Bob as they moved across the gallery to look at a very large painting of a thin lipped dark haired woman seated on what appeared to be a throne.

Sarah whispered to the sleeping baby, "Wonder what they would think if they knew that was Anne Boleyn painted from memory?" The infant stirred as if in acknowledgement, then settled back into a deep sleep.

#

It was almost closing time so Saul's had only a few customers, most seated at the counter and an occasional two or three to a booth. The late hour promoted softer voices and less clatter of dishes and cutlery so Aris and Sarah spoke in quiet conversation.

"That was quite exhilarating this evening." His untouched coffee sat in front of him.

"I'll say." She ate the last spoon of soup from her bowl before she went on. "Twenty-two-thousand dollars on the opening of your first real show? John couldn't believe it. He said it's never happened before for a new artist."

"Well Sarah, I would not call myself new." He laughed. "Rather more seasoned than that."

"How did you paint so many pieces so quickly?"

"Super powers, remember?" She did remember. He acted so human, so Carlos-like that, more often than not, she still forgot what he truly was.

"You have really brought that time in history to life for me." She tilted her head, gazing shyly at her empty bowl as she spoke. "You have brought my own existence to life for me. I can't remember what life was like before you and when I try, I feel empty." Melancholy welled up inside of her. "I would never want to be without you."

He could swear he felt his Immortal non-beating heart pulsate at her words. "You will never have to be without me." He reached across the table taking her two hands in his. "Super powers and Immortal. What can I say?" His laugh was soft as he lifted her hands, touching his lips first to one then the other.

Color rose in her cheeks as she met his gaze.

"So Sarah, how is it in your heart? Am I making any progress?"

She was honest as she spoke. "I have so many feelings I didn't know existed before and they confuse and delight me at the same time."

"Just know that I love you and I pray there will come a time when there is no confusion, only delight. I am waiting for that day. Until then I will remain your friend and will keep you safe."

CHAPTER 40

DeMarco hadn't been in touch with her since he left the country. He told her he would wait for her to contact him and he had held to his word. She missed his company yet was glad she didn't have to deal with the confusion he brought into her life. So strange that a human man confused her while one of the undead made her feel safe and secure. She stared at her laptop for several minutes before she began the email. It was time to tell him. She was sure of her heart. She had no idea where her love would lead her, but she knew it was for Aris and Aris alone.

His reply to her was brief. "I knew when I last saw you this would be your final decision. My travels to America are finished. DeMarco."

Special moments she had spent with him filled her mind. She sat quietly re-reading the words he had written. Sighing deeply, she deleted the email and closed her laptop.

CHAPTER 41

The three girlfriends sat around Colleen's coffee table sprawled on pillows on the floor. They just finished planning their yearly camping trip and were excited about their plans.

"I'm so glad we're including Maggie and Gabriela this year." Bonnie reached for a cracker, placing a small sliver of cheese and an olive slice on it before she popped it in her mouth.

"Me too. I don't know why we didn't ask Maggie before now. Do you think she'll come?" Colleen stretched her arms over her head then stood to check on her baby.

Sarah stacked the random sheets of paper and the camping magazines in neat piles on the table as she spoke. "I hope so but now that she's met Sam, I'm not so sure. She's absolutely besotted with him."

"Besotted? Where the hell did you get that word?" Colleen looked at her friend as if she had two heads.

"Just from some reading I've been doing, that's all."

"So when do you have time to read? You and Carlos seem to be joined at the hip. And I hope you are. Literally." She waited for an answer but Sarah wasn't talking. "Well, are you?"

"Honestly C, you're nosey beyond belief. I'm not sharing that info yet even with you two."

"Aha, silence is consent. You are. Finally. I was beginning to worry about you, hon."

"Nothing to worry about here, C." She spoke slowly while her thoughts raced. Soft kisses, being held tenderly. Being wrapped in strong arms. She wanted him in her bed, but she knew it was impossible. And the more she was with him, the deeper and stronger her passion grew. Sometimes she thought she would burst with desire for him. It was then her thoughts always returned to the Catacombs and her mortal life. The decision was hers and hers alone. Love had not yet become a strong enough motivator, but who can call the future. Only the Keeper of the Infinity Diaries.

#

"Well, Sarah, what do you think?" The walls of the huge room and the tall ceiling of the loft were painted white. The floor was very light thick wooden slats polished to a fine shine. She felt she was standing in the middle of a cloud. Somehow, it was so fitting for him.

"I think it's wonderful, Aris. It's enormous. What are you going to do with all the space?"

"Enjoy it while the commissions to do paintings just keep rolling in." He laughed. "It's been difficult to live in such small rooms as I have been. Remember, for centuries I lived without even the encumbrance of a body." He took her arm to guide her to a tall window overlooking the city. "This loft is the first true home I have had in your time."

A welcome warm rain shower kissed the city, washing away the dust and grime that accumulates in metropolitan life. Everything looked brand new. The Chicago skyline was filled with mirrored buildings and now they reflected the rolling clouds that surrounded them. Sarah felt as if she were floating high above the traffic and noise below.

"I will paint here. I will re-create on canvas a life I knew long ago. It makes me so happy to share it with you, to give you a glimpse of your own distant past."

"It's so strange. Since my regression work with Bonnie, I can see it. I mean you and I together at court. And Anne. And Queen Katherine. Is life so full of surprises for all humans?"

"It can be if humans open their minds to possibility. After all, Sarah, all things in life are nothing more than possibilities turned into an agreed reality, aren't they?"

She turned to him, wrapping her arms around his broad shoulders and kissed him. His mouth was warm, thick, inviting. His lush lower lip was as smooth as silk as she kissed him deeply. His taste was of no earthly man; sweet fruit and flowers, the damp warmth of clean forest air in summer. Her legs grew weak as he lifted her and carried her to the only furniture in the tremendous room, an ornate carved rosewood sofa.

He laid her back into the lush cushions. Her hair tumbled to her shoulders as he released the clip holding her curls in check. His gentle fingers traced her eyebrows, her jawline. Lifting her chin, once more his lips found hers. She gasped as the tip of his warm tongue touched the soft velvet mound of the inside of her lower lip. Shyly, it peeked in and out of her quivering mouth. Her body flushed with desire. She pulled him toward her, overwhelmed with her need to feel his weight on her. Her kiss grew demanding. She reached her hand to touch the straining hardness pressing the front of his trousers.

Grasping her wrist gently, he caressed her face. "No, my love. This intimacy is one thing that is not possible in reality. Not so long as you remain mortal." He kissed the tear that pooled just under her eye. "I desire you with a passion that has lasted hundreds of years, yet I am unable to fulfill my eternal craving. I have kept my lovemaking to gentle, casual caresses out of fear of harming you.

We must go no further. I am able to resist my need, but I cannot suffer yours. My desire to fulfill your yearning and to be unable to causes me great sorrow." He stood, taking her hands and bringing her to her feet. "A walk in the cooling rain is exactly what we need right now."

Once outside his building they progressed down the wet street holding hands, but she was the only one under the umbrella. He walked next to her, his black hair glistening in the misting rain.

CHAPTER 42

SARAH HAGAN, transcript, session 8

"Where are you Elizabeth?"

"*I am nowhere and everywhere. I am disembodied and surrounded by the reality of the universe. I am more alive than I have ever been yet without material form. Where am I? I know not. What am I? I know not.*"

"What can you see?"

"*Space. Dimensions. I see all things that were and all things that will be yet they are without form. Only thought. And yet not thought as there is no mind to think. There is only what I am and I am all, everything and nothing.*"

"Elizabeth, is this death?"

"*Death? Life? In this place, they are both one and the same as there is neither and both simultaneously.*"

"Are you alone?"

"*Since there is no me, there is no sense of alone. Since I have no body, I am all things and all things are a part of what I am.*"

"Are you afraid?"

"*In this place where I am, there is no fear, no want, no hate, no desire. There is only an all-encompassing feeling of peace that passes all human understanding. I am peace itself. I am one-ness. I am all.*

Bonnie watched her friend, waiting for her to continue. To breathe. As she stared at her, she found no rise in her chest. No inhalation. She jumped from her chair and grabbed Sarah's shoulders. "Come back to me, Sarah. Come back to real time." There was no response. "Sarah. Sarah." She was shouting, shaking her. "Come back to me!"

Suddenly, gasping, the hypnotized woman blinked. "Bonnie, Bonnie." When she opened her eyes, they were glowing with an unearthly ecstasy that terrified her friend. "Bonnie." The word was slurred as Sarah slumped back on the couch, unconscious.

#

The paramedics finished the paperwork then assured the two friends it was nothing more than a fainting spell. They left Bonnie's office as the women sat facing one another, sipping what was left of the cold tea in their cups.

"Good grief, Sarah. I thought I'd lost you."

"For a minute, I think you did. I've never felt such peace. I would have stayed in that place forever, wherever it was."

"I think we've done our last past life on you, my precious friend. I never want to go through that again."

Sarah just smiled as she thought, "I think we will all go through that once in our life, just once. At the end of it."

#

Sarah hadn't discussed her latest regression with anyone, not even Aris. It was something that was somehow sacred to her and she held it close, veiled.

She was anxious to have some quiet time to ponder her session. Her hasty good night to Gabriela was hardly civilized yet Gaby wasn't offended. She knew her human friend was in therapy and she understood that sometimes her sessions left her drained. She said her good night and went to the guest room to telephone

Richard.

Sarah nestled into the comfort of her familiar bed as she remembered the feeling of unsurpassed peace she felt floating that afternoon without a body or a mind. Where was she? Was that really what death felt like or was it simply what her mind thought death would be like? Once again, questions. Since Carlos then Aris entered her life, it had been full of mysterious, enigmatic, perplexing questions. And now this. Was it her subconscious telling her she was ready to let go? To move into everlasting life with the only man she had ever really loved? And with thoughts swirling, making her more dizzy than she had been that afternoon, she drifted off to sleep.

#

Even in sleep she recognized the room. It was Aris' loft. It was nighttime and the room was empty, devoid of furniture. The only light was from floor sconces holding huge, flaming, brightly lit candles and a full moon pouring light onto the shiny wooden floor. There were no external buildings to mar the landscape. The world outside was dark, unfathomable. From somewhere, she knew not exactly where, soft courtly music played as if from a living orchestra yet there was no one in the room except her.

She was nude beneath a soft white bathrobe. Suddenly as happens only in a dream, he was there. Tall, dark. Her beloved. He, too, was dressed in a long, white robe, his beautiful feet bare against the cool wood of the floor. He wore the hooded collar over his head as if he had just stepped from the shower, his hair still wet. He reached his arms to her. Making no sound, she moved toward him. He opened his arms to enfold her. He held her close. She could smell the sweet clean scent of him and it stirred her. He kissed her softly then stepped away, taking her in his arms to dance. The soft music led them into a gentle waltz. Her feet barely touched the floor as he whirled her around the huge room. The candles flickered as they danced past, stirring the air around them.

Faster and faster they spun until she was out of breath. She wasn't sure if it was from the dance or the desire that filled her to overflowing.

When at last they stopped the waltz, he leaned down to kiss her. She reached to slide the hood from his head. Her bitter scream filled the room when she saw that, instead of the face of her beloved beneath the hood of the robe, there was the death's head of a skeleton. Was this her future? Skulls and bones, death and horror. Even in her sleep, her subconscious fell back on her personal mantra. "I'll think about it in the morning. It will all be different in the morning." She spent the rest of the night in dreamless slumber and when she woke up, she had forgotten the nightmare.

CHAPTER 43

Aris and Sarah spent a quiet evening waiting for Gabriela to return from the airport with Richard. A hard rain had just ended and the distant thunder was just a rumble as he held her close. Sarah still hadn't told him about her session or her vision. She knew if anyone would understand, it would be Aris. She just wasn't quite ready to discuss it, to bring it from that secret place inside of her to the real world. Whatever that might be. At last she fully understood that she had no true idea what was real and what wasn't.

She thought that Aris was real. And she was real. Or was she? She was certain she was real only when she was in his presence. Human. Vampire. Immortal. What did it matter as long as she was with him.

She heard a key turn in the lock signaling their two friends were home. They both stood to welcome them.

#

He shook his head in disbelief as he spoke to his friend. "I do not know, Richard. I am not certain the time has come for me to return to the Catacombs." The rain began again and splashed against the concrete of the balcony as they sat in Sarah's cozy living room.

"Aris, if ever it was time, it is now. It has become obvious that the Spanish coven intends to lay siege to the Catacombs. Can you fathom a vampire war under the streets of modern London? Can you imagine something of that magnitude becoming public knowledge? It will end our seclusion, our very way of life. The only answer is to take the conflict to the mountains of Spain where there is no human life. If we wait, the world will be in chaos. Humanity will know of our existence. We will be hounded and tested and driven from the planet. Akira will never stand for such treatment and we will have a full scale world war between Immortals and humans. We cannot have such an occurrence. It must not happen."

"Why do you think my going to the Catacombs and speaking with Akira will change any of that? I am but one."

"You know of war. Your human life was as a warrior. Your early Immortal life was as a great warrior. You have the only experience of our kind with conflict and battle. Akira needs you, we all need you. Please Aris, consider what you are saying."

"My God Richard, we are a society without hate, without weapons. How can I change centuries of a peaceful people into an army? There is no hope of that."

Gabriela paced behind her seated mate. At last she spoke. "Aris, this is the time. Now. Sebastian says Akira will stand for you in front of the Council. They will forgive you. They will take you back into the coven. They are in great need of a general. You are our last hope. Do not turn your back on those who love you, those who need you."

Aris looked into the eyes of the woman seated beside him. "Sarah? What do you say?"

Richard stood, speaking from frustration. "She has no idea what to say. She has no true concept of the magnitude of the situation."

"Richard," Sarah spoke. "I may not be an Immortal. I may not feel what you feel, but I know anguish and sorrow. I see both in your faces. You have stood by me, protecting a human, stepping into a life that is foreign to you to make sure I'm safe. You have been the embodiment of kindness. How can I stand in the way of your survival now? What would that make me?" She turned toward Aris. "Go to London. Go to the Catacombs. Meet the Council. Aid your people. I will be here waiting when the decision is made."

Anguish rang in his voice when he spoke. "Sarah, you don't know what you are asking. The last time I left you to go to the Catacombs I lost you for centuries. I fear that loss more than I fear extinction."

"It won't happen again. We're wiser. It's a different time. No one can tear us apart. I'll be here waiting for you to share whatever we have for as long as we can share it."

"Please, Aris, at least allow Sebastian to see you, to speak with you." Richard spoke out.

"Sebastian? Here? In Chicago?"

"Yes, he returned with me. He waits at the hotel for your answer."

The room was silent except for the sound of distant thunder and rain beating down on the patio.

"Alright. I will see him."

"Shall we go now? He waits impatiently to see his brother once again."

"I will stay here with Sarah." Gabriela rose from her seat to stand behind her roommate.

"I want to go along." Sarah reached for his hand.

"No. You wait here. I may be there for many hours. You and Gabriela stay home. Have dinner. You must sleep. I will return at the end of the evening."

"No matter what time it is?"

"No matter the time." He kissed her gently. "Now rest."

The two Immortal men left her apartment and she had never felt smaller or more insignificant in her human world than she did in that moment.

CHAPTER 44

"I still don't get it Sarah. What's Carlos doing going to London?"

"I told you, C, John Marshall is trying to set up a showing for him over there. He paints English history. John thinks the timing is great. The article just came out about him and there's huge interest in his work right now. This could be an enormous break for him." She ached to tell her best friend the truth about her secret life, but she knew she would never be able to do it. Colleen could never believe her.

"Yeah?" Colleen peeled back the white paper on her hot dog as the two women sat on a park bench, the shade of a huge green maple tree sheltering them from the sun. "So, why aren't you going with him?"

Sarah asked herself that same question time and again. After his meeting with Sebastian, the decision was made. He must return. It seemed he was the only hope the Immortals had against an army; not one of them had his expertise in weaponry and hand-to-hand combat. The only way to kill a vampire was by a stake in the heart and the only way to extinguish them forever was with fire. A vampire war in the streets of London was unthinkable. It must be waged in the wilds. The Immortals had never known war. They had no weapons, no training. Every day his kind sat underground in seclusion and did nothing was a day closer to destruction.

Sebastian brought news from their spies. Their self-proclaimed enemy outnumbered them. De Flores and Mariska had first tamed them with fear and were now training them for battle. It was only a matter of time before they arrived in London; only a matter of time before the human population knew of their existence. They must ready themselves and go to Spain. It was their only chance at keeping their lives as they were.

Aris promised her he would return after his meeting with Akira. He would have to go before the Council for a formal trial but Sebastian assured him, under the current circumstances, forgiveness was the only plausible verdict. So he readied himself to leave even as Sarah sat eating a quiet lunch in Lincoln Park.

"I'm sorry, C. I spaced out for a minute. He won't be gone very long. This is just a preliminary meeting."

"Oh, by the way, Bob is really excited about Carlos' idea to bring art into the streets. He told Bob he wanted to give something back to the kids in the barrio. I don't quite know what he means by that, but I think it's great. These kids have no idea what it is to have someone who cares if they live or die. It can make all the difference in the world to them."

"Yeah, I know. He told me he was going to talk to Bob." Sarah didn't tell Colleen the real reason the Immortal wanted to develop a mentoring system. It was Aris' way of paying Carlos back for his great sacrifice, mentoring young men who had no one who cared. Just like Colleen, he wanted to pay it forward. The vampire's innate goodness made up for any of the wicked things he had done when he was first changed. Love for him welled inside her. In her eyes he was more than a man, more than an Immortal. In that moment she recognized him for what he truly was, exactly what he had been telling her all along. Her soul-mate.

She longed to explain herself to Colleen. To have her friend know what was really going on in her life, but she knew she would never, ever be able to. It was painful for her. It put a wall between them that Colleen didn't even know existed.

"When he comes home, you two will have to come to dinner and we'll figure out how to get the whole thing started."

"Yeah, I'm sure he'll want to start as soon as possible." Sarah's words, just like her life, had a double meaning.

#

"Are you busy? Is this a good time to talk?" Sarah's heart beat faster when she heard Aris' voice on the other end of the telephone.

"A perfect time. I just crawled into bed. How are you?"

"As well as can be expected being on the other side of the planet. And you, how is it with you?"

"It's good. Gabriela is doing her best to make up for you being gone." Sarah laughed. "She's constantly trying to get me to go places and do things."

"Keeping busy is very good and I will return in just a few days. Sarah, I have news; I was able to meet with Akira today."

Completely alert, Sarah sat upright in her bed. "What happened?"

"It brought me great peace to find her forgiving. I was so concerned for Sebastian and what the consequences would be for him for allowing me to continue my existence after the Council had declared me doomed. But she was so kind. She says she feels no human emotion yet sometimes it appears she is more humane than most human beings I have encountered."

"So," impatience rang in her voice, "did she forgive both of you?"

"She appeared to be joyful to see me once again. She is grateful that Sebastian saved me and knowing I lived disembodied for hundreds of years, she feels I have done penance. She knows the Catacombs is in need of me right now. She welcomed me and will stand for me at the trial."

"There is to be a trial?" Her fear for him was clear in her tone of voice. "If there is a trial, can't they choose to extinguish you?"

"Yes, however Akira believes the Council realizes the enormity of the uprising in Spain. She believes they will exonerate me and allow me to return in exchange for training and leading an army."

"When will this trial take place?"

"Soon, but first I must return to the states to meet with John Marshal. Tomorrow I meet with the owner of the gallery here in London and we begin making plans for the art showing. I must coordinate the showing with the trial. Akira has given her permission for me to continue with my human life for the time being. So the art show is the next step. It will be the perfect reason for my absence from Chicago. I found a small flat today in London so I have a place to live above ground while I am here."

"A flat? How long are you planning on being away?"

"As long as is necessary. After the showing, I will say I am staying to absorb more of the countryside and prepare for the next exhibit. It will give the Council time to reach their verdict and give me time to choose and train my commanders. Akira is calling as many Immortals to the Catacombs as the Keeper of Records can locate."

"I'm frightened for you, for all of you."

"Do not fear. We are superior in intellect and strength. Their numbers are greater than ours, but our strength is in our abilities and in our ties to one another. They have no such ties. They war among themselves and kill each other daily."

"Yes and that's what scares me. Murder means nothing to them. How will you teach your Immortals to kill when they are so against taking life?"

"Sarah, we are peaceful, but we are not cowards. This is a war of defense. We will do all we need to do to protect our coven and our way of life. And to protect the humans that live on the earth above us."

"They don't even know you exist."

"Yes, and we intend to keep it exactly like that. Now, sleep well."

Whispering into the receiver, she spoke. "Aris, my life feels so empty without you."

There was a moment of silence before he spoke. "Your words touch me deeply, Sarah."

"I've begun to realize that until now, I have seen you as a combination of two beings, Carlos and Aris. It was painful to lose Carlos, and frightening to know you were now alive. I could not imagine being anything more than your friend. I thought the price was too high to pay for more, but being away from you and having time alone to think, I have come to a different conclusion."

He waited in silence.

"You are Aris, an Immortal soul. And I love you."

His voice was soft, warm, when he spoke. "I will hold you in my arms before the week is out."

"Good night." She hung up the telephone and for the first time in months, felt complete.

CHAPTER 45

"So Gorgeous is setting the world on fire." Maggie placed the steaming cup of morning coffee on Sarah's desk then sat in the chair across from her.

"I don't know if he's doing that, but he's had a wonderful reception in London."

"He'd have a wonderful reception any place he goes as long as the women have eyes."

"Maggie, give him a break. He's more than a pretty face." Sarah laughed as she tasted the coffee, stopped, and poured two more sugar packets into the cup.

"Yeah, I know, but it sure helps to break the ice. When is he coming home?"

"Tomorrow afternoon. He has a meeting with John Marshal on Friday and they'll decide all the logistics. John has really taken a liking to him."

"Yeah, well Carlos is a definite commodity for business, isn't he? He's talented, good looking, has a sordid past and has become incredibly articulate. What's not to like? He's changed so much since he started coming here," Maggie shook her head as she spoke. "It's hard to believe he's the same guy."

"A near-death experience would change anybody, don't you think?" Sarah always became uneasy when anyone spoke of the changes in Aris. He managed to appear to evolve gradually for her friends, however, the difference in his personality, even his appearance, was noticeable. He looked older, wiser, more worldly.

"Yeah, I guess it would. I mean he always seemed to be a good guy. There's just something so much more about him now."

Sarah pulled a file from her drawer. Opening it she laid it on her desk, signifying the end of the conversation. "Well Maggie, there is so much more now."

Maggie began to speak,then thought better of it as Sarah shuffled through the file, beginning to make notes for her next session.

#

Back in Chicago, Aris toyed with a curl in Sarah's hair as he spoke. "There are Immortals arriving at the Catacombs daily. They come from all over the globe to stand for their brothers and sisters. We are a fearless breed, but I worry for them. They have never felt the stake or experienced premeditated killing. They are innocents." The couple sat on her sofa, her head on his shoulder, the evening summer breeze blowing gently through the open sliding glass door.

"Can you teach them?" Her concern for him and his family was apparent in her tone.

"I can teach them the use of weapons and the strategies of war, but to teach a peaceful people to kill is something I have yet to do."

She sat up, looking in his eyes. "But you've been a soldier, a warrior both as human and as Immortal. You've taught battle strategies before."

"Yes, but only to humans. Humans are driven by fear. They can kill one another because of an innate foreboding of death. Our kind has no fear; we have always lived in peace and can never die if we abide by the law. They have no understanding of suspicion and doubt. I despise that I must be the one to teach them such ugly concepts and yet I must. They must understand that they can be touched by the evil of the world."

"The more facts I learn about the Immortals and knowing Richard and Gabriela, I am so drawn to enter the Catacombs and really understand your way of life."

"No human may enter the Catacombs unless it is for the mating ritual. It has never been done in all of our history."

"I understand, I just meant I wouldn't be afraid. I want to know more about you, that's all."

"Just know I love you." He kissed her gently drawing her head back onto his shoulder. He hadn't mentioned her declaration of love since his return from London. She wondered if he ever would. "Now tell me, what has been happening with our human friends while I have been away.

She snuggled into his arms and began to share the day-to-day life of the long two weeks without him.

#

Richard had returned from London with Aris. He and Gabriela had gone away for the weekend while Aris was in Chicago and able to keep watch over Sarah. There had been no further visitation from the unknown intruder, but the Immortals were not ready to give up their vigilance in caring for their human friend. She was always within the sight or voice range of one of them, never without their protection.

She wondered if they left the city to feed. It was something they never discussed. Her relationship with the vampires felt so normal to her, she forgot they drank blood. She wondered where they found the animals that supplied their need then immediately put the thought from her mind. Knowing them, she was sure they took animals from the wild. Their gentle souls would never steal someone's pet. How would Aris ever be able to teach these beings to kill? Knowing he had been a great warrior in battle made her rest more easily, but she still worried about him and his Immortal family.

They sat on the breakwater, watching the sun rise over Lake Michigan. The city was just beginning to come to life. They had plans for a full day. Packing paintings to ship to London, making sure all of the small details that were always so important in the long run were complete; their list for the day was so long they decided to begin at dawn with coffee at the lake.

"Do you think you'll be gone more than a month?" Her sadness at his traveling was apparent in her voice.

He smiled as he hugged her. "At least a month. It will be difficult for me as well, however, I have no control over the Council. They will see me when they are ready and they will take as long as they wish to make a decision. Akira will do all she can to move it forward, but even as they deliberate, I will begin training."

"Will all the Immortals go into battle?"

"All who wish to. We fight for our race."

"We spoke last night of the ancient wars you fought and the weapons you used hundreds of years ago. What weapons will you use in Spain? You told me a long time ago, a vampire must be staked. Does that mean hand-to-hand combat?"

"Hand to hand. Knives and swords. Arrows. The Keeper of Records has ancient texts describing weapons brought by the Immortals to earth when Akira and Khansu first arrived. Even now they work to forge them. In appearance much like your ancient swords and arrows except these are forged through alchemy, a secret known only to the Keeper of Records. Each step in their making is accomplished by a different company of workers. No one group has any inkling of what any other group does. Once created, the weapons can never be destroyed. They have a mystical power that only Akira is able to bestow. Each weapon will always return to the hand of its owner. The creation of Nalyd weaponry is a long, tedious process."

"What weapons does De Flores have, do you know?"

"They, too, work in secret. Our fear is De Flores found the texts when he worked in the Records Hall. If they are able to reproduce them, ours will still be more powerful because of Akira's gifts. We do not fear them, Sarah, nor should you fear for us."

"How can I control that? I sit here in the middle of a modern world with planes and cars and computers while you fight an ancient war with weapons from another planet. Even saying it makes me doubt my own sanity."

"You must doubt nothing. You must believe in us. We have no choice but to win this battle."

It was as if someone turned up the volume on a radio as the teaming city came to life behind them. He stood, reaching for her hand. "Come, it is time to go. We have a full day ahead of us. If we want to spend the evening with Colleen and Bob tonight, we best begin." He helped her to her feet and they walked slowly down the breakwater toward the street.

CHAPTER 46

As always, Colleen checked the baby monitor before she closed the door to the nursery. It was the evening before Aris was to leave for London and the four friends sat around the coffee table, comfortably discussing the upcoming art show.

"How many paintings will you show, Carlos?" Colleen sipped her lemonade as Bob refreshed Sarah's wine. They had all grown accustomed to Aris' full glass of water sitting in front of him. He had never touched alcohol in front of them and no one questioned him about the water he never drank. It simply was there in case he wanted it.

"There are thirty-two for this show plus a lot of pencil sketches and ink drawings."

"Why don't you tell them what a big deal the gallery is making of you?" Pride rang in Sarah's voice as she smiled at Aris seated beside her.

"It's not such a big deal."

"Oh yes it is." She turned to Colleen and Bob. "There's a chance some of the people from the royal house may make an appearance at the gallery. Because all the paintings are of England and a lot of them of the English aristocracy from past times and from the present, the royals have taken a notice. There's a chance this guy here may even meet the Queen."

"Come on Sarah. Don't make more of it than it is. I'm proud of it, of course, but it's just a simple art show. I'll be happy if anybody shows up and doubly happy if people buy my work. John Marshal has invested a wad of money in this."

"It's because he believes in you."

Bob slapped Aris on the shoulder as he crossed the room toward the kitchen. "We're all proud of you. You've come a long way."

"Carlos," Colleen leaned toward him, a question in her voice. "I've been wondering, how can you paint dead kings and queens of England? Are you guessing what they look like?"

Sarah drew in a long breath of air as she turned toward him.

"That's pretty easy, C. I just study all the past paintings of them. Since the only visual record they had then of their families was paintings, they made sure there were a lot of them and done by the best of the best artists. I just study them and put my own slant on them."

Sarah relaxed again. He always knew what to say and it always made sense.

Bob came back into the room with a pitcher to refresh his wife's glass of lemonade. "Well, we want to buy one now, while we can still afford it." He laughed.

"How about I just do one for you as a gift? A special painting of your own little royal family."

Colleen jumped off the sofa and hugged him. "Carlos, you are the best." She beamed as he kissed her cheek.

"It's the least I can do for all that you've given to me." He wrapped his arm around Sarah as he kissed the top of her head. "You've given me a life that I never knew was possible and I am eternally grateful."

As time progressed, Sarah became more and more aware that her personal eternity had been laid out for her five centuries past. She smiled. There was no defeating destiny.

CHAPTER 47

"How was your day?" As always her mood lifted as soon as Sarah heard Aris' voice on the telephone. He had only been out of the country for little more than a day, yet she missed him desperately. She faced her office window, watching the city come to life before her. She arrived at the office early to catch up on long overdue paperwork. Gabriela sat in the outer office waiting for Maggie.

Maggie enjoyed having Gabriela join in her work. She introduced Gaby to internet shopping and chocolate chip cookies. Sarah knew Gaby really didn't enjoy eating human food, but she never let on when Maggie brought her sugary treats. Sarah's freezer was stacked with the sweet chocolate loot she took home from the office. It was an unending supply of goodies for their girl's nights in.

"Sarah? Are you still there?"

"I'm sorry, I was just thinking about Gabriela and Maggie."

"How are the ladies faring?"

"They get along great. It amazes me how easy it is for an Immortal to just 'fit in' with humans."

"You forget, we are half human. It is just another part of us."

"I miss you."

"You fill my heart with sorrow and joy with those words. I am glad you wish me with you and I am sad that you are without me." Aris laughed at his own conundrum.

"Well, you've only been gone a day. I'm sure it'll get worse before it gets better. Do you go to the gallery tomorrow?"

"Yes, the paintings are to arrive in the morning. We have a very busy week ahead of us."

"When will you go to the Catacombs?"

"After a late dinner tonight. John and I and Reginald Clinton are having a celebratory meal together before the showing. I think you would like Reginald. He's very, very British but he has a great sense of humor and he is very excited to present my work at his gallery."

"Will you spend the night at the Catacombs?"

"John thinks I'm spending the night at my flat, but I am going below. Richard and Sebastian have news of the Spanish coven. I am anxious to learn all I can."

"Will you call me tomorrow?"

"Of course I will. I must go now or I will be late picking up John. I will call you in the morning. Say hello to Maggie and Gabriela for me." He hesitated for a moment before he spoke. "I love you and I miss you." He disconnected before she had time to answer.

#

The library of the Catacombs was paneled in dark wood from the floor to the eighteen-foot ceiling. Half way up, a narrow walkway gave easy access to the books lining every wall. Tall, simply carved ladders lined the room waiting for a scholar to lay claim to a volume just out of reach. The entire room was illuminated by sconces holding glowing globes of soft yellow light, very different from the Tudor days when all was candles and fire. It had taken hundreds of years for the Catacombs scientists to decipher the ancient alchemist's text and create their own form of heat and light.

Scattered about the room, large ornately carved wooden tables doubled as desks for anyone who had need of them. Tall wing-back burgundy leather chairs surrounded the tables and the floor was covered in layer after layer of the finest silk carpets.

The large room was empty of activity except for the three handsome Immortals sitting in a corner far from the main door. They leaned their heads close, speaking in soft voices even though there was no one to hear them.

"The trial is to begin on Monday. We just received the word an hour ago." Sebastian had called a meeting as soon as he knew the schedule.

"So what do we do now?" Richard softly tapped his fingers on the table.

"I go to trial." Aris stood, pacing in front of the table. "What else is there to do?"

Sebastian spoke, "Aris, sit down. Richard, quit tapping. You two will drive me mad. Please relax. I told you, they have no choice but to allow you to go free. You must begin the training of our army. And quickly. The spies tell us they will soon begin their march to London. It must never happen. We must stop them in the mountains before the humans realize we exist.

Aris sat, Richard stopped tapping and Sebastian? He stood and paced the floor.

#

"The trial begins tomorrow." The cell phone line broke up as Aris spoke.

"I didn't get that. What?" He caught her just as she was preparing to leave her office for the day. She returned to her chair, swiveling it so she could look out the window at the evening clouds rolling in.

"Can you hear me now?"

"Yes. Much better."

"The trial begins tomorrow."

She shot out of her chair. "Tomorrow?" Panic was clear in her voice.

"It will be just fine. Sebastian is sure all will be well. It may take some days of deliberation so, in the meantime, I am going to begin training the commanders."

"Please, be careful. I'm so worried. What if they don't set you free?"

"We will deal with that if it becomes necessary. Sebastian assures me I will be acquitted and I believe his word."

"I'd feel a lot better about it if you were home already."

"Sarah, I am home." He chose his words carefully. "Don't you see, this is more my home than Chicago. These are my people. I cannot turn my back on them and I must face the Council with resignation. If it were not for you, I would spend the rest of my life in London in the Catacombs. It is where I feel I most belong."

"If it weren't for me? Am I the only reason you stay in Chicago?"

"Good heavens, Sarah. Whatever do you think could be strong enough to hold me to the three dimensional human world? Only my love for you."

Maggie leaned her head around the door. "Hey boss, Gaby's ready to go home and so am I. What say we close up shop." She realized Sarah was on her cell phone. She put her hand over her mouth. "I'm sorry, boss."

Sarah covered the mouthpiece. "That's okay. It's time to hang up anyway." Maggie shut the door when she left the room.

"Aris, I have to close the office. Please be careful and call me later. Will you?"

"Of course. I love you, Sarah."

"I'll speak with you later." Sarah pressed the 'end' button on her cell phone. Her mind was full of concern. He didn't really want to be in Chicago. She was holding him back from the life he truly wanted to live among his own kind. She understood his need, his desire. But what would she do without him? He was willing to give up his culture, his life, for her. Was she willing to give up hers for him.

CHAPTER 48

The Council sat on one side of the long carved wooden table. Sconces similar to those in the library lined the wall behind them. The light was soft, but sufficient to provide a unique clarity of vision Aris wasn't accustomed to above ground, even in direct sunlight. He stood behind a podium facing his judges.

The Chief Councilor, Bartholomew, rose from his chair rapping on a block of wood with an ancient gavel. The chatter quieted as the Council members all turned to give him their attention. They were dressed in regal robes of rich hued velvet worn over their perfectly tailored business suits. Twelve in all, there were six males and six females each with an equal say. Bartholomew was the tie-breaker and so he held the final rule among the lawmakers.

Akira paced the cold stone floor in front of the long table. Her blue velvet robe of state dragged behind her. "Will you not see reason? He has suffered his own judgment these five hundred long years. He was without embodiment. He was alone without solace. He searched for a beloved wrongly taken from him. What more can we ask of him?"

"What we ask of all our citizens. Adherence to the law."

"I care not for the law. I care for justice. This Immortal has suffered isolation and neglect. Can you not see that his debt is paid?"

"That will be decided in Chambers, your Majesty. We have heard your testimony. We will now hear his."

Exasperated by their attitude, Akira swept from the room leaving Aris to plead his case to his accusers. King Khansu and Sebastian had already given their testimony. One to exterminate Aris and one in favor of his acquittal.

The King held no favorites. He wanted Aris destroyed for his flagrant breaking of the Great Law. Taking life for revenge was the ultimate crime and not only had he done it, he had done it twice, killing both Cardinal Wolsey and Queen Katherine. Through lies and subterfuge, Anne Boleyn used his loss of Elizabeth Wyatt to manipulate his grief. Yet, he knew better. He knew the penalty.

The first time he was tried for the death of Wolsey, he was released. The second trial for the death of the shunned Queen Katherine, he was sentenced to death. Only the fearlessness of Sebastian had saved his essence from total extermination after his second sentence. The King wanted to rid the Immortals of Aris after his first transgression. He was even more determined after the second. Yet Aris escaped into the netherworld where he floated for five hundred years. It was a personal affront to King Khansu. He was determined to end the existence of Aris once and for all. He was eloquent in his testimony for the death penalty.

When it was his time to approach the Council, Sebastian stood for Aris telling of his great ability as a warrior, a leader of armies. He warned them of the Spanish coven and what would happen if they were to attack the Catacombs. He appealed to the members combined conscience as leaders of their people. Aris was an Immortal desperately needed for his experience and leadership if they were to win what must be the forthcoming battle and maintain their kingdom. He spoke only the truth.

Then, it was his time. Aris stepped before the Council. He stood quietly, his hands folded in front of him, his head bowed. When at last he spoke, it was with a confidence he did not feel. He knew the power of the King to influence the Council. He knew his own testimony was the only one that could save him. He measured his words carefully.

"I stand before you a contrite Immortal. In my folly I listened to an evil woman and broke the law of the Catacombs. Anne Boleyn used me as a weapon to murder her enemies. I killed. Twice. I was used as a pawn in a murder scheme by a woman without conscience. She manipulated my deep personal loss to incite me to murder. I lost my only love and Queen Anne made sure she turned the knife in my wound until I readily did her bidding, doing away with her rival as well as a Cardinal of the Catholic Church.

"I admit to my crime. I deserve to be eliminated from the coven, yet I beg you to forgive me, to allow me to continue. I was driven by loss and despair. The loss of my soul mate took my mind along with her. I must be honest. I am not remorseful, but I am repentant. This is my home. You are my people. I have searched for my beloved through time and space for all these past centuries, driven by eternal love. I have tried to help others during the last centuries. I am not the man you knew so long ago. I have found my love at last. I beg of you, do not take me from her. Allow us this time to be together."

Touched by what he heard, Bartholomew spoke softly. "Is this beloved female a human?"

"Yes, she is human. She was human when I found her five hundred years ago here in England and she is human today, reincarnated in a body living in America."

Bartholomew stood, leaning his hands on the smooth wood of the table. "And so what do you wish us to do Aris?"

"If you were to meet my beloved you would then understand why I was mad when I lost her. She is the embodiment of compassion. I have waited century after century for her and I beg for your mercy. Allow me to continue so that I may love her and protect her." He dropped to his knees, bowing his head.

Bartholomew crossed to his side. Speaking softly, he touched his shoulder. "Rise, Aris. We will adjourn to deliberate your fate. You spoke well for yourself. Be assured there will be at least one who will vote in your favor."

#

"At least it is over. There is nothing more to be said or done." Aris' voice was calmly resigned as he spoke into the receiver of his cell phone.

"How did you feel about it?" Sarah was anxious. It showed in the way she clipped her words. "I mean, how do you think they'll decide?"

"I honestly have no real idea. Sebastian still feels they will vote to free me. He was amazing. If anyone was my champion, it was he. I know he has been speaking to the Council members one by one in the last few weeks, reminding them of the seriousness of the Spanish coven and that I am their only military man. He is very convincing when he wants to be. Akira was on my side, but King Khansu annihilated her testimony that I am a good, solid Immortal with his, ripping me to shreds for defying the law, not once, but twice.

"When I spoke it was only of you. My wish to spend as much time with you as I can. They are in deliberation now. I have no idea how long they will be cloistered."

"Oh, Aris, I'm worried. How can Sebastian be so sure?"

"He depends on the knowledge of the Council about the Spanish coven. They need me, Sarah. Now do not worry so much. All will be well." He wished he felt the confidence he heard in his words. Khansu, after all, was the King and the King wanted to be rid of him. How would the Council vote?

CHAPTER 49

The two friends sat on Colleen's patio drinking iced tea. Colette slept in her playpen. Sarah stood to tuck the light pink blanket around the baby's legs so she wouldn't get chilled as the late afternoon sun began to sink below the horizon.

"Thanks, hon." Colleen smiled. "Sometimes I think I'm up and down more than a jack-in-the-box. She can be a handful." She stared at her baby girl. "My handful. Isn't she precious? I had no idea the feelings that I would have about my kid."

"She's pretty sweet." Sarah grinned at the changes motherhood had wrought in her friend. "What time is Bob getting home from the station?"

"He's going out with some of the guys for a beer after work so I don't know. Want to have dinner here with the girlies?"

"Sounds great." Sarah gathered the glasses and baby toys, carrying them into the living room.

Colleen cooed at the baby as she brought her inside and settled her in her bassinette by the patio door. The little girl grinned a huge toothless grin at her mother, then grabbed hold of her thumb. "She owns me when she does that."

"Yep. I can see that." Sarah laid the toys on the coffee table and took the glasses to the kitchen. "C, why don't I just whip up a simple little salad for dinner?"

"Don't you ever get tired of rabbit food? How about a big, juicy burger? Besides, I haven't been to the market this week. The pickin's may be pretty slim."

"How about I just figure it out?" Sarah pulled a stool out from beneath the tall breakfast counter. She pointed at it. "Sit. I'm fixing a salad. You can watch."

Sarah opened the refrigerator, pulling out the crisper drawers. A head of lettuce and a couple of carrots were all that could be found. "You don't have anything to make a salad. What do you feed Bob?"

"Bob's a guy and he eats guy food, Sarah. Now, how about a burger?"

"Not on your life. What's in the freezer?" She opened it and looked in. Several burger patties, a couple of packages of frozen vegetables and three frozen pizzas. Reading the label on the pizza, she turned to her friend. "It's pizza, kid. At least it's got tomatoes and mushrooms on it. We need to get you to the store." The oven pre-heated as the two women sat on the sofa watching the baby sleep.

"So, have you heard from Carlos?"

It was even more difficult for Sarah to think of Aris as Carlos now. Since spending so much time alone with him and her friendship with the Immortals from London, he had been Aris to her and Aris alone. It was just her Chicago friends who called him Carlos. Sometimes she had to catch herself not to use his true name when she spoke with them.

"Yes, he called yesterday. Things are going great. He likes the man who owns the London gallery. The owner says he's had a wonderful response to the advertising campaign. He's expecting a record crowd. Several London art magazines responded and are attending. When John Marshal decided to bring Carlos' bad-boy past out, it was like hanging out a banner. Suddenly, everybody wants to meet him."

"Yeah, and he's a damn good artist, too." The timer on the oven dinged letting the ladies know the oven was ready. Sarah went to the kitchen and popped in the pizza.

"Colleen, where's a hot pad? You moved them since I cooked here last."

"In the drawer next to the stove." The baby started fussing so as Sarah passed by on her way to the sofa, she picked her up, handing her to her mother. She sat next to Colleen.

"Sarah, I'm sort of shocked you aren't going to London to attend the show. I mean, without you, there wouldn't be a show. If you hadn't taken him home to meet your mother and your mother hadn't introduced him to John Marshal he'd still be working at the market. Anyway, doesn't he want you to come?"

"Sure. He told me more than once. I just hadn't planned on taking a vacation right now."

"And here I thought you were loosening up. Who cares if you were planning a vacation. Get Bonnie to cover your most demanding cases and go for a week. You don't have to make a life commitment, you know. Just go for the show then come home. I'm sure it would mean a lot to Carlos."

"Yeah? Well, it would mean a lot to me, too. You know, I think I'll call Bonnie tomorrow to see if she can cover for me for a week. If she can, maybe I'll go."

"Great. I'll do whatever I can to help. Want to go on-line now and look for flights?"

"Let's wait until the pizza is done. I'm not sure yet I'll go, but we can check it out after we eat."

"If you do, are you going to call him and tell him you're coming?"

"Nope. It will be a really big surprise for both of us."

#

It was late and Sarah snuggled in her bed talking on her telephone. The only light in the room was from a candle. The breeze from the open window caused the flame to dance, creating moving shadows on the bedroom walls. "How much longer before you know anything?" Sarah was anxious to know with certainty that Aris was exonerated. She waited more impatiently for the verdict that he did.

"As long as they please. I know there is some contention among them. Some feel as Khansu does that I should be eliminated. The more realistic of the Council know they need me, my expertise. I've begun to organize the Immortals into troops. There are almost twenty-five-hundred Immortals who will join in the battle. Those from the Catacombs and those who live a human life above ground. We all fight for our very existence.

"Sarah, this is an undertaking that often feels impossible. Sometimes I feel I know so little about warfare. I am accustomed to being a warrior, not a general. I am accustomed to being commanded, not being a commander. I am so grateful to have Sebastian. He is an organizer beyond belief. Without him, Gabriela and Richard, I would certainly fail."

"Aris, will you be able to create an army in time to keep the Spanish coven from coming to the Catacombs?"

"There can be no question. The battle must be fought in Spain in the mountains. We cannot allow them to come to London. If they do, there will be a blood bath in the streets above that you cannot even begin to imagine. A few thousand of our kind in battle would be like World War Three to you humans. Sarah, we must protect your kind and keep our species a secret. They must never find out about the Immortals."

"I know you're right. I know. I just wish I could be there with you."

"My dear, as a human, you could do nothing to help. You would not even be welcome in the Catacombs."

"But I'd be welcome at your art show, wouldn't I?"

"To the art show? That is different. You would be more welcome than you can ever know. Is it a possibility?"

"I'll think about it, Aris. It would be difficult right now." But not nearly as difficult as it was being away from him. Sarah knew before she hung up the telephone; she was London bound.

#

"Of course I'm happy to help if any of your clients have an emergency, but when did you decide to go to London?" Bonnie wiped the perspiration from her forehead with her towel as she turned up the resistance on the elliptical another notch.

Sarah waited until the young woman at the front desk of the gym was finished announcing a spa special over the speaker system before she answered. "Last night. I've been thinking about it all week but I just decided last night. I really want to be there for the opening at the gallery."

"Are you going to tell him or is it a surprise?"

"It's going to be a surprise. I'm pretty excited. I haven't been to London since Jeff and I were on our honeymoon and that was just a whirlwind of one tour after another. This will be a leisurely week and a half."

"Can't live without him, can you?"

"Stop it, Bon. I do miss him, but I want to be there to support him as well. He's doing great and he needs to know how proud we are of him."

"Sarah, when are you going to admit to everyone how much he means to you? Have you even admitted it to yourself?" She stopped the machine and stood next to her friend on the treadmill. "I know you didn't think you were capable of really loving but hon, you have every sign of the disease. Why don't you just admit it? We're all waiting."

"All?"

"Yeah, even Bob mentioned it at dinner the other night and for a guy like Bob to recognize and talk about love in public, it must be a pretty obvious thing. So?"

"So? You know I love Carlos. We all think he's great."

"Give me a break. I'm your shrink and your pal. Say the words, okay?"

Sarah took a deep breath. "Okay, I'm in love with A . . ." She caught herself just in time. "With Carlos. Are you happy now?"

Bonnie whooped, kissed her friend's cheek and climbed back on board the elliptical. Her legs started pumping as she laughed out loud.

#

Sarah had just stepped off the elevator when her phone rang. She heard Colleen's laughter even before the receiver was to her ear. "Hi, C."

"So, you finally said the 'L' word, huh? No more B.S. So it's declared--love at last."

"Oh shut up, C." Sarah felt light hearted at her friend's teasing. She had been lying to all of them and to herself for much too long. "Now are you all happy?"

"Yep. Bob said just the other night he wondered when you were going to pull your head out and recognize you have all the symptoms. We think it's great. You two really belong together. And now, wow. He'll be able to take care of you in the manner in which I would like to grow accustomed."

"You would like to grow accustomed?"

"Yep, this guy is going to do really well. You deserve to have someone like that in your life. It's been full of losers so far. It's time you had a real man."

"A real man. Yes, C, I've got myself a real man here alright." She felt true delight as she walked into her apartment and closed the door. "A real man."

CHAPTER 50

It was still early morning, but Richard was already behind schedule as he hurried through the door to the library. Aris and Sebastian sat in their usual meeting place in the far corner of the room talking softly about organizing the Immortals into a fighting corps.

"Sorry I am late." Richard spoke as he sat. They settled in while Aris rifled through a stack of papers sitting on the makeshift desk.

"There are ten Immortals I have chosen to be commanders. Here are their dossiers." He slid the folders across the table to the couple. "See what you think. Sebastian and I both find these ten the most able to do the job of training the rest of the coven."

Sebastian nodded his head in agreement. "Yes, we had over one hundred who volunteered, however, these were the final choice."

The friends were silent as Richard quickly read through the folders. When he was finished, he agreed the ten seemed to be perfect. Five of the chosen men and women lived in the Catacombs, five above ground. All were highly intelligent and dedicated to their kind. Each had something unique to bring to the table and had strong leadership possibilities.

"When do you intend to begin training?" Richard slid the folders back to Aris for safe keeping.

"Day after tomorrow. Akira has given us the entire lower level of the palace for a command center and training facility. Her guards prepare it even now."

"And what of your trial?" Richard was unsure if the time was right to mention his legal proceedings, but he asked anyway.

"Nothing yet. There is no rushing the Council, yet I feel very strongly that I will be exonerated. Almost every day the spies have more news about the movement of the Spanish coven. They obviously prepare for war, yet they are disorganized at best. Even De Flores as king has limited control over them. His commanders are not much better than the rest of them. They cannot agree on a plan and fight constantly among themselves. Their constant arguing gives us the time we need to train and strategize."

Sebastian stood. "Come, let us go down to the command center to see how the work is progressing."

"Good idea." Richard slid his chair back under the table and the three friends quietly left the room.

#

The corridors in the Catacombs were all made of light colored stone. They were lit by the same strange golden globes as the library, floating in sconces mounted at five-foot intervals throughout the maze of hallways. The globes gave off heat as well as light, so the air was comfortably warm, not cold and damp as would be expected. The original globes of light were brought to earth by the first star voyagers thousands of years before. Akira and the Master Keeper of Records worked with the scientists to find a way to mass produce them using earth elements and the alchemy texts. The Catacombs, while maintaining the elegance and tradition of the past millennia, was equipped with conveniences far beyond those of the humans living above the ground. It was a marvel when Aris compared it to the limited luxuries they had during Tudor times.

The palace and village covered several square miles beneath the city and descended hundreds of feet below in layer after layer of levels. Canals connected some of the more remote chambers. The four friends stepped from the elevator at the lowest level into a cavernous room bustling with activity. Large tables similar to those in the library were being arranged in rows. The guards worked quickly and in silence. An air of anticipation filled the room as they positioned chairs around the tables. Each commander would lead two hundred and fifty Immortals so the room was being set to accommodate one commander with his or her warriors at a time. There were twenty-five tables, each with ten chairs.

Aris was the first to speak. "It appears all will be ready."

"A very good sign." Relief could be heard in Sebastian's voice. "When do we meet with the commanders? I know only those who live below ground. I have yet to meet those who live above."

"We meet tonight. Akira is giving a reception for all of those who will be in charge as well as for the Council. It is a rare occurrence for Akira to mingle with the Council outside of chambers."

"This war is a rare occurrence." Richard turned to leave. "We had best return to our chambers. We have much to do before this evening." He squeezed Aris' arm as they passed through the door into the corridor. "You are doing a marvelous job. It could not be accomplished without you."

Aris hoped the Council would agree with Richard and forgive his crime. It was his only hope for a future with Sarah and without her there was no future at all for him.

CHAPTER 51

Colleen lounged on Sarah's bed while her friend packed for her trip to London. "You'll need a raincoat. From what I read in the travel book, it rains all the time over there. Bob said when he was traveling through England, they didn't have a sunny day once."

"I'll wear my trench and boots on the plane."

"You sure are packing light. One suitcase?"

"C, I'm only going to be away for eight days plus flying time and I won't change clothes on the plane." She laughed. "Not everyone needs half their household when they travel."

"Are you insinuating I over-pack?"

"Well hon, taking that little coffee maker with you on your honeymoon was kind of strange, you must admit." Sarah closed the suitcase and set it on the floor. "There, it's finished."

"Are you ready?" Colleen checked her watch. "We had better head out if we're going to be on time. Is Maggie going to be joining us?"

"No, she can't make it. It's just going to be you, Bob and me for cocktails. Bonnie and her fireman will get there in time for dinner at eight. It's so great to be having a send-off dinner. It makes the trip seem even more special."

"Yeah, well, just don't up and get married while you're there. We all want to be at the ceremony when it happens."

"You're thinking way ahead of yourself here, kiddo." As she turned out the bedroom light, thoughts of a future with Aris filled her mind, a future as an Immortal.

#

She had just snuggled into her bed after a pleasant evening spent with her friends when the telephone rang. She looked at the clock. It was late.

"Hello?" There was a smile in her voice. She knew who was calling before he spoke.

"Sarah. How was your evening out?" Aris' question was sincere. He missed her and he had become accustomed to their group of friends. He missed them as well.

"It was fun. We ate at the Bistro and Maggie stopped by on her way to the theatre. Her new guy seems nice." She propped her pillows against the headboard and sat up. "How about you? What is going on in the Catacombs?"

"We prepare for war. How I wish this were not so. I have chosen the commanders and we meet soon for our first planning session. No one knows what to expect and they are all a bit nervous. Other than the Council, there have never been leaders among our kind. It is a new position for these Immortals and none is sure how the yoke of leadership will fit around their necks. As a leader, one is trapped with the care of those under their command. For humans, it seems easy. For us? We have no responsibilities other than the law. To take on the responsibility for two hundred and fifty beings is an enormous task for an Immortal."

"I know you will be able to train them. I have complete faith in you."

"Without Richard and Sebastian, I would flounder. It is three minds working together that will bring victory."

"And the Council, Aris? When will they give their decision? Have you received any further word?"

"It seems that all but one has decided in my favor. It must be unanimous before I am free. I do not know who is against me, but it is one who does not understand the severity of the Spaniards' declaration of war. Until they all agree, I am in limbo."

"Yet you work for them, training their army."

"There is no 'them.' There is only us. These are my people. I care what happens to our society regardless of what happens to me."

She swung her legs off the bed, heading to the kitchen to make a cup of tea while she talked. "And the art show? How is that coming along?" She smiled when she thought of how surprised he would be when she showed up in London.

"The gallery is prepared, my paintings hanging and ready. So much is happening both above ground and below." He laughed. "It is good that I do not need to sleep."

"How is John?"

"He is well and he has arranged for me to meet every important art critic in town. They are all interested in my life as a gang member. What is so fascinating about that, I do not know but I'm doing my best to learn. I have added study about Chicago gangs to my daily chores. When I speak with these people, they will expect me to have lived a gang-banger life. I had best know something about it."

She carried her tea back to her bedroom. "It isn't your past that is fascinating. It's you." Placing the cup on the bedside table, she crawled beneath the covers once again.

"Tonight Akira is having a reception for the commanders and the Council members. It will be a very important meeting. Perhaps the one event that will turn the single vote to extinguish me into a vote to let me continue. When the severity of the problem with Spain is so obvious that even Queen Akria is taking part in the planning, how can anyone hold out to destroy their only hope." He laughed. "I know she will make it perfectly clear what her desire is for my future. It will be difficult for anyone to turn away from that under the circumstances. Please, have no worries. All will be well."

"I am sure you're right." She finished her cup of tea.

"Now, my dear, I must say good night. I must prepare for the reception. My wish is that you could be here beside me, but for now, I am just thankful there is such a thing as a telephone."

"As am I. Goodnight, Aris. Shall we talk tomorrow?"

"Of course. Sweet dreams." She heard the sound of the receiver being hung up before she ended the call. She always felt empty when he left her presence, whether it was in person or just his voice on the phone.

#

Sarah had a sense that a new erotic vision might surface in her dreams that night as she settled into her bed. Drifting from wakefulness to slumber, she cuddled beneath the covers feeling safe and warm. She welcomed her nocturnal adventures. They fulfilled a sensual need that her waking self denied. The feather bed beneath her seemed to caress the curves of her body, the pillows to create a sensual cradle for her head. As she drifted deeper into the sea of slumber, she felt the dream weight of a heavy body climbing beneath the covers behind her. She knew the feel of Aris and relished his hard muscles as they wrapped around her, drawing her into him, holding her safe. The back of her body melded into the front of his. She was unable to tell where he ended and she began.

One arm wrapped under her, his hand coming to rest on the mound of her warm, tender breast. His fingers caressed her erect nipple. His other arm draped over her, his free hand seeking the garden of soft sweet blond hair protecting the sacred opening to her soul. He relished in the softness of her inner thigh, pressing gently then releasing the warm, tender lips of her secret woman's place. She swelled and moistened to welcome his seeking touch. He lovingly caressed the warm, wet velvet between her legs, his long fingers sliding in and out of the veiled tunnel to her heart.

As he caressed her, she pressed her round smooth bottom into his hard member and he groaned. Reaching for his hand, she slid his fingers from inside her. Turning slowly toward him, feeling every cell of his skin against hers, she wrapped her legs around his back drawing him toward her. His eyes were closed, his head thrown back and his perfect mouth tight as he fought his need.

"No, Sarah. No, my love." Her lips sought his to silence his denial. They disappeared into the kiss, their lips caressing, their tongues tasting. The fragrance of their desire was honey and musk as it wrapped around them. In her dream, he was unable to deny her any longer. He reached his loving hands to lift her to him. She opened her legs as a blossom opens in the sun. He was her solar disk, the center of her existence. Slowly, lovingly, he entered her. Her eyes closed to heighten her physical experience. Her back arched as she strove to devour him, to feast on the powerful maleness of him.

Strong fingers gripped her shoulders as he buried himself again and again in the hot, welcoming darkness inside her body. She groaned with pleasure as her dream Aris made wonderful love to her. Stronger and stronger were his thrusts until they no longer gave her pleasure. She cried out for him to stop, but he was lost in passion. His hands on her shoulders bruised her flesh. His weight on top of her crushed the air from her lungs. Still he consumed her.

She couldn't draw her breath from the great weight of him and just as the room began to spin, he threw his head back and roared as he found his release. He collapsed on top of her panting into her throat. When he raised his head to look at her, it was not Aris that had taken her so forcefully in her dream. It was the face of the gypsy, Diego, staring back at her. She began to cry softly as he rose and left her to her solitary bed.

When she woke in the morning, her pillow was still wet with her tears. She watched the dust mites in the sunlight streaming in through her window and longed for her Immortal.

CHAPTER 52

The sound of chamber music filled the audience hall. Lighting was soft as was the conversation light. Akira was in attendance, however, her mate, Khansu, was not. He was withdrawing more and more from the governing of the Catacombs coven and spending a great deal of his time in seclusion.

The Council and the commanders were in attendance as were several of the higher courtiers. Aris was speaking with Bartholomew about Spain when he noticed a young woman enter the chamber. What drew his attention wasn't her lovely face and figure, but the rather enormous white wolf that walked by her side.

"Bartholomew, who is the woman with the wolf? I have never seen a pet below ground."

"Ah yes, Jane Howard. Her's is an unusual story."

"Please tell." Aris stepped closer, not wanting to miss a word.

"She was brought into the Catacombs by the wolf you see at her side. She was mortally injured and half dead with fear. We never found how Hawke was able to bring her to us, how he knew of the Catacombs, and how he was able to enter."

"Hawke?" Aris asked, mesmerized by the story being told by the Head Council.

"Hawke is the name she calls the wolf."

They both turned to watch as the female bowed before Akira then walked away to sit quietly in the dark shadows beneath an archway. The wolf stood vigilantly at her side.

"She is from the time of Elizabeth I. She had been a maid-in-waiting to her Queen. As you can see, she is very fair and attracted the attention of Essex, the Queen's young lover."

Watching her, Aris could see Jane Howard had the same coloring as Sarah, blond hair and light eyes. She was smaller than his love, but just as comely.

Bartholomew continued, "Essex was a rogue among the ladies of the court, yet the Queen was so totally besotted with him she turned her eyes away, seeing nothing. Jane remembers little of what happened to her just before she was brought to the Catacombs, but she does remember Essex was involved. She remembers him finding her away from the rest of the riders of the royal hunt. She remembers him approaching her. There, her memories end.

"She was torn and bleeding when brought to us and there was no time for deliberation. We would either change her or let her die. The Council voted immediately to save her and she was changed.

"She is kind and gentle and well loved by all, but she keeps to herself, rarely appearing in court. Her only companion, the wolf."

Aris continued to stare at Jane Howard. "What an unusual story. Is she grateful for her immortality?"

"She says she is grateful, but there is a deep sorrow within her that keeps her separate from the rest of us. One can see it in her eyes. She seems to find solace only in the company of the white animal."

"An unusual story to be sure."

Their attention was called as a fanfare played. Akira stood to speak. As all those in the room rose, Aris looked over his shoulder. The young woman and the white wolf were nowhere to be seen.

CHAPTER 53

The deli was relatively empty for a Tuesday morning. Sarah, Gabriela and Colleen sat at Sarah's usual booth eating a quick bon voyage breakfast.

"Well, it looks like you are going to London after all." Colleen spoke to Gabriela through a mouth-full of pancakes and syrup.

"Yes, I am. It will only be for a short while, but I will be able to see some of my friends, whom I haven't seen for some time."

Sarah knew her vampire friend was thinking of her mate. While Gaby seldom mentioned it, Sarah was aware she missed him very much. "It won't be long now." She sipped her last drop of coffee then placed her credit card on the table, signaling the waitress they were ready to leave.

\#

Colleen dropped the roommates off at the airport. She smiled as they turned to wave, one tall and dark, her exotic beauty mesmerizing, and the other small and blond, beaming like a light-bulb. They waved back as they disappeared into the building.

"I'm really glad you're going with me. I know you've missed Richard." Sarah reached into her purse to withdraw her passport.

"Time is different for us but yes, I do miss him. I look forward to being with him again."

The two friends went through security quickly, making their way toward the first class lounge. They settled in to people watch, chatting amiably as they waited to board.

Sarah lowered her voice when she spoke. "I heard part of your conversation with Richard this morning. I've waited until we had some time to talk to ask you about it. It sounded like he had more information about the Spanish coven."

"Yes, he and Sebastian have been gathering all that they can about the way they live and what they do to prepare for the confrontation with us. Our spies have recently had much better luck infiltrating their higher ranks. We now know a great deal more about Mariska and De Flores."

Sarah settled into a comfortable armchair as they leaned closer to one another. Gabriela spoke softly. "As we already knew, De Flores showed up in Spain sometime in the sixteenth century. We have not been able to find the exact time however, it appears it was during the time of Henry VIII or Elizabeth I. He was searching for something or someone. Again, it has been kept a well-hidden secret what the treasure might have been. He was attacked by the same coven that changed Richard and me and lived in obscurity within their ranks for centuries. The Master Keeper of Records has very little information about the Spanish coven, so we know nothing of him before he became king. It is just recently that he has found notoriety among them. Mariska also came to Spain in that same timeframe. She, too, was searching. There is a legend of a wild woman living in the forest who was written about by some of the monks who lived there. We feel it might have been her. She was changed by the same evil vampires that attacked De Flores. It seems that even though they were brought to the coven within a short time of one another, they went for centuries without any acknowledgement of each other. It is just recently that De

Flores has shown interest in her. The two of them together are formidable. They were recluses, unaccustomed to interacting with even those of their own kind. In their chosen isolation, they built a mystique around themselves. Our Council feels it is because of their seclusion, their great beauty and their powerful intellect that it has been quite easy for them to step to the front of the coven and declare themselves rulers."

"Does Sebastian have any idea why, after all this time, they suddenly have decided to attack the Catacombs?"

"It appears that it is De Flores who has made the decision. He gives no reason to his coven. They simply follow him without thought or question. We have not been able to ascertain his purpose other than to take over our kingdom. The feeding ground of London is much more verdant than that of the Spanish countryside. It seems to be the purpose, yet we are not sure. Remember, De Flores is aware of the Infinity Diaries. Within his hand, they become a weapon of mass destruction."

"Gabriela, I know the Diaries contain the evolution of every soul that has ever been. I don't understand that at all. How can past, present and future be written before it happens?"

"Sarah, this is something only the Master Keeper of Records is able to discern. Only those who work on the Diaries are exposed to any of their secrets and only in small bits. No one except the Master knows all."

"Does the work relate only to mortal lore?"

"No, Sarah, it is all souls in all dimensions."

"I don't understand what that means." Sarah shook her head as if to clear her mind. "It's just more than my brain can absorb."

"It is more than any human can ever comprehend, even more than the superior mind of the Immortal is able to perceive. Only the Master is able to penetrate the secrets. We of the Catacombs live outside of your time and space. We see through dimensional space. We access the infinite with our Immortal minds, yet only the Master is able to fully interpret the Diaries."

"This Master must be a pretty important guy."

"Yes. And he is Master for all eternity."

"How was he chosen? How did the Diaries begin?"

"A long story best left for a future time."

It was obvious Gaby wasn't going to discuss the inception of the Diaries so Sarah moved on with her questions. "I remember Richard said the writings weren't finished."

"That is true. As long as there is human time, the Diaries will continue to grow."

Sarah was about to ask another question when a female voice over the loud speaker announced their boarding sequence.

"Come Sarah, let us take our seats. You will find the more you learn about eternity, the more you realize the world you humans inhabit is but a shadow of true reality." She stood placing her hand under her friend's elbow and guiding her toward the red carpet of the first class travelers. After all, when you have the secrets of the ages within you, why fly economy?

CHAPTER 54

Sarah stared out the window of her hotel on Threadneedle Street. The evening sky was dark and foreboding as she looked down on the rain spattered pavement below her third story suite. Huge water drops hit the glass and ran in streams down the smooth surface. The topsides of several umbrellas open against the rain resembled a caterpillar inching along under the soft light of the yellow street lamps.

When Gabriela mentioned Richard had booked a reservation at an historical hotel in London, Sarah never imagined anything as opulent as the rooms she occupied.

The enormous sitting room was decorated in soft shades of sage green and white. Carved crown molding a foot thick encircled the twelve foot ceiling. Tall windows lined one wall. Sage green velvet drapes pooled in soft ripples of cloth on the thick oriental carpet. White velvet wing-backed chairs sat facing the fireplace and the fragrance from a huge bouquet of lilies sitting on the table between them filled the room.

"I'm so sorry it's raining on your first evening in London," Gabriela spoke as she entered the door. She noticed the dark circles under Sarah's eyes. Silently, she wondered, "*Is it jet lag or is she worried about the outcome of Aris' trial?"*

"Why don't you rest for a while?" The Immortal turned Sarah to face her sleeping quarters and guided her through the open door. Exhaustion enveloped Sarah as soon as she stepped across the threshold and saw the queen-sized bed drowning in a sea of white down. Stripping off her wrinkled traveling clothes, Sarah slid her tired body beneath the cool soft sheets. She was asleep before her head hit the pillow.

Gaby closed the door without making a sound, then returned to the window, standing silently watching the movement of the traffic in the street below.

#

Rain was still falling through the dim dawning light as Sarah's eyes fluttered open. She felt disoriented as she gazed at the unfamiliar surroundings. Her thoughts, rising from her jet-lagged brain, seemed to surface at half speed. Slowly she recalled the flight into Heathrow, the taxi ride to their hotel. She remembered gazing from her sitting room window at the wet streets and black umbrellas shiny with rain-drops, the sweet scent of the sheets and the feeling of the soft bedclothes against her bare skin as she fell asleep. She yawned, stretching her arms over head.

"How long did I sleep?" she wondered. Sliding from beneath the covers, she dressed in the fleecy white robe draped across the foot of her bed. When she opened the bedroom door, she was surprised to see Gabriela still in her traveling clothes standing in front of the window, still gazing at the street below.

Since the day the Immortal moved in with the human, she fully lived her human side, fitting flawlessly into her surroundings. She ate meals and slept nights. Her habits were so human even Sarah forgot she was a vampire. Yet there she stood unmoving, undead, still as a mannequin and just as beautiful.

At the sound of Sarah's breath, Gabriela turned. Her carved

features animated in delight at seeing her friend awake and looking more refreshed. "Did you sleep well?" Gabriela sat in one of the chairs facing the fireplace. Reaching toward the breakfast tray sitting on the table, she poured a cup of steaming, rich coffee. The inviting aroma floated across the room.

Sarah wrapped her robe around her as she settled in across from her friend. "It's still raining."

"Yes and it may keep up for the next few days." Gaby crossed her long legs and relaxed into the pillowy padding of the white chair.

After dropping two lumps of sugar into her coffee, Sarah stirred it slowly with one of the ornately carved small spoons lined up on the breakfast tray. "I like the rain." She turned her head to glance at the dark clouds out the window. "We have lots of days like this in Chicago."

"I, too, enjoy rainy weather." Gaby smiled as she shared her news. "While you were sleeping, Richard telephoned."

"Yes?" Sarah leaned forward, placing her cup and saucer back on the table.

"He didn't tell Aris we were here so it will still be a surprise."

"How soon will we be able to see them?" Excitement at being with Aris again was obvious in Sarah's tone.

"Soon. Aris is unable to leave the Catacombs without the consent of the Council while they are still in deliberation so they wait. Richard will telephone as soon as they receive the authorization."

"Does he think it will be a problem?"

"No, it seems the Council is beginning to understand just how important Aris is for their safety should there actually be a confrontation with the Spanish coven. Still, it is the law that until he is exonerated he will be under their jurisdiction and must have their approval to visit the streets of London other than for his human work."

She refreshed Sarah's coffee. "Why don't you take your time with your coffee. I must shower and change from these rumpled clothes. Would you like to go sight-seeing today rather than just sitting here waiting for a telephone call?"

"That sounds great." Still feeling jet lagged, Sarah drank the last sip of liquid in the cup then returned it to the table. After a huge yawn she stood and stretched. "I might as well shower and dress too. It will make me feel like a new woman."

"What would you like to see?"

"Since this is your turf, why don't you choose?"

Gabriela thought only a moment before responding. "How about Tower Hill? There is so much history surrounding that one spot, I think it would a perfect place to begin."

"Sounds wonderful." She spoke over her shoulder as she disappeared into her bedroom. "I'm really looking forward to the day."

#

The damp grass was blue green against the wet stones of the buildings. Rain had stopped falling, but still threatening dark clouds covered the sky. In the distance the tall twin spires of Tower Bridge were outlined against the gloom. Sarah was surprised by the number of people milling around Tower Green, umbrellas in hand. Gabriela held her elbow, guiding her easily through the crowd.

As they wandered around the Green, history surrounded their every step. Sarah was captured by it as she listened to the costumed guides explaining historic legends to the tourists. It amazed her that the Ceremony of the Keys had been carried on every day without fail since the 14th century at precisely 9:53pm. Only once since it began was it even late. During World War II, just as the Yeoman and his escort passed through the Bloody Tower Archway, a number of incendiary bombs fell on the guardroom. The shock and noise blew the men off their feet, but they stood up, brushed themselves off and carried on. Tradition seemed the lifeblood of

England. She relished the thought that the same words have been spoken by generation after generation of Chief Yeomen Warders dressed for centuries in identical Tudor Watchcoats.

If human traditions are so strongly rooted, how much more impervious to change must be the traditions of the Immortals? Sarah was worried. How would the Council ever allow Aris to step beyond their law to go free?

#

Aris began to run toward her the moment he saw Sarah standing on Tower Green. He was laughing out loud when he reached her, wrapping his arms around her and swinging her in a gentle circle. "You came. You came to London." His words were muffled by her warm lips as she reached to kiss him. The scent of him heated her body as the cool rain began to sprinkle on their heads. Their hair was soaked before the kiss ended.

"Of course I came. Did you think I'd miss your art show?"

"I feel complete again." He whispered against her damp temple. "Thank you."

"Enough." Richard smiled as he wrapped his arm around his mate. "Let's step out of the rain before we are drenched. We will continue our reunion where it is warm and dry." He guided them across the green and into the White Tower.

#

They sat in the front room of Aris' London flat to dry off and warm up by the fireplace. Richard poked the fire to raise the flames while Gaby and Sarah sat on the sofa, their stockinged feet resting on the coffee table. Aris entered the room carrying a bottle of wine and four glasses.

"This calls for a toast. We all will join in welcoming Sarah to London." He placed the bottle and glasses on the table, then kissed her on the top of the head before he poured the wine. It was a deep, red Bordeaux, which sparkled in the light of the dancing flames.

"To Sarah." They all raised their glasses in salute.

She laughed as she sipped her wine. She knew the Immortals drank only to be polite, but she appreciated their little tribute to her.

"I just wish I could come below into the Catacombs," she said.

"I know. I am so sorry, but you know it is not possible." Aris sat next to her, taking her hand in his. He could hardly believe she was actually sitting next to him in his flat of rooms. "But there are many other things to see while you are here. When I am not training for battle, I will be with you."

Her eyes clouded at his words. "How is the training going? You haven't mentioned it today."

Richard spoke up. "We wanted this to be a day of joy for you, a day of reunion. Not a day to discuss war."

"I know and I appreciate that, but I'm concerned."

"All goes well, Sarah." Aris took the wine glass from Sarah, set it on the table and grasped both her hands firmly in his. "The commanders are doing splendidly and the troops are responding more rapidly than we had hoped. We will be ready to travel to Spain very soon."

"How in the world will twenty-five-hundred Immortals travel to Spain without anyone noticing?"

"We will travel in separate small groups, some driving, some flying. We will meet in the forest near the Spanish coven and march on their fortress."

"Fortress?"

"The royal court holds up in a medieval castle and the rest of the coven in the forest that surrounds it. The spies report they have no idea we are coming to their kingdom for the fight."

"Yes." Richard spoke. "We will have the element of surprise on our side."

"What about the weapons? Aris, you said your arsenal of weapons had not been completed."

"The Nalyd weapons have been forged. They are waiting for Akira to use alchemy for the finish. It will be only a few days before they are ready. We hope to have the training and the weapons accomplished at the same time, then we travel."

He placed her hands in her lap and reached for her wine glass. "Here, a toast to tomorrow and Stonehenge."

She took the glass and sipped the wine. She thought, "*Stonehenge. I wonder if those Druids weren't really Immortals in long black robes.*" She chuckled at the thought of her three friends cavorting around the monoliths in the full moon.

#

They circled the chiseled boulders, holding hands and talking softly. "I really thought they would be much larger." Sarah said looking at the top of one of the tallest.

"Are you disappointed?" Aris asked, truly concerned.

"No, how could I be disappointed. I am here with you. It's just I somehow had the impression they were skyscraper size. I don't know why."

"Many people feel that way, however, it isn't the size of the stones. It's the magic." He turned her toward him. "Can you not feel the mystical power of this place?"

"A little. Do the Catacombs have mystical power?"

"You have such interest in the life below ground. You know, Sarah, there is only one way you may ever see our way of life."

She looked at her feet as they continued along the walkway. "I know. I'm just interested."

"Sarah, you know I would perform the ritual with you, take you for my eternal mate."

She was silent as they continued their walk.

"Would you do such a thing for love, Sarah?"

She turned from him without answering, took his hand again and continued to walk the path surrounding the stones.

CHAPTER 55

The gallery looked much the same as John Marshal's in Chicago. Lovely carpets and heavy, comfortable furniture was scattered in seating arrangements around the large rooms. A buffet table was laden with cocktails and finger foods. Well-dressed patrons roamed from painting to painting making comments and taking notes.

Sarah watched as Aris stood, surrounded by attractive women full of questions. He smiled as he answered each one. Occasionally he would glance at Sarah, wink and smile, then go back to being gracious.

"He really is made to be in the public eye." John Marshal stood next to her, a huge smile covering his face. "He's won over every journalist in the room, male and female. See that tall red-headed woman with her hand on his arm vying for his attention?"

It was hard to miss a woman over six-feet tall in stilettos who was fawning over the man she loved. Sarah relished the fact she felt no jealousy. She knew Aris was hers and hers alone for as long as she lived. *"How long will that be?"* she thought.

"Sarah, are you alright?" John gently touched her shoulder.

"Yes. I was just thinking about Carlos' success."

"That's what I'm trying to tell you. That tall woman is the most prominent artist's agent in London. While she was oohing and aahing over Reginald's choice of Carlos as his showcase artist, she mentioned she was going to ask him if he had representation. Sarah, if she takes him on, he's in the royal house--no doubt of it. With his talent, looks and personality, he could win over the devil."

"I don't know about the devil, but he sure has won over that agent." She smiled as Aris looked at her, rolling his eyes and laughing at all the attention he was getting.

CHAPTER 56

The four friends were sitting in front of Aris' fireplace. His flat had become their favorite place to meet just as Sarah's apartment had been in America. The autumn winds were blowing and whistling around the corner of the building making the room feel even more cozy.

Their meeting was yet another celebration. Just that afternoon Aris had been called into the audience chamber to meet with Akira and the Council. He had been forgiven. He was once again a functioning member of the Catacombs free to come and go, to live above ground or below.

Sarah had waited in his flat for him to return with the decision. She asked him not to call her but to come to her. Whether the news was good or bad, she wanted to hear the verdict from him in person.

She paced the floor most of the morning, sitting occasionally on the sofa and doing her best to read a magazine. She sat for only a moment at a time before she was on her feet again, wearing a trail through the thick carpet.

She felt him outside the door before she heard his key. Rushing to meet him, she opened the door before he did. A huge smile on his face answered her unspoken question. He picked her up off the ground in a joyous hug and a passionate kiss.

"I am free." They both laughed out loud. "I am forgiven and a full member of the coven." He kissed her again as he spun her in a circle.

She was overwhelmed with joy knowing he was safe. Glancing around the room at her friends, she was so grateful to have become a part of a living fantasy. "I'm so glad I came here, that I can be a part of such a wonderful week. First the art show; now this is the frosting on the cake. Exonerated. I'm so relieved." She sat on the arm of his chair with her arm draped over the tall wing-back. They had laughed and congratulated Aris and toasted one another for over an hour and were now ready to relax and simply enjoy spending the evening together.

"I must admit, I, too, am relieved. I was sure they would understand their need for me, still it is much more pleasant to have it all behind me." He smiled. "Let's celebrate tonight. We can engage our stomachs for a change and take Sarah out to dinner."

"Splendid idea." Richard helped Gabriela into her coat as Aris made sure the fire was out. They spilled out the door hurrying down the street, pushed along by the strong, determined wind.

#

Gentle rumblings of thunder could be heard in the distance and diminishing dark clouds barely blocked the light of the moon and stars. Gabriela sat, curling cat-like, in one of the chairs by the fire reading Shakespeare. Determined to memorize all his works, she treasured quiet time to study. She was hard at work on *Hamlet* as the clock ticked past midnight.

Behind the closed bedroom door, Sarah slept soundly in her fluffy white bed, lulled to sleep by the sound of the retreating storm. Silently, one of the French windows swung open. A shadow crept soundlessly over the windowsill and to her bedside. A strong sweet smell filled the room as the figure opened a small glass phial and held it beneath the sleeping woman's nose. Her breath grew shallow, her body limp. The shadow lifted her as if she were weightless. The dark apparition carried her out the window and down the wall, disappearing into the dark garden below.

#.

Sarah regained consciousness on the hard leather seat of a jeep as it bounced through ruts and ridges carved in what had once been a usable road. Her shoulders ached from her arms being secured behind her back and the cold metal of the handcuffs cut into her wrists. Light was barely visible through the black silk scarf tied around her eyes. Techno music reverberated through the cab.

"This is just a dream." She told herself over and over. "A bad dream. I shouldn't have had those anchovies." After only a moment she had to face the hard realization she wasn't dreaming. She had no idea where she was or who had kidnapped her. Or why. Her heart raced in her chest as she strained against her bonds.

"Stop that." A low female voice snarled as a gloved hand cracked across her cheek. "If you cut yourself you'll bleed and I assure you, you don't want to bleed now." Her Latin accent was thick.

Drugs clouded her mind and silent sobs of terror shook Sarah's body. She managed to stutter single syllable words in between gasps for air, "Who are you? Where am I?"

"Shut up you stupid human." Another stinging slap. Fear ran ice cold in Sarah's veins and she curled into a tight ball on the seat. A familiar sweet smell permeated the air and before she could exhale, she was once again unconscious.

#

Gabriela paced frantically in front of the fireplace in the hotel suite. "How could I have let this happen?" If Immortals could cry, she would have wept. Richard reached for her hand, drawing her to sit on the sofa between he and Aris.

"You thought she was safe. Gabriela, we all thought she was safe. You did nothing wrong." His hand caressed her shoulder as he wrapped his arm around her. "What we need to do now is find her. Quickly."

Standing, Aris resumed Gabriela's pacing. "We know it was someone from the Spanish coven." He turned to look at Richard as he spoke to him. "Was Sebastian sure De Flores is still in Spain?"

"Yes, and will you please sit down. Between the two of you, you will wear a hole in the carpet." Aris dropped onto the sofa, leaned forward and placed his elbows on his knees to rest his head in his hands.

"Sorry." Lifting his head, he looked at his friend. "I know it is of no help if I lose my mind, but the hour we must wait for our flight to Spain is longer than all the centuries of my existence." He was silent for a moment before he leaped to his feet once more, moving to stare out the window at the late afternoon light. "Why would they want her? What can she possibly be to them?"

"We can't be sure, my friend. Could it be somehow the king found out about you? That you were a warrior and will train our army?"

"But how? Unless there is a traitor in the Catacombs, a spy for De Flores. And how would kidnapping Sarah change any of that?"

"Perhaps they plan to use her to lure you to Spain? If you were out of the way, their path to London would be clear."

"That does make sense." He crossed the room to sit again. "There does not seem to be any other plausible answer."

A look of fear passed between Gabriela and Richard. Unfortunately, they both could think of another reason, but neither chose to bring it up to Aris.

#

In the vast room the only piece of furniture was a thin sleeping pallet. The cold stone floor and walls smelled musty and damp.

Sarah lay curled under several threadbare blankets to keep warm in what appeared to be a deserted medieval castle. She slept a great deal of the time, kept in a stupor by the drugs her captors put in the meager food allotment she received. She had no idea how long she had been confined. Days? Weeks?

Her sleeping eyes fluttered at the sound of the huge, heavy wooden door to her dungeon scraping against the stone floor as it swung open.

"Wake up. You must eat and clean yourself. Theresa will attend you shortly. Eat." The handsome young man wheeled a cart carrying food in covered dishes. He wore jeans and a black short sleeved tee shirt even though the room was so cold Sarah could see her breath. His dark auburn hair was shoulder length and wild. She vaguely remembered him bringing her food at least once before. She was sure he wouldn't hurt her or he already would have.

She knew she was being held captive in a cold miserable old castle somewhere far out in the country. In what country, she wasn't sure. She tried to sit up but she was too shaky from the drugs to succeed. The young man reached to help her. His hands on her shoulders weren't friendly, but they weren't rough.

"Sit. Eat. You will feel better." His voice was soft, but demanding. "Now."

"Where am I?"

"I told you yesterday, that is something you are not to know." His words were accented the same as the woman's in the car.

"*Spanish? Italian?*" she thought.

"Who are you and why am I here?"

"More questions? Are all humans so full of questions?"

She lifted the lid on one of the dishes. Two fried eggs and a piece of dark bread looked back at her. "If you're not human, what are you?"

He smiled a wicked smile. "You will find out soon enough."

She didn't need to wait. She already knew the answer. A vampire.

#

Gabriela read the map and gave Aris directions as he maneuvered the red rental car they had picked up at the Spanish airport through the deep ruts in the loose dirt and gravel. Richard leaned over the back of his mate's seat to talk to his friend.

"Sebastian said to leave the car at the edge of the forest and go forward on foot. There are vampires that live in the forest and it will be easier to remain unseen if we travel without a vehicle. It should take less than an hour to reach the castle compound."

"I do not like this, Richard. If they can sense us coming, they may kill her."

"No Aris, they want her alive. She is their weapon against us. I am sure of that."

"But what if you are wrong. What if they have her for some other reason. They must not harm her." His foot pushed the accelerator closer to the floor and the car leapt forward, bouncing hard over a deep furrow.

#.

Sarah didn't like the way Theresa looked at her as the young vampire peeled away her dirty clothes. She held them at arm's length as she walked to the fire and tossed them in. "These cannot be saved." Theresa resembled the young man who had brought her food. The same age, same coloring. *"Could they be brother and sister?"* she wondered.

There was no bathroom in the deserted keep so a huge copper tub was brought into the room and filled with steaming water. *"Why are they treating me so well,"* she wondered. *"Is Theresa the prep cook?"* She shuddered as she stepped into the warm, welcoming bath. Sinking to her neck, she closed her eyes, pretending she was at home in her own tub.

Her imagination was hard at work when Theresa spoke again. "Hurry up. You have a special audience today."

"What?" Her eyes flew open. "Who is coming?" She hoped it would not be the woman who had slapped her during the torturous ride to the castle. She hoped it would be someone who would give her some information about where she was. "What do they want of me?"

Theresa smiled a wicked smile. "You will just have to wait to find out, won't you?"

#

The woman who walked through the door was tall and lean. Her pitch black hair was clipped short and slicked off her face. She wore dark red lipstick; her vicious smile showed large straight white teeth. Her tailored black suit was made of the finest wool and her black stilettos clicked on the stone floor as she entered the chamber. She was as beautiful as the wicked queen in Snow White. Sarah was afraid, but she willed herself to be strong. She failed miserably. Her legs trembled where she stood.

"So human, are you frightened?" An evil smile lit her eyes.

Sarah tried to speak but her tongue wouldn't cooperate. Her mind was clear. They hadn't drugged her all day preparing her for her meeting. Words came into her mind, but they wouldn't come out her mouth.

"I see, you are. You should be. I have plans for your future. You will regret what you did to me." As she leaned close to Sarah, the stench of her breath made her prisoner's stomach turn. "You will beg me to end it, but your agony will go on and on. And now human, I will leave you to ponder your prospects. And do not worry. You will not be lonely for long. I will return very, very soon to spend some quality time with you." A sinister chuckle sounded deep in her throat as she crossed the room to leave. The huge door banged shut as Sarah moved to the window.

She was imprisoned in a high, narrow tower. A pile of sharp stones had fallen from the crumbling foundation creating a dangerous barrier between her and ground. The castle was nestled into a high mountain range and covered the entire top of a flattened hill. The hill was surrounded by a thick forest. She couldn't see very far in the distance because of a dense fog creeping through the trees and up the hillside. She tugged at the bars separating her from her freedom. "I've got to find a way to get out of here." She didn't even realize she was speaking out loud as she repeated the phrase over and over again.

CHAPTER 57

"So, you have been introduced to our Queen?"

It was early in the evening when the serving boy entered. Sarah was on her pallet beneath the blankets to get warm. She had spent the rest of the day after her audience examining the room. There were no cracks or crevices in any of the stones that she could see. She tried to pull up one that seemed a bit loose but she failed. It wouldn't budge. She tried digging around the bars on the windows with her fingers but those stones, too, were immovable.

"I spoke to you, woman. Are you made mute with fear?" The serving boy brought her last meal of the day. Cold meat and one potato. "Why are you always balled up on your bed? Do you find solace there?"

"There's no solace anywhere in this miserable place. I'm just cold." She sat up. "Why does she hate me? What can I have done? I've never seen her before." She wrapped one of the ragged blankets around her shoulders. "Why am I here? And, for God's sake, why does she want to torture me?"

"Come, eat. You will need all of your strength for tomorrow."

"Tomorrow?" Her voice was thin, hollow. "Oh, yes. Tomorrow." As she reached for the plate of food, she thought, "*that means somehow I have to get out of here tonight."*

#

They covered their car with brush and left it. Richard pointed the way as the three friends took off at a steady run deeper into the forest. Their feet flew over broken branches and leaves as if they were nonexistent. They ran in silence, each lost in their own thoughts. To Aris it seemed as if they ran in slow motion.

#

The sky was still pitch black when the door to her chamber slammed open crashing into the stone wall. The noise was loud enough to be an explosion. Sarah sat bolt upright instantly awake. She laid down for only a moment after she ate and must have fallen asleep.Her mind was groggy.

"Out of bed. Now." The loud voice of the lead guard seemed to bounce off the unyielding walls. "I said now."

She struggled to rise. Her mouth was dry and she realized there must have been drugs in her food again. The room was dark except for the light from the bright kerosene lanterns that two of the vampires carried. She stumbled as she crossed to the door. Hard, cold hands gripped her arm to keep her from falling. She wanted to cry out, but she was struck dumb with fear. The frost from her breath was visible as they made their way down the long corridor of the castle.

After what seemed an endless time spent winding through the maze of hallways they stopped before a huge ancient wooden door. Her captor leaned hard against it and it opened slowly into a cavernous dark chamber. Candle sconces provided the only light. She could see the back of a tall male figure standing in front of a tall window on the other side of the enormous room.

"On your knees." The guard shoved her and she fell, bruising her bones on the stones of the floor. "Lower your head, human. You are before the King." He pushed her down until her forehead touched the floor. As she cowered on the cold stone the only sound was the footsteps of the guards as they left the room. Then all was silent. She fought for breath.

His words were spoken softly as the King moved to her side. "Lift your gaze to look at me."

She was unmoving.

"I said look at me," he demanded.

Slowly she raised her eyes to meet his. Jumping to her feet in disbelief she stiffened, unable to move. She spoke one word and one word only. "DeMarco!"

THE END

Aris Reigns

The Kingdom Of Vampires

AN INFINITY DIARIES SERIES: Book 3

PROLOGUE

His back was stiff and his stride furious as he paced in front of Sarah. "DeMarco. Yes." He turned to face her, his eyes daring her to look away. "DeMarco. And De Flores." Menacingly, he stepped closer. His breath was hot, his skin white, all of the golden tones, gone. His wavy black hair hung in tangles down the back of his neck and over his forehead into his eyes. The boots on his feet were soft black leather and his jeans were tight and well worn. In the dim light of the lanterns, she could see he wore a dark knitted sweater under his black leather jacket. "And, yet another man. One you seem to have forgotten altogether." He spoke softly in a threatening whisper. "Diego."

"Diego?"

"Yes. Diego." Raising his voice until it bounced and echoed against the stone walls. "The gypsy you pledged your undying love. The gypsy whose heart you entranced, whose body and soul you possessed."

Sarah realized she wasn't breathing just before he lunged at her. She gasped for air as he grabbed her by the shoulders; he shoved her toward the window with such force she feared he might throw her through the glass onto the stones below. Gratefully she realized he was pushing her toward a tall wing-back chair hidden in the shadows in the corner of the enormous room. Unceremoniously he threw her onto the chair as he shouted. "Sit." He restrained himself from striking her and, again, began to pace. When he spoke, his voice was low. Dangerous. "Do not move."

She couldn't move if she wanted to. The shock of being brought before the evil vampire king in his throne room in the heart of a medieval castle only to find that the bloodsucker holding her prisoner was none other than her Italian ex-boyfriend from Chicago was more than her motor centers could handle. She was frozen to the spot. Unable to face him, she stared at her shoes. Her addled brain wondered how her captors knew what size she wore. When she was kidnapped by the vampire Queen, she was in bed in London, barefooted.

DeMarco raved on. "When your father snatched you from Diego, from me, I went mad. I roamed the woods like an animal mourning your loss. When, at last, I returned to the gypsy camp my grandmother told of a vision she had of you in the court of Henry VIII. I set out to follow you to London and there I found you at court. Do you remember?" He stopped in front of her, stooping down, resting his hands on the tufted arms of the chair where she sat. She felt like a trapped animal. A trapped wolf will chew off its own leg to get free. She vowed she would do whatever it took to get her out of this God-forsaken place. She remained silent in fear that any word from her might drive him over the edge.

"Yes, I found you at court in London. I came to you. You shunned me. You turned me away. You told me you loved another." There was madness in his eyes as he gripped her face in between his huge hands, forcing her to look at him. "But I loved you still." His eyes softened. He pulled her to her feet. Repelled by his sudden urge to hold her, he tossed her down onto the chair once again.

He slowly circled her as he spoke. "I watched the palace. I

followed you to the ship on the day you set sail for Spain. I stowed away, but before the ship cast off, a sailor found me. He gave me over to the captain. Beaten and whipped, I nearly died from the great loss of blood and the infection that set into my wounds." He tore the jacket from his shoulders, pulled the sweater over his head and threw both of them on the floor. His muscles strained with anger. His body looked powerful, invincible. "See this?" He spun on his heel, exposing his nude back to her.

Even in the soft light from the lanterns she could see the long silver scars running from shoulder to shoulder, crisscrossing his spine to his waist and below.

Turning to face her, he picked up his jacket and put it on, his pale chest a striking contrast to the black leather. "I took a thrashing for you because you said you loved me. The wounds on my back healed, but the wound in my heart stayed open and bleeding. I vowed I would find you, win you back. I was obsessed to have you for my own.

"When I healed sufficiently to work, I signed on to a ship's crew bound for Spain. They drove us like dogs and I grew strong once more in spite of my ordeal. It was only after we landed that I found you were dead, killed by a storm at sea. Again, I mourned my loss of you.

"Desiring solace, I traveled the countryside unaccompanied and on foot, learning the lay of the land. It was then I found this very castle occupied, in those days, by minor royalty. I secured work inside its walls as an apprentice to the lord's blacksmith. I lived a quiet life, alone and finally at peace, for more than two decades. Then in my forty-second year, the blacksmith died without a wife or child; he willed me his small house and his work shed. I took pride in my work and made a decent living." He stared out the window, possessed for a moment by human memories. His face softened and Sarah could finally see DeMarco, the man she had cared for, in this vampire King standing before her.

His countenance changed; his spine stiffened. His voice grew gruff as he continued. "One evening as I walked in the forest, I was set upon by two of the fabled undead. I had heard of vampires before but I did not know they truly existed. The two males dragged me to their encampment and there, took my human life." DeMarco paused, staring into a far distant past. After a moment, he continued his story, his voice now a soft whisper. "For three days I suffered the fires of hell. When the pain stopped, I knew that I was the same as they."

Again, he stooped down before her, his eyes level with her own, pain clearly visible in his gaze. "I knew there was no turning back, no way out, so I quietly accepted what I had become." Tearing his eyes from hers, he stood and began anew to pace. "I lived within the coven, yet apart from it. I learned all I could about vampire lore. As the years passed, I heard tales of the Catacombs. The legends said the Catacombs was a place of great learning; their libraries contained books with the secrets of life and death. Never forgetting for a moment my only true love, my Elizabeth, I realized if I could get my hands on those books, I might be able to find her. My deep love for her was my last vestige of humanity, all that was left of my human life and I clung to it like a drowning man.

"I plotted my journey to the vampire underground kingdom in London, concocting a plausible story as to why they should admit me to their society. I heard of others who left Spain for London who had been welcomed and lived there still.

"I set sail to England, working my way across the sea on a merchant ship. It took weeks before I reached my destination, but to a vampire, there is no such thing as time and so I was patient.

"I appealed to the great Council." He sneered when he spoke the word 'great.' "I told them I longed for a peaceful life, a life without being a beast of human prey. They believed me and, after much time and testing, I was accepted. I worked diligently, building a reputation as an honorable Immortal." He laughed and it was an ugly sound as it reverberated off the stone walls. "It took centuries, but, at last, I managed my way into the most elite circle, those who work on the Infinity Diaries, the books of life and death. I was given primary responsibilities that I readily accepted and fulfilled. After decades of pristine work, I gained the trust of the Master Keeper of Records. He gave me what I was looking for, access to the ancient scrolls. The delicate job of updating and copying the ancient scrolls was delegated to me; transferring them into current volumes representing each soul that had ever walked the earth.

"Working with determination, I searched until I found the soul-chart of Elizabeth Wyatt. It was there I learned about Sarah Hagan of Chicago. Research is quick and most accurate on the internet so I found out everything I could about the author from Illinois. I devised a plan to win you once again.

"I arrived in Chicago where I found you and courted you. I hoped you would feel something when you saw me, remember me. But you did not."

His eyes radiated something more terrible than hate. She shivered as he whispered, "I became everything you could ever want. DeMarco Brassi deserved your love, but you gave it to another. You turned from me yet again and for that, Sarah Hagan, you will die."

CHAPTER 1

The sound of the door scraping on the stones as it opened sent a shiver of dread through Sarah's body. The beautiful female vampire still wearing a black business suit, stepped into the room, high heels clicking on the stones as she crossed the floor to stand next to the King. Even in her fear Sarah marveled at the dark beauty of the evil pair.

Mariska stepped closer to their captive as she spoke. "You do not remember me from your past, do you human?"

Her mind cloudy with a thousand disjointed thoughts, Sarah couldn't remember ever seeing the female vampire before. She shook her head 'no.'

Now it was the Queen who paced in front of her. Sarah found herself mesmerized by her movement, breathing in rhythm with her tapping steps.

"Long ago in the gypsy camp you thought you bested me. You used your long, fair hair and pale skin to steal my betrothed." Her black eyes burned a hole through Sarah, a sinister laugh curved Mariska's crimson lips. "Soon I will begin using my dark powers to steal your mortal life. Slowly. Painfully." Her last words were softly whispered and even more frightening because of it.

Sarah's head swam as she did her best to recall some memory of the female vampire who was standing before her. Suddenly, she had a flashback to one of the hypnotic dreams she had had during the time she was doing past-life regressions with her psychotherapist, Bonnie Petrillo. In the dream it was the sixteenth century and a maiden named Elizabeth Wyatt was fighting in the dust with a young gypsy woman. Sarah's mind began to clear. During her hypnotherapy sessions, Sarah discovered Elizabeth Wyatt had been the name of one of her past life incarnations. Somehow this vampire thought Elizabeth Wyatt had stolen her man in that past life. Then Sarah recalled why the two women were fighting. Elizabeth, in fact, had stolen her opponent's man. They were battling over Diego and Elizabeth won. She remembered the curse the bruised and defeated gypsy threw on her as she crept away from the midnight fire.

And now, here she stood, Mariska, Queen of the Spanish Coven. Sarah knew it was going to be a long night.

#

Three manservants entered the chamber carrying two comfortable chairs and a round, carved wooden table. One built a glowing fire while the other two placed the furniture at a comfortable distance from the blaze. They were followed by a lovely young female vampire carrying two jewel encrusted golden goblets on a matching tray. As she placed them on the table, the gems glistened in the firelight.

Turning from Sarah as if they had forgotten she was there, Mariska and DeMarco moved across the room to sit in the chairs. They raised the goblets to toast one another, then drank; neither paused while there was a drop left. Sarah shuddered thinking what must have been in the goblets. Her captors sat quietly for a moment, staring into the fire. Then, as one, they rose to approach her.

The Queen was the first to speak. "You, human, will die a slow and tortuous death." The shadows the firelight cast on Mariska made her face appear to be an eyeless skull. When she spoke, the words came from the mouth of a death's head. "And then the true carnage begins. We march on the Catacombs. We will slaughter their King and Queen. Our army will eliminate every Immortal citizen." She spoke as an afterthought. "Ah, yes, and DeMarco and I will personally take care of those who mean the most to you. One by one we will slowly eliminate your loved ones. I want you to ponder that as you wait for your own death. And I assure you, human, we will take the greatest care with your precious love, Aris." Sarah's heart raced. She knew she had to escape, to find a way to warn the Immortals.

Mariska drew DeMarco to her side. "We will rule in the Catacombs. We will own the Infinity Diaries. We will know the secret workings of the universe. With the power of that knowledge and our fearlessness, we will rule the human world and feed on them openly like the sheep that they are." Mariska stared at Sarah for a moment more, then shouted toward the door. "Guard."

As the soldiers entered the room, DeMarco turned to stare out the window at the star studded sky. Without looking toward Sarah, he lifted his arm to wave her away, condemning her to her chamber to await her death. She heard the muffled tapping of stilettoes on the stone floor as the soldiers took her into the hallway and closed the door behind them.

#

"Escape. Escape. Escape." Her mind ran in circles as they marched her through the vast hallway. *"But how? How? I only know I'm somewhere in the mountains in Spain. If I can get away, where do I go? I've got to get away. How can I get away? And where the hell do I get away to?"* Her mind ran like a hamster on a wheel, continuously moving, going in circles and reaching no conclusions. *"The bars. I've got to get the bars loose. I'll figure out where to go once I get out of*

here. "At least she had the beginning of a plan as the door to her prison loomed in front of her. It crashed against the wall as the soldiers slammed it open, shoving her inside. Stumbling and falling, she hit her head on the cold stone floor. She lay unconscious, a trickle of blood pooling beneath her forehead.

#

Aris, Richard and Gabriela quickly concealed the car they rented at the Barcelona airport with loose brush, then raced through the forest, effortlessly leaping over huge fallen branches and trees. They were determined to reach Sarah before it was too late. At last the three Immortals could see the top of the castle tower in the pale light of a crescent moon. Richard touched Aris on the shoulder signaling him to stop. At the same moment a tall dark figure stepped from behind a tree.

"Simon." Gabriela embraced the spy from the Catacombs. It had been years since she last saw him, his recent life spent in subterfuge in the evil coven. He held her for a brief moment then turned to embrace the males. "Aris. Richard."

Frantic to secure Sarah's safety, Aris ignored the niceties of his ally's greeting. "Is Sarah alright? Where are they keeping her?" It took all of his patience to stand still and wait for a reply. He ached to storm the castle, but knew rash actions would bring him no victory.

"She is being lodged in the only tower left standing." He pointed toward a stone wall atop the stark rocky crest of the hill separating them from her prison.

Aris made to leave but Richard held him fast. "Wait. We are in need of more information."

"I am in need of nothing." He tore out of his friend's grasp. "I am going to find her."

"No, Aris." Simon stepped in front of him. "She's been taken for an audience with the King and Queen. Wait until she returns to her chambers. The castle is close by, we must take care."

"Wait? I wait for nothing." He turned from them, racing in the direction Simon had directed them.

#

Sarah groaned as she opened her eyes. The huge lump on her forehead was throbbing and she was shaky on her feet as she staggered toward the window. She had no idea how long she had lain on the floor, but the sky was still dark. She still had time before morning. Her hand was shaking as she reached to grasp the windowsill. The wind whistled through the bars and echoed throughout the chamber. Sarah's imagination played cruel tricks; she swore the wind called her name. Leaning her aching forehead against the cold metal separating her from her freedom, she heard it more clearly.

"Sarah. Sarah."

Suddenly, long powerful fingers wrapped around the bars and quietly lifted them from their foundation, bending them as if they were made of soft wood. Sarah knew she must be dreaming as Aris leaped through the opening, landing silently before her.

"Aris." It was a whisper.

"Come." Lifting her as if she were weightless, he wrapped her arms and legs around him. "Hold on tight. The only way out is down." She breathed in his fragrance as he climbed out the window. Leaning her cheek against his powerful shoulder, all of her fears fell away as he made his way, spider-like, down the ancient stones of the tower to the ground. He carried her as he ran through the forest to safety and the waiting circle of her Immortal friends.

#